LAST CALL

Revelation Revealed in the 21st Century

Third in a Trilogy of End-Time Prophecy Novels

KEN KELLY

LifeRich Publishing is a registered trademark of The Reader's Digest Association, Inc.

LifeRich Publishing books may be ordered through booksellers or by contacting:

LifeRich Publishing
1663 Liberty Drive
Bloomington, IN 47403
www.liferichpublishing.com
844-686-9607

ISBN: 978-1-4897-3598-0 (sc)
ISBN: 978-1-4897-3597-3 (hc)
ISBN: 978-1-4897-3596-6 (e)

Library of Congress Control Number: 2021909837

Print information available on the last page.

LifeRich Publishing rev. date: 05/11/2021

For my brother Gary

I wish to thank all who have supported me
through prayer an encouragement
throughout this trilogy journey!

I want to offer a warm thank you to
Judy and Amanda Kelly
for their suggestions and input.
And
Gale Peck
with Iceberg Strategic Creative graphics design
for the book cover and KLK Ministries logo

CHARACTERS

Level Seven (Heaven)

God Almighty is the creator and ruler of heaven and earth. He gave Satan (Abaddon) the right to influence and rule over level three (earth) after Adam's decision to choose sin rather than to obey the creator. The Almighty's goal is to recreate the heaven and earth back to his original purpose of peace and tranquility.

Jesus Christ is God in the flesh who came to earth. Being the only sacrifice pure enough to redeem mankind, Jesus has promised to return to level three and remove sin for all time. He is all knowing and understands that Abaddon's goal on earth is to stop Jesus from completing the prophecies of his second coming. Jesus, referred to as the carpenter by his nemesis, Abaddon, has directed his archangels to protect the Jews and Christians from the coming calamities that have been foretold. He has chosen the four members of the A-Team to be key players in achieving the completion of the redemption of mankind through salvation.

Archangel Michael is assigned by Jesus to be the protector of the Jewish nation and the chosen offspring, the Christians.

Archangel Gabriel assists Jesus in carrying out the prophecies from the Bible, and he supports Michael in protecting the Christians in level three.

Chris O'Malley was best friends with James Lucas, Cindy Sparks, and Aaron Rubin since they were fifteen years old. He overcame his addiction to drugs, received his PhD in Theology at Wheaton College, and became pastor of a congregation in Wheaton, Illinois, and part-time instructor at Wheaton College. After being called by God to be an end-time preacher, he was raptured, along with his daughter Michelle and James Lucas's wife, Annette. Chris is in heaven with his son, Paul, who died at birth; his wife Caroline, who died of cancer; and Cindy Sparks' daughter, Penny, who died of SIDs as an infant. The Lord still has plans for Chris in level three.

Level Three (Earth)

Nefas Quietus (Nef) has promoted himself to "Global Order Director" (G.O.D.). He was appointed by the western world leaders as the diplomat and negotiator for Middle East peace. Charismatic, intelligent, well-spoken and handsome, he has risen to world dominance by causing a worldwide war and then bringing peace. Possessed by Abaddon and mentored as the coming Antichrist, he has established a global society, one-world religion, and a global economic plan. He is preparing to eliminate any nonconformists to his rule—Jews and Christians who are members of the underground church of Smyrna, a congregation that Nef has coined as the "undergrounders."

James Bradley Lucas is a graduate of West Point, Supreme General of the Middle Eastern and Western armies and is under the direct command of Nefas Quietus. He has been best friends with Chris O'Malley, Cindy Sparks, and Aaron Rubin—the A-Team—since childhood and has dedicated himself to protecting his loved ones. As a world-renowned war hero and member of the inner circle of Nefas Quietus, he is the undercover spy for his son, Brad Lucas (Pastor BL), and the underground Christian church.

Cindy Sparks has been a member of the A-Team since childhood, lost her daughter, Penny, as a young baby to SIDS, divorced, recovering alcoholic and completely infatuated with Nef. She is a graduate of Stanford University and earned her master's degree in political science from Northwestern University. As a successful aide to an Illinois senator, she was promoted to diplomatic liaison to the Director of Middle Eastern Affairs, Nefas Quietus. She is now a consultant and top aide to the director and is part of his inner circle.

Aaron Rubin, who at fifteen, was saved from an attack by Abaddon's demons when James, Chris, and Cindy came to his rescue, and he became an integral part of the A-Team. Aaron graduated from Jerusalem University, earned his PhD in engineering, and became a noted Rabbi. He co-developed the sophisticated defense system surrounding Israel and was elected to be a member of the Knesset, serving as Director of International Policy Institute for Counterterrorism. He has maintained a close friendship with Nef and appreciates Nef's role in getting the holy Jewish Temple built. He is blind to the real identity of Nef and Nef's true intentions for his country.

Christopher James O'Malley (CJ) is the son of Chris and Caroline O'Malley and attended Northwestern University on a football scholarship. He is best friends with Brad Lucas, the son of James Lucas. Not sharing his father or sister's faith in Jesus, he was not included in the rapture. Jesus appeared to him in a vision. CJ repented and is now the founding pastor of the underground church of Smyrna. He is using his father and sister's notes to teach on Revelation via the Internet. His goal is to warn fellow committed believers, also left behind after the Rapture, of coming prophecies and to evangelize the world. He has set out on a mission given to him by God to visit the two witnesses in Jerusalem and to learn what God has called him to do next.

Bradley Christopher Lucas (Brad) is the son of James and Annette Lucas and attended Northwestern University with CJ on a football scholarship. Like CJ, he did not share his mother's faith in Jesus and was not included in the Rapture. Brad has become CJ's right-hand advisor in the underground church of Smyrna and director of logistics. He is in secret contact with his father, James Lucas, and his continual prayer is for his dad's salvation. He is currently in charge of the Church of Smyrna's ministry.

Stacey Lucas was part of the drug culture instead of attending college. The daughter of James and Annette Lucas and older sister to Brad, she hated her father because he separated from her mother. She had blamed her dad and God for her mother's disappearance in the Rapture until she accepted the Lord and joined the undergrounders after her horrific experience surviving the seven thunders. She is now with her brother, Brad, and is the director of supply for the underground church of Smyrna. She is married to Larry Quinn and expecting their child.

Larry Quinn was an army sergeant and assistant to General Lucas. He lost his mother in the Rapture, accepted Jesus, and became a follower of the church of Smyrna. He was sent by James to join the undergrounders to oversee hydroponic food development and is now married to Stacey Lucas.

Spurious Shuham (Spry) has a PhD in theology, was the past chair of the theology faculty at Oxford University and is the current spiritual teacher under Nefas Quietus. He propagates that all religions believe in the same god, now called the supreme being. Head of the new one-world religion, Spry is a member of the inner circle of Nefas Quietus and is possessed by Abaddon's archangel, Decedre, an unholy spirit member of the unholy trinity.

Archangel Nergal was the commander of Hades who was called to level three to participate as a member of the unholy trinity.

Level Six (Hell or Hades)

General Raze is the head demon of destruction and commander of the demonic armies. He does Abaddon's direct bidding and is a member of Abaddon's inner circle.

Colonel Odium is the head demon of hatred and is second in command to General Raze.

SUMMARY

The first half of tribulation has proved challenging for the A-Team. James, the general of all armies and member of the coveted inner circle of Nefas Quietus, is beginning to recognize some unusual personality traits that have him convinced that Nef is not who he claims to be. James's recall ability has brought to light many of the end-time teachings of his best friend, Chris O'Malley. He has stepped up his clandestine activities with his son Brad, who is co-leader of the Smyrna church, the church that Nef has coined as the undergrounders. James has directed the defense of the western community during the release of the four horses, seven seals, and six of the seven trumpets introduced in the first half of tribulation. He is even more suspicious of Nef now that peace has come to the world community and James has been introduced to the new economic plan and the one-world religion's commandments. He relishes in playing the Judas of the twelve disciples of Nef. James's profound apprehension for the safety of his family has caused concern about Nef's tenacious and demanding search for the undergrounders' headquarters and leaders.

Cindy also has noticed a distinct alteration to Nef's personality. His quick explosion of anger and dismissive and grandiose attitude have made Cindy anxious. However, her loyalty toward Nef has not wavered. She remains his faithful administrator, confidant, and member of Nef's inner circle.

Aaron has guided his constituents through the building of the Temple and has held his place on the Israeli Knesset. He considers Nef a true friend and appreciated his contribution in obtaining peace in the Middle East so that the Temple could be built. He is in contact with both James and Cindy on a regular basis.

Chris has been in Heaven since the time he was raptured. He has petitioned Jesus to allow him to have an integral part in the fulfillment of prophecies and to help bring the rest of his A-Team family to the realization that eternity is only available through Jesus, the true Christ.

At the close of *The Rise of Abaddon* we saw CJ being called by God to a mission in Israel.

CHAPTER 1

"Uncle Aaron, it's so wonderful to see you." CJ said, with a wide smile. He enjoyed the look of shock on his Dad's friend's face as he stepped through the door and gave Aaron a hug.

CJ moved back and Aaron still had not said anything. "Where are the kids?"

Aaron stood with his mouth agape at the door looking into CJ's face. "CJ, you look great! What do you mean, kids? They aren't much younger than you. Come in, come in, my son." Aaron yelled toward the kitchen. "Ruth, we have an unexpected guest. CJ O'Malley has come calling."

As CJ walked into Aaron's house he said, "Dad always referred to them as 'the kids.' Anyway, I just happen to be passing through and thought I would drop by."

"Just passing through. Very funny. With all that has been going on in the Middle East and Europe, not to mention the horrible stinging sensation and poisoned waterways, I am shocked you would leave the United States."

"We have the same problem there. Some of us were able to avoid the stinging pain and contaminated water, though."

Aaron tilted his head and sighed. "You needn't be coy with me, son. I know you must be a Christian. I listened to your dad for most of my life speaking about his Lord, and during the later years he was obsessed with a book called Revelations."

CJ said timidly, "The book is called Revelation, not Revelations;

1

but, yes, that was his passion, and I have picked up the baton, so to speak."

"Well, I am a Jewish rabbi, so don't waste your time on me. After all, I had the greatest, your dad, taking his best shots at me for years, although I must admit that your pop and I had some prodigious debates. He did have an uncanny understanding of the Jewish faith. We believe in the same God, which some are calling the "supreme being," but your dad and I totally disagreed about the Messiah."

Aaron showed CJ over to the sofa. CJ took a deep breath as he leaned back into the soft cushion. "Perhaps you should think about all that Dad shared with you and just look around. I'll bet you would see a lot of the prophecies he spoke about coming to fruition."

CJ felt at home. He took note that the living room was sparse yet comfortable. The sofa was old, but it felt like a soft cloud. He snuggled in and glanced at the Star of David on the wall and the menorah on the table in front of the picture window. The carpet was relatively new and very supple. He had removed his shoes at the door and enjoyed the soothing feel of the fibers.

Ruth entered the living room and walked over to CJ, leaned down and gave him a motherly hug. She stood up straight and looked at her guest and then stepped back. Looking at Aaron and back at CJ, she laughed and said, "Okay, boys, enough about religion. Aaron, you two haven't been together for five minutes and it sounds like you and Chris all over again."

The phone rang. Aaron glanced at the LCD to see who was calling, excused himself, and went into the kitchen while CJ visited with Ruth.

Aaron pushed "Talk." "Hi, Cindy, guess who dropped in for dinner?"
"Hi, Aaron. Who?"
"CJ. We thought he had dropped off the face of the Earth or disappeared with his dad and sister, but here he is. What say you catch

a ride with James and come over and see him? He looks like Chris and talks like him too. It's uncanny."

Cindy tilted her head, raised her eyebrows, and said, "I'm in the middle of final touches for the ceremony at the end of the week; but I could wrap it up sooner, so why not? I'll call James and see if he can leave a few days early. Maybe we could come in and show CJ around Jerusalem together before the big celebration."

Cindy heard silence. She knew Aaron was concerned that Nef had decided to perform his award ceremony on the Temple grounds in Jerusalem and was against the idea. She wished she hadn't mentioned it.

Aaron said, "I still don't understand why Nef is doing this presentation in the Temple's inner courtyard. Why couldn't he have the award ceremony in Rome?"

Cindy knew how tenacious Aaron could be. She rolled her eyes and responded, "Now, now, Aaron, we have discussed this already, and Nef's mind is made up. There is no need to get him upset again over this. It is his award, and he wants to receive it in Jerusalem by the Temple. After all, the Temple is one of his greatest achievements and one of yours too. He did all he could to protect the Temple during the war, and it is still standing in perfect shape. At least you, and your cohorts, could give him that."

"We appreciate it, but we don't like bringing attention to our holy place and allowing potential radicals into the area."

"Aaron, you know that Nef has a good handle on things. No one would dare harm the Temple or any Jews, especially while he is in the area."

"Yeah, I suppose so, but we will still be on high alert."

Cindy figured she had better change the subject. "Okay, back to a little family time. I will contact James about coming early to see CJ, and I'll call you back." Cindy ended the call.

Cindy's room seemed brighter and her heart was lighter knowing that she would see CJ. She had often thought about Chris and wondered what happened to his family. She reflected on her last conversation with CJ, which was after the disappearance. He was so upset, and she never heard from him again. She even thought he could have possibly disappeared as well. She briefly sat back in her chair. Cindy pondered on the times she had held CJ as a baby and played with him as a child. He always called her "Aunt Cindy," and he was as close to a son as she would ever have. She excitedly picked up her phone and said, "Call James." She heard a ring, and then James's voice spoke on the other end. Cindy skipped the normal niceties. "James, guess what?"

"Hi, Cindy, what's up?" James said like he used to in junior high.

"Aaron would like us to come out a few days early to visit with his unexpected guest."

"Unexpected guest?"

"Yes. CJ just popped in for dinner. Aaron and Ruth want us to join them and the kids for dinner tomorrow night and then take CJ on a city tour the next day. We have to go there for the ceremony anyway and if you can get away early, then let's go!"

James's face turned white, and his lungs seemed to burn. "Cindy, are you calling from the office?"

"Yes, why?"

"Oh." James took a breath. "I was about to call you, because I need to talk to the Director."

"You mean the Global Order Director, don't you?" Cindy corrected James.

"Yes, but first I think your idea of going early is a great one. Why don't we meet at my airport hangar at noon tomorrow? We can fly over in my jet."

"Splendid. I will put you through to the Global Order Director now. I have to run so that I can get ready to leave."

James had to think quickly. He knew that Nef had the communications bugged and that if Aaron called Cindy and she called James, then Nef would know where CJ was. *I must gain control of this and get CJ in my custody,* James thought as his jaw tightened. *If I don't, he will be detained and will be forced to give up Brad and Stacey and the*

*rest of the undergrounders. Nef is probably ready to call Sterns right now.
I can't let that happen!*

James's heard Nef say, "Hello, General Lucas."

"Hello, Mr. Global Order Director, sir. I wanted to alert you to some fantastic news. I just learned the whereabouts of one of the leaders of the undergrounders. In fact, I have arranged a rendezvous with him.

"Very interesting. Who?"

"It's CJ O'Malley, Chris O'Malley's son." James rushed his speech and feigned excitement. "He suspects nothing and foolishly thinks that my old friendship with his father will save him. Maybe he is coming in because he sees the error of his ways. Can you imagine what it would do to the underground movement if their leader converted to the one-world religion?"

"That's an interesting visual."

"I will spend a day with him in casual conversation, and I will see what I can learn. Then I will show him my headquarters in Jerusalem and see that the last room he views is the interrogation cell. He will be locked up until after the celebration. Then you can personally interview him, and with your amazing power of persuasion you can help him see the true advantage of following the supreme being. If nothing else, together we will learn all the information he possesses about the undergrounders. I'm not surprised he showed up. I felt sure that their main headquarters was in the European region."

Nef, of course, knew that CJ was in Jerusalem. His communication's director notified him while Cindy was talking to Aaron. Nef was patched in to listen to the conversation between Cindy and Aaron and with James. "Great work, James. I had no idea that the undergrounders' leader had surfaced. I will have General Sterns return from the U.S. region as soon as he can to help out in the interrogation, if needed." Nef disconnected and leaned back in his chair. He thought that he had won a great victory. To get James to turn on his own was a tribute to Nef's power and to James's devotion to him. *Although I am impressed with James's action, I will still have them watched closely,* he thought.

Nef called General Sterns. "General, I want you to conclude the U.S. search and return from the Midwest. The undergrounders' leader, CJ O'Malley, has surfaced in Jerusalem. General Lucas is flying there to take charge. I want you to have your men watch the general and his entourage tomorrow and the next day. If the suspect does not end up in the interrogation cell at headquarters that evening, or if the general deviates from the plan at all, have your men lock them both up."

Nef was sure that General Sterns would like the sound of that.

James gave a weak smile as he noted how excited CJ was as he and Cindy entered Aaron's home. James's mind was on something else. What James didn't know was that CJ had already been to the Temple grounds the day before.

"Wow, what a day! The Temple was amazing, even though I couldn't go inside—I got to walk where Jesus walked."

The feeling that James had when Cindy called about CJ in Jerusalem hadn't subsided in the least. He couldn't eat much and told the others that he had a bit of a stomachache. "Perhaps I am nervous about the upcoming ceremony since I am in charge of security."

James noted that Aaron frowned. Aaron said, "I thought General Sterns of the GSS had that responsibility."

"Well, Aaron, we both have to share such a big job."

Aaron showed signs of agreement. "I like and admire Nef, but I don't know where he found this Sterns guy. He is a real jerk if you ask me. He obviously doesn't like Jews, and he makes no bones about it."

"The guy tries, and he is fiercely loyal to the Director." James defended Sterns for Cindy's sake.

"The Global Order Director." Cindy corrected James again as she raised her eyebrow to emphasize that James must refer to his commander with the proper title.

"Come on Cindy, that's a mouthful."

CJ entered the conversation. "Soon he will demand to be called by the acronym—G.O.D." No one laughed.

James looked at CJ and said, "CJ, let's go for another ride. I have one more thing to show you."

"I know, Uncle James."

James looked at CJ kind of funny. "I want to show you where I work." James slid his chair back from the table, and CJ did the same. James continued, "Aaron, thanks for a great day. I'm going to take CJ and show him some more sites alone. We'll be back later."

Aaron stood and said, "Sure, see you when we see you."

"Can I come too?" Cindy asked.

"Nah, we need a little male bonding time," James said as he put his arm around CJ's shoulders.

✝

CJ sensed warmth, love, and understanding from his dad's best friend. They walked to the front door and opened it. James let CJ exit first, then followed.

The daylight was bright; and the heat was intense but felt good on CJ's skin. He stepped off the porch and walked briskly to James's military car. James got in and started the engine. CJ was unusually calm. He knew his calling and where he was about to be taken. His stomach had a few butterflies dancing around, not from nervousness but from the thrill of doing God's work.

CJ raised his hand and gave a quick wave as Aaron and Cindy returned his wave.

CJ and James drove away.

✝

James was taking CJ on a tour of his headquarters. "This is my office and that is the main hub of the security section and…"

CJ interrupted. "How long before you take me to the interrogation room?"

James's mouth dropped open. He was always amazed when he talked to his son Brad from his hidden room, and Brad seemed to know exactly what James was going to suggest before he could say it. Brad would claim that he had had a vision or a visit from God. It always baffled James. "Well, I guess I have stalled long enough. We need to talk, and the interrogation center is a good place to do it."

CJ looked James in the eyes and said, "You mean the interrogation cell, right?"

"Right," James said as he grimaced as if to say "Sorry."

The two men entered the cell. James shut the door and flipped a switch. He told CJ to sit down and sat in a chair facing him. "CJ, what on earth are you doing? The Director has his two army branches searching the world for you and the undergrounders. I'm in charge of one, and General Sterns oversees the other. What were you thinking to show up in Jerusalem, now of all times?"

CJ raised and dropped his shoulders and said, "I'm where the Lord wants me."

James looked incredulous. "You mean the Lord wants you dead?"

CJ appeared at total peace. "I will follow his direction anywhere I am called. Uncle James, I am just a man and not essential to any movement. If God wants to take me home—I'm ready."

James was nearly speechless at CJ's lackadaisical response, but he did feel a respect for CJ that caught him off guard. James stood up. "I have shut the recordings down for now; but if anyone else gets to you, you will be forced to disclose the new headquarters."

"Uncle James, please don't worry. There is nothing anyone can do to me to get to Brad, Stacey, Larry, or your future grandchild. I promise!"

"You know, don't you? Did Brad tell you?"

CJ shook his head. "No, he never had to. The information and intelligence he kept coming up with was too detailed to come from a lower-level office. Besides, I always knew that the Lord was going to use you for great things. You were more than a friend to Dad. He loved you more than a brother; heck, he probably loved you as much, if not more, than his family. I can tell you right now, he is before the Lord begging him to intercede in your life and do whatever it takes to get you to admit your love for Jesus and accept his forgiveness. The end is near, and you are going to have to make some critical decisions that will affect your eternal existence. You can choose to be with the family you have so fiercely protected along with your best friend, or not. The choice is yours, and I'm praying you make the right one!"

James felt a tear running down his cheek. He discreetly wiped it away as he said, "I have to go for now. I must be sure that the area is secure for the Director, and then I will deal with you." He leaned forward and looked intently at CJ. "You cannot be interrogated by Sterns." James stood and left. The cell door locked behind him. James turned and momentarily stared at the door with a sad and pensive look. *I love that kid and adore his dad. How can I save him?* He placed a guard at the cell door and rushed up the stairs.

James was finalizing security and racking his brain as to how he was going to orchestrate CJ's escape and remain in good standing with the Director. Cindy's wellbeing could also depend on it. James knew that Nef could eliminate Cindy in a heartbeat if Nef couldn't use her to control James. He decided that he couldn't do anything until right after the celebration. *Perhaps in all the confusion I could slip away, get CJ out, and somehow blame Sterns. Now, that would be a perfect outcome.*

CHAPTER 2

As CJ sat in the interrogation cell, he had never felt so calm. He stood, moved around the table and knelt. Thanking the Lord for his love and forgiveness, he asked for wisdom, strength, and guidance.

The desk sergeant stood up quickly as he saw two men briskly walking through the headquarters' main entrance. They obviously had a set purpose as they approached the front desk. "Sergeant, we have come to pick up the prisoner," the colonel said as he handed the desk sergeant signed orders. The sergeant snapped to attention and saluted the colonel. The officer was from the GSS.

"At ease, Sergeant. As you can see, General William Sterns has ordered the retrieval of the young man in the interrogation cell. Now, please take us to him."

"Yes, sir. First, please sign him out. It is SOP."

"Certainly, Sergeant." The colonel signed.

The soldier led the two men to the cellblock. Each guard stood at attention and saluted the colonel as he passed. The colonel's sergeant major was accompanying him. They stopped at the cell door. The desk sergeant ordered it unlocked. The colonel stepped in and commanded the prisoner to stand. He had the sergeant major place hand restraints on CJ. The colonel, his sergeant major, and the prisoner left without any fanfare.

CJ was ordered into a transportation vehicle.

Two hours later General Sterns walked into the headquarters and ordered the sergeant to take him to the prisoner.

"But, General, you had him transferred already. He was removed two hours ago by your colonel and his sergeant major."

"What are you talking about, soldier? I didn't give any such order!" General Sterns barked.

"But, sir, he had the orders with your signature on them to release the prisoner into their custody. Here, look!"

Bill Sterns grabbed the paper out of the sergeant's hand. The signature was a forgery, but even he would have been fooled had he not known better.

"Who is this 'Colonel A. Michael?' I have never heard of the guy." Sterns's face crunched up as he growled, "Believe me, I know my own officers! Where did they say they were transferring him to?"

"They didn't say, sir. He was GSS so we didn't feel free to ask."

"You better pray to the supreme being that we find this kid, or you will be the one facing an angry director. Now, get on the communication line and find him!" Sterns did an about face and stormed out. He needed to get over to the ceremony.

†

The sky was clear and the excitement in the audience was electrifying. The great celebration and recognition for the man responsible for global peace and security had finally arrived. Guests appeared from all over the world, and the front section was populated with high-ranking followers of the one-world religion and their families. The seating area was full, and the people in the standing-room only sections were shoulder to shoulder.

The crowd settled down as the members of the Director's "inner twelve" appeared at the back of the stage facing the audience. Dignitaries had been seated onstage where there was a wide aisle down the middle of the seats. The onlookers watched the two files of six "disciples" slowly walk side by side down the center aisle to the front of the stage. The two files broke off with one group filing to the seats on the left and the other group to the right. Spry was at the end of one line, and James, was at the end of the other, so they ended up sitting on the aisle seats to the right and left of the podium. The color guard appeared at the back of the stage, marched smartly down the aisle to the third row, and stopped.

James turned to look at the twelve soldiers. Their dress blues with gold shoulder braids were impressive, and their white caps with black bills and red bands were striking. He was pleased with his design of the new dress uniforms for the Global Military. He had incorporated a red stripe, representing blood, down the trouser sides to honor their fallen comrades and a red stripe down the placket of the jacket to signify the willingness to shed blood for the global community. James heard the sergeant major give the command, "Right face, present arms." They were carrying the traditional sabers of the Global Military. The swords had gold caps and guards and donned pearl white handles. The braids that hung down were gold, and the razor-sharp blades were a dazzling silver. When the color guard held the sabers at "present arms," the tips of the blades touched the noses of the guardsmen. As James turned his attention back to the front, everyone sat down and the sergeant major said, "Parade rest." Spry approached the podium.

The crowd arose from their chairs and applauded. Spry raised his arms, motioning for the audience to be seated and to quiet down. "My fellow global members, it is a privilege that you cannot imagine, for me to be here today and to introduce our special guest and honoree. He is a man who has worked tirelessly to bring the world peace and prosperity. You have all heard the new economic standards…" The crowd jumped to their feet, cheered, and clapped. Spry raised his hands again, and they sat down. "Yes, that announcement does deserve a good cheer. For the first time in the history of the earth, humankind will be at peace and will experience a standard of living open to only a few in the past. Our illustrious leader has brought us peace by uniting his followers under a one-religion banner that focuses on service, love, sharing, and pleasure!"

Again, the crowd broke out in spontaneous applause. Spry let them go a bit longer and then regained control. "I have witnessed this special and unique person sacrifice sleep to attend meeting after meeting with hostile leaders to win their support for the betterment of the whole community. He has propagated that it is better to give than receive, and it is better to care more about your neighbor than your own pocketbook. His philosophy is that it is best for all to care for one another in the same way they would take care of themselves or their biological family. Yes, he has made us his family, and he is our father and leader. The ten regional leaders, myself, and our general of the Global Security and the Global Military, General James Lucas…"—Spry dipped his head toward James who returned the gesture,—"…have unanimously selected this supernatural man, to receive the Global Medal of Peace and Honor!"

The crowd again gave a resounding standing ovation as James heard the sergeant major say, "Ten-hut, present arms, cross blades." The saber tips touched, forming a tunnel of gleaming steel for Nefas Quietus to pass through.

As Nef started for the podium, Spry raised his voice, "Ladies and Gentlemen, our Global Order Director!" The crowd went crazy, clapping and cheering. Some were crying with excitement and showed an expression of true love for their leader.

James turned to watch Nef pass through the tunnel of sabers as he approached the podium. Everyone sat down when Nef raised his hands in a humble gesture for quiet.

As James sat, he had a strange feeling and turned toward the soldiers as the sergeant major brought the squad to parade rest. He was unable to get a clear look at the sergeant major's face, but there was something about him that seemed familiar. The director started to speak, and James turned back to face him. He had no desire to bring attention to himself while sitting just to the right of the podium. The last thing he wanted was to undergo the wrath of the director for taking any limelight away from him while he was giving his address.

Nef droned on for over an hour. James knew that the color guardsmen must be getting tired of standing, but he quickly dismissed the thought. After all, they were fighting men and women and standing for long periods was simply part of the job. Finally, James noticed Spry nodding at him, so he stood as Spry stood. James turned on his microphone. They joined at the center of the aisle behind Nef and walked together to the right of the Global Order Director. Facing Nef,

Spry opened a beautiful blue velvet case. James removed the medal that hung from a gold ribbon.

James spoke loudly into his remote microphone. "It gives me great pleasure to have the privilege to place this Global Medal of Peace and Honor around the neck of the one man who has brought this world community so much. I do it as a representative of the ten regional leaders; the leader of the one-world religion, my friend, Dr. Spurious Shuham; the global security and global military which I direct; and the entire global community!" James faced Nef. "You have created the first global peace treaty and the most homogenous society ever known to humankind. In just over three years, you have built a new order, a one-world religion, and a new way of life for the entire world!" James placed the medal around Nef's neck as the crowd again reacted with thunderous applause.

James had memorized his lines well, which were given to him by Spry. He wasn't sure he believed any of it, but Nef probably wrote it. The two presenters started to return to their seats, and James took another quick glance at the sergeant major on his left side. His face was still obstructed, but James was sure he knew the soldier. He sat down as he heard the sergeant major give the orders in succession to form the honor canopy for the director to pass through as he left the stage.

The entire group of dignitaries and leaders were told to remain in their seats as the director left, followed by the color guard. After the director exited, Spry was again to address the crowd and invite them to join him, the other eleven leaders, and the Global Order Director at the courtyard of the Temple for a reception. There would also be an unveiling of a special tribute to their Global Order Director. He was then to guide the rest of the leaders off the stage in the same manner that they had entered.

As Nef turned and started up the center aisle, he nodded to Spry as if to say, "Job well done." He then nodded at James as he passed by. As a show of resect, James turned in his seat to follow the Director's exit. As Nef passed under the canopy of sabers, James saw one saber come down hard. To his horror, he saw blood splatter up in the air. He ran down the aisle. The other soldiers seemed frozen in place as James saw one guardsman pull his saber out of Nef's head, thrusting it into his side and driving it to his heart. James yelled, "No!" but it was too late.

The other guardsman started to hack at the assailant. Another guardsman yelled for the rest to hold the assassin down as he dragged his sword's blade through the neck of the attacker, severing his head. James grabbed the guardsman's arm and flung him to one side. "You idiot! How can I interrogate the killer if he has no head?" Blood had covered the area around the body. James slipped and fell onto the director's body. Looked ahead, he was staring at the severed head of the aggressor. It was CJ's head. James thought he was going to vomit and turned away. He gathered himself, grabbed the head, and held it. James glanced over at the position of the sergeant major. He noticed a pile of clothing and a saber lying on the stage in the very spot that the sergeant major had been standing. It looked like he had been sucked out of his uniform. It then became clear—the sergeant major was his lifelong friend, Chris, an angel of God. He was here with his son, C.J.

Spry slipped and slid to James's side. "James, you're crying. Don't cry for Nef. He will be back. You mark my word—nothing can kill him. I know he is more than a mere mortal. You wait and see." Spry wept.

James looked at Spry. *What a fool. I'm not crying for Nef,* he thought. James stood and ordered five members of the squad to collect the remains of the murderer and to secure the body and head safely from everyone. "I need his remains so I can search them for clues as to who is actually behind this assassination. Get him out of here and take him back to my Jerusalem headquarters now! Spry, you accompany the Global Order Director's body to the hospital, and I will be there in one hour. I must get back to headquarters and be sure that you, Cindy, and the rest of the leaders are not in danger as well. The rest of you guardsmen go with Dr. Shuham. You other soldiers, accompany these men and be sure that Dr. Shuham and the other ten leaders are safe."

James noticed General Sterns at the back of the stage. Covered in blood, James walked over to the General. He looked at Bill and said through clenched teeth, "Bill, how did my prisoner get out of the interrogation cell?"

Bill looked shocked and said, "I have no idea. When I arrived at headquarters he was gone!"

James moved closer to Bill's face. "Why were you at headquarters, anyway? You were to be here to protect the Director."

Bill stepped back and said in defense of his actions, "I was searching for the escapee."

"Well, you found him. He is the one who killed the Global Order Director, who is now headless and being transported back to headquarters."

Bill looked scared for the first time. "James, I had nothing to do with his escape. I simply wanted to talk to him."

James paused to collect himself. "He was under my jurisdiction, and you should have asked my permission before going there."

"I realize that now, but please don't be swayed by some incriminating evidence at the scene of his escape. Believe me, I can explain."

"I don't have time now to listen to excuses. Make sure that all of the leaders are secure and then meet me at headquarters," James ordered.

"Yes, sir," Bill responded, standing at attention and quickly saluting.

†

No one could see the three figures hovering over the pandemonium below. Archangel Michael looked at CJ. "I know that what we asked you to do was incredibly hard. The Lord's prophecy: 'One of the heads of the beast seemed to have had a fatal wound, but the fatal wound had been healed.' Jesus, through John in Revelation 13:3, prophesied that 'the whole world was astonished and followed the beast.' It must be fulfilled."

Michael looked down at the confused crowd below and then back at CJ and Chris. "Spry, the Unholy Beast, is right. Abaddon will rise again. Man cannot kill pure evil. Our Lord and Savior will deal with him soon."

Chris hugged CJ. "Job well done, Son, you have taught the undergrounders with the Lord's leading and fulfilled his calling."

Michael looked at the two hugging and said, "Well, our Lord and Savior is waiting for us. Chris, you will now be able to personally introduce your son to Jesus."

Michael, Chris, and CJ headed toward the light that shined from level seven.

Greeting the three was the Son of Man, whose face shone like the sun, and his clothes were of white light. His feet were like bronze glowing in a furnace, his legs were like fiery pillars, and above his head was a rainbow.

CHAPTER 3

James let his air out slowly with a satisfaction as he glanced up toward the heaven. Knowing CJ was with Chris gave him an uncanny peace.

James headed back to headquarters with CJ's body bag. He had no intention of searching the contents, and he didn't want an angry crowd further mangling the body. James, followed by his detail carrying the corpse, approached the desk sergeant. "Sergeant, you and the corporal take these remains to the morgue. I will personally search them for clues, and then we will move forward with cremation. I don't want anyone to have access to the remains but me. Is that clear?"

"Yes, sir, General," the sergeant said as he saluted.

James started to leave, stopped abruptly, and turned to face the sergeant again. "Sergeant, how did my prisoner get out of here?"

"Sir, a GSS colonel presented orders signed by General William Sterns to release him into the colonel's custody. I couldn't contact you because communications were down..."

"Communications were down?"

"Yes, sir, I don't know why, but we are investigating it now. Anyway, this colonel and his sergeant major took the prisoner out."

"Did they say where they were taking him?" James asked.

"No, sir, and because it was GSS, I didn't ask."

"Let me see the orders," James demanded.

The sergeant rifled through a stack of papers, pulled out a sheet, and handed it to James. "See sir, there is the general's signature," the sergeant said as he pointed to the line at the bottom of the orders. "I had our analysis department run confirmation. It checked out as authentic. General Sterns denies that it is his signature. He claims it's a forgery."

"When did the general see this?"

"When he came to interrogate the prisoner. It was about three hours ago, sir."

"So the general came to talk with the prisoner after the prisoner was released to the GSS colonel?"

"Yes, sir."

"I want this signature ran again, and I want a confirmation in writing on my desk within the next thirty minutes. Understand, Sergeant?"

"Yes, sir."

James thought for a second and then asked, "How about this Colonel Michael. Have you found him?"

"No, sir. He doesn't seem to exist in our database. His sergeant major doesn't either."

"You have his sergeant major's name?"

"Yes, sir. It was C. O'Malley, sir. See, we had him sign as well," the sergeant said as he showed James the logbook.

"Very interesting. When General Sterns arrives, send him to my office and notify me. I will be at the morgue."

"Yes, sir!" the sergeant said as he snapped to attention.

"And get on that signature!" James barked. James went down to the morgue and closed the door. He turned off the surveillance before entering the room and then picked up CJ's head. "What were you thinking?" He felt a sense of peace again. "You had the best support team known to man. You had your dad. Colonel Michael? Colonel A. Michael. Could it be? I remember Chris talking about the Archangel Michael, the protector of the chosen. Wow."

Thirty minutes later the intercom crackled, "General Lucas, General Sterns is in your office."

"Bill, this is your signature. We have had it analyzed and re-analyzed and it is authentic."

"I did not sign any such order. If I had signed the order, why would I come to interrogate the prisoner here?"

"Good point. That you attempted to usurp my authority will be a subject for another time."

"Please James, you must believe me. It had to be a plot perpetrated by the undergrounders," Bill pleaded.

"Perhaps you're right, but until I can get all the facts and get to the bottom of this, you will have to be confined to quarters."

"Confined? I need to be helping you prove what happened."

"Bill, if word gets out, and it will, that you signed the document releasing the assassin of our Global Order Director from prison, there is no telling what the angry mobs would do. I am confining you for your own protection." James pressed down his intercom button. "Sergeant, please come in here and take the general to his quarters. You won't need anyone else; General Sterns will be most cooperative; right, General?"

"Yes, sir," Sterns said with resignation.

After they left, James let his shoulders relax and smirked. *Good work guys,* he thought to himself. *Director eliminated and Sterns confined. What a successful day.*

Abaddon morphed out of Nef's mortally wounded body. As the great serpent emerged, he appeared as a leopard but had feet like a bear and a mouth like that of a lion. His archangel, Decedre, followed suit by morphing out of Spry. "I will return soon. In the meantime, I give you my power, my throne, and great authority for a limited time. You will work wondrous miracles and magic on my behalf." Decedre bowed to his master. Abaddon and Decedre heard Spry say that he felt exhausted as he sat down to rest.

Abaddon's lion mouth sneered and said, "Pathetic, all of them!"

Decedre scoffed, "Yes, especially this one. Lord and master, now what do you wish of me?"

"Come with me. I have some undone business to take care of before we take total control of level three. We are going to pay the carpenter a friendly visit in level seven."

"I thought we were banished from level seven for all of eternity."

Abaddon looked boldly at Decedre. "Don't be silly. Just for now. We will be back. No question about it!" The two unholy demons passed over to level seven.

As Abaddon and Decedre approached heaven, the gates closed. Two archangels appeared. Gabriel spoke, "Abaddon, why have you come here? You are banished forever from this place."

"Ah, Michael and Gabriel, it is so good to see you two losers again."

"It seems to us that it is you who are the loser," Gabriel said.

"Oh, Gabriel, my banishment will be short lived, believe me."

Jesus appeared. Abaddon laughed at Jesus and said, "Again, you have stumbled into my plan for level three. I want to thank you for having that young fool kill that idiot Nef. I was wondering how to slay him."

Jesus ignored Abaddon's statement and said, "You are no longer allowed here. We have banished you for all eternity. Do not come here again!"

"Oh, I assure you that I will be back, but right now I want to inform you that I am very close to taking total control of level three. All of the Almighty's precious creations will worship me. If you want to save them, you will have to come to level three and try to stop me on *my* turf."

"It will be my pleasure to put you back where you belong—in the Abyss!" Jesus said as he stared at Abaddon.

"I can't wait for you to try. See you when I see you." Abaddon turned with Decedre and headed back to level three.

†

As Abaddon and Decedre entered level six, Abaddon stopped and took a deep breath. The heat of Hades and distress of the inhabitants were a pleasure and comfort for the serpent of old. Abaddon called for Nergal to come to him.

Nergal was a commanding angel when Abaddon rebelled against the Almighty. He stood by Abaddon's side, fought, and was protecting his back as they were swept from heaven. For his service, Abaddon made Nergal an archangel. His drive was wrath—it was insatiable and best put to use in level six. However, Abaddon needed complete loyalty from his replacement in order to control Nef. "Archangel Nergal, you have run Hades well. I now want to address the souls that reside in this den of pain, and then you will accompany me to level three for your new assignment. You will possess the new Messiah, Nefas Quietus. Archangel Decedre will continue to possess the idiot Dr. Shuham. I shall assume my rightful place as god on earth and will roam freely and demonstrate my great powers."

"Yes, my lord and master," Nergal said as he bowed to Abaddon. "Have you someone in mind to take over Hades?"

"Yes, Odium and Madid have faithfully served me. They will be promoted to archangels and will govern jointly until all who prove loyal to me are released to level three to rule with me."

"You mean all that worship you unconditionally," Decedre interjected.

"Yes, I have heard that when Jesus came here, there were some who repented but could not leave. They will stay."

"When will Madid and Odium arrive?" Nergal asked.

"They are coming. I want to address the millions who suffer now."

Abaddon turned to face the occupants of level six. He raised his hand into the air. The crying and moaning stopped. "My fellow fallen believers, some of you are here because of your insubordination, but most of you are here because of that spiteful man, the carpenter. He claimed that you had to accept him as your savior to avoid this place and to enter level seven. You chose me. Well, I am here today to inform you that you chose right and what the carpenter says is a load of deceitful lies. I will soon turn this level around, and most of you will be released back into level three to reign with me for eternity. My time has come, and those in level seven will be taking your place here for not following and accepting me as their true savior."

Level six broke out in celebration. For many inhabitants, Abaddon's statement was the first thing to be pleased about in centuries. Abaddon raised his hand again and silence followed. "I cannot let you out now, but it will be soon, I promise!"

The millions listening cheered. Madid and Odium appeared, and the control over Hades was relegated to the two new archangels.

Abaddon made his last statement to those that had rejected the carpenter while in level three and to those who had chosen to join Abaddon's rebellion in heaven.

Abaddon, Decedre and Nergal, the three members of the newly formed unholy trinity, left, and the sounds of pain and moaning began again throughout level six.

✝

The hospital was in an uproar when James entered. He noticed the dazed look on the staffs' faces—everyone rushing about. *The king is dead*, James thought to himself, *and all of his men are in panic mode.* "Where is Dr. Shuham?" he shouted to an orderly.

Raising her shaky hand to her forehead, Cindy kept pacing as she waited for James to arrive. Seeing James, she ran to him sobbing and hugged him. "What are we going to do? He is our future. He was not evil, nor was he the Antichrist like Chris hinted. Nef is dead and we know the Antichrist cannot be killed."

James held Cindy. "Spry seems to think Nef is going to come back to life," James said matter-of-factly.

Cindy stepped back and looked at James. "Spry is a fool. Even Nef said that," Cindy responded defiantly.

"Speaking of our friend, where is he and where is Nef's body?" James asked, ignoring Cindy's comment and avoiding any conflict.

"Come with me. Spry has him in the morgue." James could sense Cindy's confusion, frustration and anger. "They are trying to fix his head so that we can have a proper viewing. Spry wants to place his body at the base of the statue and..."

James interrupted. "What statue?"

"He and Nef had a statue carved out of stone to honor the great contributions that Nef had brought to the world community. Nef had wanted it in the Temple's courtyard, and Spry will not be detoured. Spry says that since negotiating the building of the Temple was Nef's first great achievement the statue must be placed where Nef wanted it. Anyway, Spry is searching for a proper casket for Nef's body and says he has a plan given to him by Nef. He wants to unveil the statue and declare Nef a martyr worthy of worship."

"What makes Spry think that he is in charge?" James said, somewhat disgusted.

Cindy sneered and then continued, "He says that Nef told him he was to run things if something were to happen to incapacitate him."

"That is Spry's story. Nef was far too smart to put that kind of responsibility on Spry's shoulders." James hesitated. He knew he needed to try to manage Spry. "I want to talk to Spry."

Cindy stopped and faced James. "James, do you know who killed Nef?"

James suddenly felt trapped. "I could evade your question, but it will come out eventually. You should hear it from me. It was CJ."

"Our CJ?" Cindy asked as she caught her breath.

"Yes, the Director ordered me to detain him for questioning."

Cindy looked confused. "Wait. How did Nef know that we were seeing CJ? I didn't mention it. I knew he was suspicious of CJ and thought that he had something to do with the undergrounders, but I would never put CJ in harm's way."

"I know, but something you didn't realize is that Nef had all our communication phones bugged. He knew everything we ever said to each other."

"So he knew about our meeting with CJ and wanted him arrested?" Cindy asked.

"Yes, and I had no choice but to obey."

"Of course, but how did he get on the stage as a color guard?"

"No real idea, but I am in the process of sorting out the details. I will let you know what I know when it is no longer a hypothesis," James promised as they entered the morgue.

"Spry, what are you planning?" James asked as he walked up to Spry who was holding Nef's head in his hands.

"I'm quite sure that Cindy has filled you in, so don't play coy with me. The body will be prepared to my specifications…"—Spry looked at the mortician who looked back with concern—"…or I will have someone else's head chopped off. I have sent some priests out of the Jewish area to find a proper casket. These foolish Jews have only common pine boxes. They believe that all that are buried should be placed in a pine box so as not to embarrass the poor who can't afford a lavish funeral. Ridiculous! Our martyred saint deserves a casket of gold and a nineteen-foot monument. He will have the casket, and it will be placed on the Temple grounds at the foot of the monument. Call your buddy, Aaron Rubin, and inform him that no interference will be tolerated, and he better keep those magicians in their place. If anyone defies our directives, the Global Order Director was prepared to tell you to shoot anyone who gave us trouble. You will carry out that order. Do you understand?"

"So, when did the Director put you in charge?" James asked defiantly.

"The Global Order Director's living spirit put me in charge and has given me supreme powers! As a casket was brought into the morgue, their discussion ceased. The casket was not solid gold, but it would have to do. "Is the body ready?" Spry asked the mortician.

"Dr. Shuham, the cut was deep into the brain matter, but I have filled it with a compound and covered it as best I can. I had a wig brought in that is similar to the hairstyle that the Global Order Director had. I think he looks pretty normal, if I don't say so myself."

"It will have to do. Place his body in the casket and leave the lid open for personal viewing when we move it upstairs to the main lobby of the hospital."

Spry turned to James. "Have the hospital lobby cleared and call in all of the Global Order Director's leaders for a personal time with the body."

Spry looked at Cindy. "Cindy, arrange for the casket to be moved at 10:00 a.m. tomorrow morning to the foot of the statue on the Temple grounds. I want a procession from the hospital to the Temple that will be fitting to honor this great man. Find a flat-bed wagon that horses can pull. I will walk behind the horse-drawn casket with my three priests behind me. Then you two followed by the ten regional leaders, then the rest of the staff, and so on. The distance is not so great that we can't walk it. Cindy, see to it that the procession is on Cybervision. I want the entire event televised so that the world can mourn with us. Have the cameras rolling for as long as it takes for all to witness G.O.D.'s eventual resurrection."

James looked at Cindy as they turned around. James said under his breath, "I'm not going to hold my breath until Nef stands up and smiles." Cindy looked back at James and replied, "Spry is just being Spry."

CHAPTER 4

The procession went as planned. The streets were lined eight to ten people deep with mourners trying to rush out and touch the casket as it passed. James's security guards that lined both sides of the caisson did their best to restrain mourners.

James was in excellent shape but walking slowly and pretending to be in mourning was exhausting. "Thank God," James uttered under his breath as the procession finally reached the courtyard of the Temple.

James looked up at the nineteen-foot sheet flapping in the slight breeze. His eyes followed the sheet to the bottom where there were four steps at the base made of carefully placed marble. The foundation of the huge monument was 15 feet by 15 feet marble square. James could feel his pulse in his throat as he gazed at the marble glistening in the sunlight.

Ceremoniously, the casket was removed from the caisson, carried up the steps to the base, and placed in front of the sheet. Spry mounted the steps and stood aside the casket. He bowed his head facing his dead mentor. The horses pulling the caisson were led out of sight as Spry turned to face the throng of mourners. James and the rest of the dignitaries filed in and sat facing Spry in the front row of chairs. The outer court leisurely filled. Sobbing and groaning could be heard. As a hush spread over the viewers, Spry turned back toward the casket and opened the lid.

James was not at all surprised when Spry hesitated, leaned over, and kissed the forehead of his fallen leader. Reverently, Spry moved to the microphone, looked out, and surveyed the crowd. The onlookers were murmuring and praying for their fallen world hero.

James sighed and thought, *Spry, you are such a showboat.*

As silence fell over the proceedings, Spry began to speak. "Dearly beloved, we are gathered here this beautiful morning not to mourn a man but to celebrate a martyr—one who was not a mere mortal. To have accomplished what he did in such a short time was nothing less than miraculous. He lies before you now to view openly and see clearly that his dead mortal body is at rest in this casket. I propose that you watch our Global Order Director's body closely in the coming days. You will see such miracles happen that there will be no doubt as to who this man really is. Yesterday, we heard his incredible speech a few blocks away from where we stand today. His achievements were many, and our love and gratefulness are enormous.

A member of the crowd stood and yelled, "We love you, Global Order Director. Please come back to us!"

Spry smiled broadly as the man sat down and the crowd applauded. Spry continued, "He spoke to me after his assassination." Some in the crowd looked confused, and others stared in disbelief. "Our G.O.D. told me that he has given me his powers while he's waiting for his flock to call him back to life. He is not only worthy to be worshiped as the one true Messiah but is god with us." Spry raised his hand and the sky lit up with a firestorm. As his arm slowly dropped, the fire started to fall toward the followers. People screamed and ducked for cover. Spry then stopped his downward motion and the fire hovered just over the crowd's heads. The people gazed in amazement. Spry made the fire disappear and proceeded to stage more miraculous occurrences. As the world community watched on Cybervision, they saw the miracles Spry performed in the name of Nef. Many in the audience believed that the man lying in the casket was truly the supreme being and would return to them.

James, feeling disgusted, could tell that Spry was enjoying his newfound abilities.

Spry beamed at his congregation. "I will be asking you to pray for his return! To help inspire us, I have had a statue created for dedication today to mark the greatness of our Global Order Director. I had planned to unveil it this morning with our true leader standing next to it, but things have changed. Although he is lying in the casket now, I believe that he will be standing again!" With that, Spry pulled on a cord and the cloth fell to the ground. The crowd gasped at the magnificent sight.

The statue was nineteen feet high and looked like the Director. It had a white robe and was barefoot, like a Greek god. In his right hand was a replica of the Global Medal of Peace, and in his left hand was a scale balancing an olive branch and a sword. The belt was solid gold, and the sash was the new banner of the one-world religion. A gold wreath-like crown was atop the head.

Spry stood solemnly looking up at the face of the statue. He turned and scanned the crowd once more. We need our G.O.D. to return to us! Now, I want everyone here, and all of those watching these proceedings, to bow down and pray with me for the return of our wonderful leader and Messiah."

Most kneeled down, but some stood instead. The Jews in the crowd were not about to bow in any venue where there was a statue. Even though many appreciated, and even some loved, the Global Order Director for negotiating the building of the Holy Temple, they could never bow before a false god. Aaron rose to his feet. James did not quite know what to do. He realized that if he did not join Spry on his knees, his days as Global Security Director would end abruptly. He would not be able to help his children survive the coming onslaught. James obeyed. He dropped to his knees, as did Cindy and the rest of the hierarchy.

Spry waited until all, except Aaron and the smattering of Jews, were paying their proper respect to the supreme being. He began to pray, "All mighty supreme being, we bow before you and ask that you return to us as our beloved Global Order Director as our true Messiah. We ask that you bring him back from the dead so that we can recognize and worship him as such. We ask for a sign that you are in charge and hear our prayers!"

Some in the crowd looked up at Spry when a booming voice said, "You shall not misuse the name of the Lord, your supreme being, for the Lord will not hold anyone guiltless who misuses his name.

Remember the worship time by keeping it holy. Six days you shall labor and do your work for the global community's survival, and the seventh day will be a Sabbath to the Lord, your supreme being. On the seventh day you shall not do any work, neither you, nor your partner, nor son or daughter. It will be a day of unrestrained pleasure..." Everyone looked up, realizing that it was not Dr. Shuham speaking. It was the statue. The crowd gasped, but no one moved or dared to stand. Many of the Jews instinctively kneeled. The statue completed the new one-world religion's Ten Commandments and then there was silence. James thought to himself, *This is another prediction by Chris about the prophecies in Revelation to come true —a speaking statue. I hope what Chris taught about what is prophesied next doesn't happen!*

A voice filled the air with such volume it made the audience's chests vibrate making it hard for them to breathe. "You will worship no other god before me! I will send you your Messiah very soon to rule over you with an iron scepter. If you can see me or hear me, then bow down. Repent of your sinful doubts about me, accept me as your only supreme being, and I will accept you openly. Now bow down!" The statue's head turned as if to look over the crowd. If anyone thought this was a trick being perpetrated by Spry, they did not show it. People were openly crying, and many were shaking with both fear and loving emotion experienced only by hearing the voice of the supreme being.

Yet, some did not bow, Aaron among them.

The statue continued, "I said to bow before me and accept me for who I am because I Am who I Am." The Jews knew exactly what he meant by saying "I Am who I Am." It was what God said to Moses at the burning bush so that Moses would know he was talking directly to God the Almighty. The statue was proclaiming that God possessed it. "From now on when you come on this holy ground, you will remove any covering on your feet, and you will cover your head to show me honor. I say for the third and final time, bow down before me and worship me!"

James had inched his way over to where Aaron remained standing. He grabbed Aaron's hand and whispered, "Get down. Don't be a fool. You don't have to really accept, just bow for now!" Aaron pulled his hand away, turned his back on the statue, and started to walk down the aisle to leave. Other Jews saw him and began to follow. The statue demanded, "Stop!" The Jews did not stop. The statue stared at the three friends of Aaron's who had turned to follow and said, "So be it."

†

The area where the three defiant Jews were following Aaron exploded into flames. Aaron's closest Jewish friend and partner, Daniel, and the two others were incinerated. Those who were watching saw the statue's mouth blow—as they had seen one of the prophets on the other side of the Temple do when setting someone on fire. Aaron was unharmed. As Aaron moved toward his friends, he looked at the statue. He still refused to bow down.

Members of the crowd were afraid to stand and run, so they crawled away as fast as possible from the flames. Many were scorched. Aaron did an about face and continued to walk away slowly as if he were in no hurry.

The statue repeated his act on several more who refused to bow but did not try to harm Aaron. Abaddon knew he could not kill the stubborn Jew. He could see Michael and Gabriel standing around him. Only Michael and Gabriel could hear Abaddon say, "Still protecting that little Jewish dog?"

Aaron walked the long way around the Temple to the other side. Being in psychological pain, having witnessed his friends' deaths, he paused, feeling as if he would pass out. *Yahweh, you led me into talking Ruth, Naomi and Benjamin out of attending. Thank you, I knew there was possible danger awaiting my family. I wish I had been able to keep Daniel from coming, but he wouldn't hear of it. He said he had to be there to help protect me, if needed.* Aaron's heart was broken. Other than the A-Team, Daniel was his closest friend, and he could not imagine going on without him.

Aaron observed that there were several people standing, listening to the prophets. News of the statue burning Jews who would not bow down before it traveled quickly to the crowd on the prophet side of the

Temple. Aaron walked to the fence and began to pray—he rocked, touching his forehead to the fence as he often had done on the old Wailing Wall.

"It is time for you to listen to the prophets that our Lord has sent to you and the other chosen. You have remained stiff-necked long enough. You must accept the truth." Aaron stopped and looked to see who was talking to him. One of the prophets had moved close to Aaron. Aaron glanced around and saw that the guards had retreated several yards out of fear. "I am he who brought plagues on the Pharaoh and led God's people out of bondage. Because of their stubbornness, I had to lead them for forty years through the desert until the sinful generation passed away. You have wandered long enough, and it is time for you to accept the truth explained to you by your friend, Chris O'Malley, while he was with you on earth. We have come to witness to the truth. The one your ancestors put to death and called a false teacher sent us. He was, and is, the truth. It is through him only that you can enter the eternal Promised Land. He has chosen to protect you, and now you are to lead your people to safety. Archangel Michael will keep you safe, but first you must accept Jesus as your Messiah, for he was, and is, and is to be. Repent and allow his Holy Spirit to enter you. The time is growing critically short!"

Moses turned and walked back to his place by the Wall. Elijah called out to Aaron and said, "I called down fire on the pagans who worshiped Baal and was later taken to heaven without dying. I have come back to warn and to call you and your brothers and sisters to the true Messiah. It will be time for us to leave soon, and you must encourage them to accept the truth, for he is the true light and the only way." Elijah turned and sat down. Aaron bent forward. With a trembling chin, he laid his head on his arms while pressed up against the fence.

✝

People from all over the globe were arranging to travel to Jerusalem to see the talking statue, pay homage to it, and to pray over the remains of their Global Order Director. On the third day following the assassination, a woman who had approached the casket to lay a rose on the chest of her fallen hero screamed and fell to her knees and began to cry with glee. She saw the eyes of the Director open and felt his touch before she dropped to her knees. Nef sat up as the crowd all bowed down instinctively. He stood up in the casket with a regal expression as he looked over the thousands who were staring at him in shock.

A woman cried out, "He's alive! Our Messiah has come back!"

Spry ran out of the temporary headquarters to investigate all the commotion. He ran toward the casket to greet his G.O.D. Nef saw him coming, followed closely by Cindy and James. "My friends, I have returned. The supreme being heard your prayers; and because of your belief, he has sent me back to be your Messiah." When Nef spoke, all could hear what he was saying, even without a microphone. Nef turned to face the crowd and removed his wig. The gash in his head was prominent. It was obvious to all that Nefas Quietus had come back to life. "Now, come help me out of this box. I no longer have need for it!"

CHAPTER 5

After Nef blessed his followers, he turned to his inner circle and said, "It is time to retreat to the Temple."

Spry, Cindy, and James followed Nef as he walked to the entrance. The Jewish high priest stood in the doorway to block Nef from entering because the holy place was only for priestly Jews from the tribe of Levite. Having viewed the inner Temple structure at its first opening before it was consecrated and the Ark of the Covenant was placed in the Holy of Holies, Nef was never allowed to enter again. Nef waved the high priest away as if to warn him that the statue might turn him into a burning candle. The high priest stood his ground. Nef stopped and moved to within an inch of the Jewish spiritual leader's nose. "I am the Messiah that you and your chosen people have been waiting for since you were given the promise thousands of years ago. Now step out of the way of my home!" Nef's voice sounded unnatural and godlike. The priest stepped aside—not being ready to die.

Nef entered and told the rest of the Levite priests to leave the building. After clearing all the rooms of Jews, he sat down with Spry, Cindy and James and began to explain his new plan. "It is time to bring change. All followers will accept my 'mark' within 60 days." Nef looked directly at James. Let it be clear that anyone who is offered my mark and openly denies it will not be permitted to purchase food or products. If anyone is found aiding these pagans, they will be shot on sight. You, General Lucas, will see to it that my orders are carried out to the letter." Nef squinted and asked, "Where is General Sterns?"

James cleared his throat. "He is confined to his quarters until I can determine who perpetrated your killing. General Sterns's signature is on the orders that released the man from detention who ultimately struck the fatal blow to your head."

Nef's eyebrows rose as he looked at James. "Are you saying that Sterns was behind my assassination?"

"No, sir. He claims that the signature was forged."

"So, then, who actually took custody of CJ?"

Nef took James aback mentioning CJ.

"Colonel A. Michael, sir, of GSS."

"A. Michael?" Nef repeated with a questioning voice.

"Yes, Nef."

"Well, that explains everything. Let General Sterns go immediately and have him here as soon as possible. I want him to control these crowds as we administer the mark."

James's eyes widened and he opened his hands upward as he asked, "So drop all charges just like that?"

"I said to let him go, and there is no need to waste time doing any further investigation." Again, Nef turned to face James directly and moved very close to his face. "First, General, never question one of my orders again. Second, you will refer to me as 'my messiah' in public and 'lord and master' when with me in private or while we are meeting in the inner circle. Do I make myself clear?"

"Sir, yes, sir!" James answered in his military voice.

"Good. That goes for you two as well, understand?"

Spry smirked with enjoyment at the thought, and he and Cindy nodded in the affirmative.

Nef looked each inner circle member in the eyes and then nodded his head as if to emphasize his order and to let them know that he would not tolerate any acts of insubordination. Addressing Cindy, he said, "You will organize the 'chips' distribution…"

"What do you mean by chips?" Cindy asked.

Nef sat back in his chair. "For months I have been having microchips produced that can be implanted under the skin. Several manufacturing facilities in the U.S. region have been working around the clock. You will need to have them delivered to every one-world religion center as soon as possible along with injection and labeling devices that will add the numbers 666 at the beginning of each person's individual Global Security Number which is embedded in the microchip. Make it clear to the priests that only converts are eligible to receive the microchip as the mark to designate their loyalty to me and the one-world religion. I want the shipments completed within two weeks. Have several thousand shipped here. We will start the implantations in six days. You, my dear, will be among the first to receive the chip. You will follow the one-world religion Supreme Teacher…"—Nef smiled at Spry—"…along with General Lucas. I want you all to set a good example. The event will take place in front of the statue."

Nef peered out from the door at the statue. "Spry, did you get the smaller replicas of the statue shipped out to the religious centers as we discussed?"

"Yes, my lord and master."

"Good. I want you to make a list of priority recipients to receive my mark. The GSS and security force should have priority, but the ten regional directors should follow Cindy and General Lucas. Let me see the list when you are done. Also, contact Cybernews. Have them announce several times a day that all members of the one-world religion are to rush to their nearest one-world religion worship center to receive their microchip. Add that they will immediately begin to enjoy the benefits that come with being a member. Also, mention that after sixty days no one will be able to purchase food or products with currency. All monetary forms will be invalid at that time. Be sure they stress how this will tighten security and eliminate identity theft. Global members can go to their global bank branch and turn in any currency for credit as long as they have the proper credentials as a one-world religion associate. In addition, Spry, I want you to stay with me. We are going to plan a sacrifice to the supreme being on Saturday. It will be here at the Temple, and we shall perform it on the Temple proper and bring the sacrifice into the holy sanctuary."

Spry bowed his head and said, "Yes, my lord and master."

Nef faced James again and continued, "General, first set Sterns free, and then commandeer the top floor of the hotel overlooking this site—I want the entire top floor—and then determine the offices and living quarters for all." Nef hesitated as if reflecting on his future needs. He continued, "Actually, it may take several floors. Yes, evacuate the entire hotel. I am sure we will find good use for all the rooms. Have the offices set up accordingly and have my personal effects transferred from Rome. You need to have the same done from your Gaeta headquarters. It will now be a secondary facility. I will move into temporary quarters tonight, so have my office and living quarters ready ASAP."

†

James walked into Bill's quarters and sat down. "Well, Bill, you're free to go. I am sure you heard the news—Nef's back." James turned his palms up and shrugged his shoulders. "All is forgiven."

Bill walked over to James and stuck his hand out. "James, thank you for your help. I am sure your input is what cleared my name and I am grateful!"

"Don't thank me. We military men must stick together."

"Nonetheless, James, thank you."

James stood and took Bill's hand and shook it. James decided to take the credit; that way Bill would owe him. "Bill, you are to report to the Temple courtyard and begin setting up the stations to administer the mark of the supreme being." James had to catch himself because he almost said "beast."

"Can I receive the mark first?" Bill asked.

"No, my friend, that privilege will go to Spry, then Cindy and then me, but you are welcome to talk to Spry and ask to be next."

"Great, and thanks again." General Sterns walked out of his quarters with James.

†

The two archangels of Abaddon morphed out of their assigned

vessels—Decedre from Spry and Nergal from Nef. They began to talk. "Well, Decedre, I have been in Hades for so long that I forgot how much fun it is to manipulate these humans. I plan to enjoy it to the fullest. Wrath against these weaklings is my favorite vice, and I plan on making up for lost time."

"Nergal, you have been brought here from Hades to control Nef for his day-to-day activities. That will free up our master to move about freely and manipulate his minions around the globe as he pleases. Abaddon gave you carte blanche as long as you have the humans worshiping the supreme being—Abaddon—and giving him their allegiance. Remember that you are the messiah who has come to bring peace and to rule, but it is the supreme being that is to be worshiped. Don't forget, or Abaddon can demote you as easily as he promoted you," Decedre warned.

"I'll enjoy my assignment, but I will keep your warning in mind. If I get out of line, let me know, okay?" He realized that Decedre had much more experience in this possessing thing than he did.

Decedre bobbed his head and raised his left eyebrow. "Yeah, sure, but remember that Abaddon possessed your vessel first, and he was very diplomatic about all things and manipulated everyone to his way of thinking."

"Maybe, but that was before he put the fear of himself in them. Life will be much easier for me. If they don't like what I say or do, I'll kill them," Nergal said matter-of-factly.

"Do as you like but be careful that it is the will of Abaddon." Decedre tilted his forehead toward Nergal for emphasis as he said, "He is still your lord and master."

After Nef's first week back from the dead, he called Cindy's phone. "Cindy, would you mind coming to my office? I need something from you."

Cindy hung up the line, and the butterflies began to dance in her stomach. Nef had not summoned her since his resurrection, and he had been distant. Cindy felt lightness in her chest at the thought of being Nef's most intimate counselor and advisor again. She realized that Nef needed his space, now that he was the messiah. She understood that a messiah was more holy than a mere man, and he probably wanted to be alone to gather his thoughts as he communed with the supreme being. Cindy knocked on Nef's door.

"Get in here!"

Cindy blinked and her head snapped back. She entered and stopped dead in her tracks. Nef was standing in front of his desk. His nostrils were flared, and his eyes looked cold and empty.

Cindy had never seen Nef like this. She drew her arms to her chest and leaned back away from Nef.

Nef ranted, "Your friends have done this! That stupid pastor and his son are dead and gone, yet the undergrounders are still interfering with my plans. They are growing in numbers even though their leader has been cut to pieces!" Nef walked over to Cindy and hit her with the back of his hand.

Cindy fell back and grabbed her cheek.

Sneering, Nef pointed his finger into Cindy's face. Through clenched teeth he said, "Now get your friend, James, on the phone and have him and Sterns find these carpenter followers and destroy them all! I don't care how late it is. After he eliminates the underground terrorists, I will have him deal with Aaron. Get it done!"

Carpenter followers? Cindy thought. She turned and stumbled toward her desk, hand to her cheek. She heard Nef's office door slam shut. Out of loyalty, fear, or just stupid blind obedience, Cindy managed to contact James and relay the message. She slowly got up from her desk and walked back to the elevator to return to her room. Her legs felt weak, and the bruise on her cheek was beginning to sting. *I'd better get some ice on the way back to my room,* she thought.

As she entered her room, Cindy fell back on her bed and began to sob. Ten minutes later her crying stopped. Anger was starting to replace her pain.

Nef knocked on Cindy's door twice and opened the door. She was surprised to see him standing in her doorway but not shocked that he could enter at will. She had noticed the night before that she was unable to lock her door from the inside. The deadbolt had been removed. When she called the hotel desk, she was told that the messiah had ordered all locks removed except, for his.

"Sorry to barge in on you, but I realized that I wasn't done with you yet. I called you on the intercom, but you did not answer. Sorry if that little request earlier made you a bit uncomfortable, but your undying loyalty must lie with me—not with your old friends! Is that clear?"

Cindy stared at Nef blankly for a few seconds. "Yes. But attacking me will not get things done any sooner. It is humiliating to be treated that way," Cindy said with a pouting voice. "Now, can you please go?"

"You dare speak to the messiah that way? Do you really think it is acceptable for you to dismiss *me*?" Nef took another step toward Cindy and raised his hand as if he were going to deliver another blow.

Cindy cowered back and sat down on her bed. She covered her face and began to cry.

Nef stopped and took a deep breath as he gathered his emotions. "Stop acting like a weak little girl," he scolded. "Now, grow a backbone and try to be a good secretary. Be at your desk in the morning. I will give you further orders then." Nef turned and slammed the door as he left.

✝

Cindy had been sitting at her desk and staring into space trying to gather her thoughts to make sense of the "new" Nef. She finally picked up her phone to call James. He answered. Cindy said with feigned excitement, "James, I would like to get together to celebrate our upcoming placement of the microchip."

Because James had known Cindy for so many years, she was positive that he could sense the slightest voice inflection and interpret the meaning with uncanny accuracy. She was now aware that Nef listened in on her conversations, so James would assume that she needed to talk without Nef suspecting anything.

"Sure, how about I pick you up tonight at eight o'clock?"

"Great," Cindy said as her phone beeped. "Have to go. Nef's calling. See you at eight."

"Cindy, I would like for you to come in here."

"Yes, my messiah," Cindy responded with a hint of sarcasm.

Cindy appeared at the door but seemed hesitant about entering. Her cheek was still red. She looked around to see if anyone else was in the office. After all, Nef could attack at any moment, but if someone were there he might think twice. "Oh, stop being silly. I won't give you a punishment unless you deserve it. Come in here now! Update me on the plans for delivering the chip to all of my followers and be sure to keep me posted on James and Sterns's progress with the hunt for the undergrounders."

Cindy returned to her desk without incident and reviewed the process for administering the chips once again for Nef's approval.

Two hours later, Spry showed up and entered Nef's office. Cindy kept on hearing the two of them laughing. She was surprised. It seemed that Nef never respected Spry all that much and certainly had never treated him like a close friend. Now they appeared inseparable. *Maybe Spry's unwavering belief and constant pleas for prayers while Nef was dead caused Nef to feel closer to him,* she thought. *We all maintained that belief and prayed as well, yet he is treating me with contempt, just because I am a woman? He never treated me that way before.*

Nef yelled out to Cindy, "Could you please come in and see me and my friend?" Cindy heard them giggle.

She went to the door and opened it. "Yes, messiah?"

"Please come in. I am starting a new rule for my subjects, okay?"

"What do you mean?" Cindy asked with apprehension.

"From now on when you enter my presence, you will bow down on both knees and not look at my face until I say it is permitted. You will then do exactly what I tell you to do, no matter what. Do you understand?"

"I guess so." Cindy's stomach turned.

"Well, then, go back out of the office and close the door. I will call you in, and we will practice." The two men beamed. Cindy didn't know what to do but to obey. Her insides began to shake.

Nef raised his voice to be heard. "Cindy, my loyal secretary, please come in here." Cindy took a deep breath, opened the door, bowed her head and kneeled on both knees.

"Good. Now, for the obeying part. I want you to crawl on your hands and knees over to my bare feet and kiss them." She obeyed. "You may now look up." Cindy looked up. "You may now stand." Cindy stood. "Now, my good and faithful friend here is curious whether you respect him. Now that he is the Holy Spirit in the flesh, I would like you to kneel down and kiss his feet."

"What? You want me to kiss Spry's feet?" Cindy asked as tears started to form in her eyes.

Nef jumped to his feet. "That is 'Reverend Shuham' to you!" Nef screamed with almost uncontrollable rage. Cindy felt Nef's spit spray from his mouth.

Cindy couldn't breathe, and her hands began to tremble. She dropped to her knees hard—it hurt.

Nef raised his head a little and said, "Now, that's better."

Cindy began to cry as she lowered her head.

"Don't be shy. Pucker up and give his feet a good slobbering kiss."

Cindy was shaking with fear and embarrassment as she leaned forward. She could not hold it any longer. The vomit spewed all over Spry's feet.

Nef broke out in hilarious laughter as Spry pulled his feet back. "Now, Spry, go clean yourself. Cindy, get something to clean up this smelly old mess. What a show! We must do that again soon."

Cindy quickly returned to her desk and called for someone to clean the carpet. She hung up the phone, turned, and ran to the stairs.

†

Cindy was still shaking inside as she sat down with James for dinner.

"What's wrong? Come on spill. I can see that you are ready to explode," James said encouragingly.

Cindy's head slumped as she told James everything that happened. "That pig made me feel like I was thirteen and back with Uncle Dan. He is a monster. He is everything a messiah shouldn't be."

James's face was ashen. He told her to be careful and not to do anything drastic. Reaching across the table and putting his hand on Cindy's, he said solemnly, "Please give me time to work out a solution."

CHAPTER 6

Cindy didn't show up for work. Nef was irritated at her absence but otherwise distracted. He was busy finalizing the proceedings for the next day. "Is the sow ready?"

Spry was excited. "Yes, my lord and master, it is quite ready. I have even come up with an outfit." Spry rushed on, "You will love it. It looks like the garments that the high priest wears, and this sow is probably the largest pig in the nation. You could ride it; it is so big."

"Good. I want it delivered in the darkness of night so that no one sees it. Then tomorrow you will lead it out of the tent to the altar, and there I will do my thing—I will commit the last allowed sacrifice in Jerusalem. It will be pork!" They both laughed.

Nef looked up and saw Cindy standing in the doorway staring at him. "Well, nice of you to decide to show up today." Nef furrowed his brow. "Where have you been?"

"You have humiliated me for the last time. I know that I can't run from you, but I have no intention of attending your stupid sacrifice ceremony tomorrow; and I certainly can, and will, reject the microchip."

Nef squinted his eyes. He stood up as Cindy turned and ran toward the elevator. "Guards! Guards!" He grabbed the phone and yelled into it, "GUARDS!"

†

Cindy pushed the down button. She pushed it several times. She

44

could hear Nef calling out for his henchmen. She turned and ran for the stairs.

It was like a bad dream. Heart pounding, the corridor seemed to grow longer as Cindy ran. Beads of sweat formed on her upper lip as her breath burst in and out. She fought off the humiliation and choked on the realization that she had been a stubborn fool—deceived by the false messiah. Now she had to pay with her life. *How will I face death?* she thought as she raced into her hotel room. *I know that his robotic forces of evil will soon invade my false sanctuary. I have seen them in action firsthand and even condoned their deeds on innocent people. I am sure Nef has ordered my quiet but excruciatingly painful end. He has never accepted rejection from anyone, especially his well-known second in command. To ignore his demands in front of others is a certain death sentence, but what choice did I have? To obediently surrender to his orders would have been even worse. Chris was right, I should have listened when I had the chance; but, no, my stubborn and self-centered streak won out, and now, to use the old cliché, I am "a dead woman walking."*

Cindy slammed the door. She knew that it was a false sense of security. All doors in the hotel, except for Nef's, could only be latched from the outside. Cindy had never considered her room a cell, but now it was. She retrieved her phone and breathlessly said, "Aaron." She had to speak to Aaron and James before the assassin squad arrived. Cindy knew she had a little time since the false messiah would anticipate her fear and would relish in it. He would drag out the time and punishment as long as possible.

Aaron's secretary answered. Cindy said with a rush, "Rabbi Rubin, please, hurry. This is the Global Order Director's personal aide, Cindy Sparks, calling." Her name struck fear in anyone hearing it because of her relationship with the one true messiah.

Aaron's voice came on. She interrupted his hello and charged on, "Aaron, I only have a few minutes left on this earth."

"What are you talk..."

Cindy glanced at the door. She cut Aaron off. "Never mind. You know that I love you and your family, so please listen very carefully. Tomorrow something horrible will happen, and you must remember when we were at the reunion what Chris said the Bible predicted. I know that was a long time ago, but you will know what I am talking about. You must save yourself and your family. Just remember, don't be fooled. I must call and warn James. Remember, your eternity depends on it." Cindy disconnected.

She listened again. Her time was running out. Cindy loudly spoke into her phone, "James."

James's personal assistant answered, "General Lucas's office. May I help you?"

"Cindy Sparks, personal aide to the messiah, calling for General Lucas. Please tell him that it is an emergency." The sense of urgency was at its peak. Cindy thought, *what a colossal fool I have been! They say loyalty can be blind. Combine blind loyalty with the thirst for power, and here I am—in a deep black hole going to Hades.* Cindy regretted so much of her life now and the destructive decisions that she had made. She was glad that her name carried so much power but realized that the end would be crashing through her door at any second. She moaned as she thought about Penny; she would never get to see her again.

Cindy heard James's voice. He answered with a high pitch of concern. "Cindy, what's up?"

"I have no time," Cindy said hoarsely. "Please listen carefully. Remember what Chris was saying at the reunion? I know that you did your best, just like I did, to ignore his sermon, but did you hear anything he said?"

James said pleadingly, "I know you feel bad about CJ and about what Nef did to you, but you have to let it go. Your place right now is with the messiah and to serve him" James was sure that Nef was listening in.

"That's just it, James, I can't serve that monster, and you must stop as well. What Chris said scripture prophesied will come true tomorrow. You must save yourself and do what Chris said to do." Cindy felt a calm come over her.

"Cindy, please don't do anything crazy."

"You think I am being hysterical, but I am not. I have calmed down, and I know what I must do. I am sure that it is too late for me after what I have been a party to, but I am going to do it anyway. I know how important your position is—and that you have proven to be a great general—but this is far more crucial."

"Cindy, please…"

"No, James, please don't dismiss me. You know what I am saying. You intimated it earlier when we were together. Don't harden your heart. I am telling you; I have seen the real person claiming to be the messiah, and he is not who he claims to be. This could be your last chance. Oh no, I hear them coming. I must go. I love you James, and God loves you even more."

Cindy felt the bile in her throat as she fought off the urge to vomit. As she kneeled, she began to pray out loud, "Oh God. I am so sorry for being such a fool and such a sinner. I know it is probably too late, but please forgive me."

The door exploded open, and two guardsmen ran in looking very smug. One carried an automatic pistol. The other had a machete in his right hand. He lifted the implement of death and said, "The Messiah says that if you crawl from this point back to his office and show proper repentance that he may consider forgiving you."

"I am asking for forgiveness, but not from that liar," Cindy said defiantly. She saw the look of enjoyment on the guards' faces. She knew that they would relish beheading the queen shrew, as she was known to the soldiers.

One of the guardsmen stepped forward. "We hoped you would answer that way." He raised his machete. "The messiah also said that if you refused his benevolent offer then your head would be just as acceptable."

Cindy turned her head slightly and instinctively raised her hand to block the blow as she watched the guard start to bring his machete down to sever her head from her body.

The room filled with a strange bright light. Cindy's mouth dropped open, and she blinked hard. The assassin's arm stopped in midair as if someone extremely strong had grabbed it. The guard's head turned slowly with a look of confusion. He hit the floor with a thud.

Cindy flinched as her executioner dropped next to her. She squinted with her right eye at the unconscious guard. He wasn't moving. His partner was lying close to him, just as comatose.

Cindy looked up. There were two men standing over her. "We have come to take you away from this place of torment. Your prayers have been heard."

Cindy didn't know what to think. *I feel alive but perhaps this is what death is like and these are angels who have come to escort me to my eternal damnation,* she thought.

One of the strange men held out his hand and said, "Cindy, please stand so we can leave."

"Who are you?"

"Please stand and follow us. Don't say anything!" The two soldiers moved to each side of Cindy and escorted her out of the room.

Several people had entered the hall to see what the commotion was about. None of them seemed to notice the three as they walked by. Cindy heard someone yell, "Two guards are down in Ms. Sparks' room, and they appear to be asleep."

As the three left the headquarters, a high-ranking GSS officer approached them. "Where are you taking Ms. Sparks?"

Cindy spoke up. "Since when do you question my movements? Would you like me to discuss this with the messiah, or perhaps with General Sterns? Now move aside and let us pass!"

The officer timidly stepped to one side as the three walked through the checkpoint. Cindy heard the officer answer his phone. "What? Yes, she just went through. Yes, sir, right away."

The escapees picked up their pace and moved into a crowd of people milling about outside. As the officer and two of his men ran after Cindy and her protectors, they pulled out their guns and started yelling for them to stop. The crowd closed in and blocked the guards' pursuit. Cindy noticed something strange about the crowd as she passed. They all had a weird mark or something on their foreheads. It was not an implanted chip but a definite mark that glowed.

Cindy recognized some of the faces as employees in the headquarters but had never seen that mark on them before. "What is with the shiny mark on everyone's forehead?" she said to the officer holding her right arm.

The officer smiled and responded, "It is the mark of the Holy Spirit. All the Lord's believers have one, but only fellow believers can see them. It is our Lord and Savior's way of keeping us safe until he calls us home." Cindy understood. She put her hand to her own forehead but felt nothing. "You have one as well. Now, please hurry."

Her prayer of repentance was heard, and for some reason Jesus had chosen to allow her to live for a while longer. As they entered a waiting car, Cindy looked at the soldier on her left. "Who are you? You seem terribly familiar. Where is your mark?"

As the soldier's appearance began to morph, two fellow believers appeared in the front seat. Cindy was distracted as the officer on her right said, "Take good care of her. She will join the rest of the chosen soon."

Cindy turned to thank the soldier on her left as his face became clear. It was Chris. He had come to her rescue once again, like he did when they were teenagers and he and James saved her from her abusive uncle. "Chris, thank you!"

He warmly looked into Cindy's eyes and said, "See you soon." Chris and the archangel Michael disappeared.

✝

"Now what have you done, Nergal?" Abaddon's eyes were hot with anger.

"What do you mean, lord and master?"

"Your uncontrolled wrath has driven Cindy into the enemy's camp. You fool! We need her here to have leverage over General Lucas. His men love him more than me, and now we have no threat for him to consider. Find Cindy and grovel if you have to but get her back here; and then you can lock her up."

Nergal, who had morphed out of Nef, bowed his head as low as he could. His hands were shaking as he said, "Yes, lord and master. I will have her back by nightfall."

"How did you let her slip through your tight security, anyway? Perhaps I should promote Madid and demote you back to six. What about that?" Abaddon said with a snake's hiss.

"No, please, my lord and master, let me make this up to you! I will find her! In the meantime, I have our fantastic sacrifice ready. It will humiliate these pigs—get it, pigs?—and show them who their messiah really is."

"Don't change the subject. I do not have time to be chasing that stupid trader, so you better pull this off and keep General Lucas in check as well!"

"Yes, lord and master. I promise!"

CHAPTER 7

After Cindy's phone call and disappearance and Aaron's open defiance of the new messiah, James was concerned about his two friends. "Aaron, do you have some time to meet tonight? How about dinner on me?"

"I would love to. Where and when?"

"I think an out-of-the-way place would be best. We can discuss the new world that the messiah is planning."

Following CJ's abduction, the funeral, and Daniel's death, James had warned Aaron that Nef had someone listening in on his and Cindy's calls.

The "out of the way" phrase was code for "be careful what you say." James assumed that Aaron knew that he wanted to meet in secret. "How about that same quaint place we met at last year. The one where you commented about the great fish?"

"Yes, that will be good. How about the same time as then?"

"Sure, I will call and make reservations and ask for our special table. See you when I see you." Aaron disconnected.

James suspected that with Cindy's disappearance he would be watched very closely. The messiah's spies didn't know where or when he was going to meet with Aaron. James smiled at the thought. He and Aaron may have outfoxed the monster this time. He was glad that he had warned Aaron so that he understood when to be nebulous and not ask specific questions. James decided to develop a highly active day with several stops around the city so that his movements could be explained but hard to track. He hoped Aaron would do the same. James would claim he was searching for Cindy. The phone rang. He could see that it was Sterns calling. He had no doubt that Nef had called General Sterns and ordered him to find out where James was going and at what time. He ignored the call.

James hadn't heard from Cindy since she had called to warn him, but news had come to him that the GSS was on an all-out alert searching for Ms. Sparks. The word on the street was that she had been kidnapped. James thought, *How in the world could she have slipped past the tight security? Guards were almost in her room to arrest her, or even worse.* He remembered his son telling him that crunch time was fast approaching. *Cindy said that the sacrifice Nef and Spry were planning for tomorrow would be another prophecy fulfilled. I need to discuss it with Aaron.*

"Aaron," James said as he hugged his longtime friend. "We have come a long way since those bullies tried to end your life in the alley so long ago."

"I have never forgotten that day, not even for a moment. It was my A-team and God that saved me, and I may need them again."

"I know what you mean. I have been briefed on tomorrow's activities by his majesty. Tomorrow Nef will be performing the last allowed sacrifice. It will be a huge sow, and Nef plans on taking it into the Temple and killing it on a new altar erected over the Temple's old alter."

Aaron's face turned white. He could barely catch his breath. "That is an abomination. Antiochus Epiphanes erected a pagan altar to Zeus in the Temple in 168 BC. It was a desolation of the holy place in scripture. It is referred to as the 'abomination that causes desolation.'"

"Didn't Chris refer to that when talking about Revelation?" James asked.

"Yes, and Cindy told me to try to remember all that Chris had said at the reunion. Chris made me promise to pay close attention to the actions and prophecies in the event he disappeared. I must confess to you, my brother—and I call you that with all the love of a true blood brother—I spoke with the prophet Moses yesterday at the Temple. He told me to accept Jesus as the true Christ and to repent and ask him to enter my life. I did that last night!"

"You're no longer a Jew?" James asked.

"Of course, I am a Jew. I am now what they call a Christian or completed Jew."

"Then you must run! Nef will destroy you before you can take another breath if he hears that you have converted."

"I am sharing this with you because you must join me. You know as well as I do that this monster is the Antichrist that Chris preached about. I heard the news today, and I can only believe that Cindy escaped because she realized the same thing and accepted Jesus. She is out there somewhere, now as a Christian. I feel it. I'm having my children over later tonight, and I plan on witnessing to them and Ruth. I am sure that they will be persuaded to seek Jesus as their Savior and as the true Messiah. I want to share my newfound faith with fellow Jews who have rejected the microchip, which is 'the mark of the beast' spoken of in Revelation 13. I must share the wealth of information that Chris shared with us. I have been secretly studying Revelation and Chris's study notes for several weeks. Too many things were happening to ignore that fell into step with Chris's teachings. Sorry that I didn't tell you, but you understand, right?"

"Of course. I admit that I have been rethinking my loyalty to Nef for some time. I confess that I have been helping the undergrounders for over three years. My son and daughter are the current leaders."

"Pastor BL. Of course. It's Brad! I have been listening to his teachings as well. You must repent, accept, and join them. Do you really think that in this current environment you can continue helping them?"

"Not really, I am sure that I'm fooling myself. With Cindy gone, Nef will double his watch over me and my actions."

"Well, let's eat and see where this dilemma leads us, shall we?"

Aaron raised his head after bowing and giving thanks to the Lord. His mouth curled as he saw the look on James's face.

"Wow, you really are into this Christian thing."

"Yep, for eternity."

†

The light intensified around the Archangel Gabriel as Jesus walked up and embraced him. "Gabriel, so, you are watching the earthlings react to the Unholy Trinity?"

"Yes, my Lord. Look at the great deceivers. To so many of the inhabitants of level three they appear to be full of love and caring. They present themselves as the Almighty, the Messiah, and the Holy Teacher. From this vantage we see the true beings—the red dragon of deception and his beasts who falsely speak soft words to the ears of the hearers on earth. Their utterances are a dragon's pack of lies."

"Yes, I know," Jesus said sadly. "It is my chosen followers' purpose to open the eyes and ears of the nonbelievers so that they accept me for who I am and reject the others for who they really are. Now watch and see what the dragon does to help drive many of my stiffed-necked chosen to their senses."

Michael came up alongside Gabriel. Behind him was a host of angels dressed for battle. The Lord looked at him. "You are prepared, I see."

Michael lowered down on one knee, bowing his head as he replied, "Yes, my Lord. When they need me, I will be there."

Jesus put his right hand on Michael's head and simply said, "Good."

†

Spry walked into the tent outside the courtyard of the Temple. The tent aroma attacked his sense of smell. The twenty foot by twenty-foot square was divided into three compartments, or rooms. Spry wanted areas for dressing and a place to keep the morning's sacrifice hidden. With eyes squinting and straining to see in the dark, he called out, "My lord and master, are you in here?"

"Yes" was heard coming from a corner of the tent.

"Are you all right?"

"Of course I am all right. We happen to prefer the dark."

Spry reached out and grabbed the handle of a lantern. He felt for the knob and turned it on. He sat it on a table and looked about as the shadows danced on the walls. His eyes opened wide as Nef casually walked over to him. Spry quickly said, "I have everything in place. Here are your garments for tomorrow morning." Spry was excited. He felt like a child that was giving his father his first gift. "Go ahead and open the case."

Nergal leapt with excitement from within Nef as Nef opened the box. Decedre glanced over at Abaddon, who was still in the dark corner looking on.

The box was filled with several items folded neatly. Spry's anticipation was written all over his face. Nef reached in and pulled out the ephod. It was made of gold, blue, purple, and scarlet yarn and of finely twisted linen. It had two shoulder pieces attached to two corners so that it could be fastened to a beautifully woven waistband made of the same yarn and linen. There were two onyx stones affixed. One stone displayed the names of his ten leaders. The other stone presented the seven regions, one-world religion, and Dr. Shuham which was engraved in fine block letters. They were attached to the shoulder pieces along with two stunning gold braided chains.

Nef held up the ephod, and Spry's chest expanded as he commented on how he had ordered the garment with Nef's world dominance in mind. To Spry's satisfaction, Nef smiled, laid it down, and reached in the box again.

The next item Spry referred to as the "breast piece." Spry began his description with great pride. "Look how striking this is! It is the same color and style as the ephod, but it is in a square that is folded in half and will cover your chest and stomach. See the four rows of precious stones? All are mounted in gold filigree settings." Spry hesitated, pointing to each and raising his eyebrows to emphasize their beauty. "Notice that there are seven around the area of your heart. Those represent the seven regions. Look at the braided chains of pure gold that will be attached to the ephod and the waistband."

"Yes, it is quite lovely," Nef said as he bent over and unfolded an elegant purple robe.

Spry pointed again and said, "Look at the hem with the pomegranates in blue, purple, and scarlet yarn with gold bells between them."

Nef pulled on the robe over his head and admired his reflection.

Spry pulled out the crown. It was a turban with a gold plate hanging in the front by two blue cords. "The plate will hang over your forehead. Notice what is engraved on it."

Nef turned the plate to read its inscription. "'Holy is the lord and master. I like that! I am holy."

Spry placed the turban on Nef's head, then pulled out the final item—a sash of fine linen and attractive gold braids.

Spry and Nef got the garments in place, and Spry suggested that Nef turn around. Nef turned and admired himself in a full-length mirror.

Decedre morphed out of Spry and turned his head as he watched Abaddon float over to him and Nergal, who had morphed out of Nef. "I love what you have done. It looks like a Jewish high priest's outfit. The Jews will understand that they now have a new high priest and that this will be the last sacrifice," Abaddon said as he looked at Nergal. Nergal and Decedre bowed as they re-entered their earthling subjects.

Spry smiled with satisfaction. "Oh, I almost forgot the sacrifice!" Spry ran to the tent opening and ordered the sacrifice to be brought in. "As you requested, instead of a bull I have this little replacement." Two men led in the largest so that could be found in all of Israel. It weighed over five hundred pounds, and as soon as Nef saw it, he broke out into laughter. The pig was dressed in a purple robe with a breastplate, belt, and sash that matched Nef's. A turban was tied to its head, and a plate hung over its forehead.

Nef looked at Spry and exclaimed, "Perfect! We will slaughter it on the altar and distribute it inside the Temple.".

"Are you going to lay the remains in the Holy of Holies with the sacred items?" Spry asked after he dismissed the two that had introduced the sow to Nef.

"No, we will put it in a wing of the Temple," Nergal responded.

Decedre understood. Abaddon had to control his pride and was not going to directly offend the true Almighty.

CHAPTER 8

Nef's disciples and followers that were coming from all over the globe had grown to several hundred thousand.

The level of anticipation was at a fever pitch.

Members of the Jewish community had come to see what the last sacrifice would be like. Many were skeptical. They had heard the warnings from the two witnesses and the one hundred and forty-four thousand Christian Jews that were preaching throughout Israel. Several Jews were curious to see if the two witnesses' predictions were coming to fruition.

Only the invited guests were close enough to witness the ceremony firsthand. The televised spectacle was viewed by millions across the globe.

Many gathered around several big screens placed strategically outside the Temple area. The one area void of transmission was near the old Wailing Wall that was still inhabited by the two prophets.

The trumpets sounded and the crowd grew silent. The tent doors opened. Nef appeared as the crowd cheered and clapped. Dressed in priestly attire, he strolled to the outer court gate and raised his hands. The crowd quieted down. "My children, my one-world religion believers, I am here today to perform for you the last sacrifice to be committed on the Temple grounds. As your messiah, I am who will usher you into a world of safety, prosperity, and health. It is I, and I alone, who will take you with me into eternity!" The onlookers quickly rose to their feet and screamed with exuberance. Many began to cry and fell to their knees to worship their new ruler.

Nef had them settle down and return to their seats. "Your faithful holy teacher, Dr. Shuham, has presented me with my ceremonial attire. It is befitting for your new high priest to wear these symbolic garments at this celebration. I would now like your teacher to bring forth the sacrificial animal." The trumpets again blew as the tent doors opened. Dr. Shuham walked out in a similar but less ostentatious set of ritual garments. Following Spry was an enormous sow being guided and prodded by its two handlers.

The crowd broke out in applause and laughter when they saw how the last sacrifice was dressed. The Jews uttered a collective gasp. A sow was an abomination to God, and they knew it. Many yelled out that it was a disgrace to sacrifice such an unclean animal near the Temple, let alone inside. Several in the crowd told the rebellious Jews to be quiet and to respect the decision and office of the messiah. Fighting broke out. People stood up to get a better look. Supporters of the one-world religion began to throw rocks at the band of Jews that had come together.

Nef raised his hand admonishing the crowd to stop. When Nef's voice rang out it had the power and blast of thunder. "I am here to bring love and pleasure to you all. There are still some who are resisting the new order, but they will soon see the light. Please, let us continue. Ignore those who are cemented in the old and fruitless ways. General Sterns and General Lucas will clear out the troublemakers." With that, the security troops moved into place and the non-one-world religion members were herded out at gunpoint.

The original outer court altar of the Jerusalem Temple is in the area of the Muslims' sacred Dome of the Rock, so to keep peace the Jews had built a new altar close to the Temple itself. Still, it was of the same dimensions as in King Herod's time and had a ramp up to the altar in keeping with the instructions given in the book of Exodus.

Nef, who was followed by Spry, slowly mounted the outer altar. The handlers then tied ropes around its four hoofs as Dr. Shuham held the pig by the head. Nef reached over and quickly slit the sow's throat, and the blood drained down into the trough below. As the pig bled out, it collapsed onto a stretcher. Dr. Shuham ordered six of his priests to join them on the outer altar. Each grasped a handle that protruded from the stretcher and proceeded to pick up the lifeless sow and solemnly carry it into the Temple to place it on the altar inside.

As the sow disappeared into the Temple, Nef turned to the crowd and said, "Today you have witnessed the last and final sacrifice. I proclaim today a holiday—to be celebrated from now through eternity. You may party and seek pleasure throughout the rest of this week in honor of me and my gift to you." The crowd roared with excitement, and music broke out as the audience began to dance and shout.

Nef entered the Temple. He sneered as he looked at the dead pig on the Jews' precious altar. Nef had two butchers at the ready that began to dress the carcass. He then ordered the one-world religion priests to take the dead sow's parts to a wing where he had instructed that the pig was to be roasted.

The next day, Nef communed and cajoled with his inner circle and leaders until the servers appeared. He had all his dignitaries join him, and they were served the sacrificed meal.

At dinner, Nef noticed that Aaron was absent and asked James where their good friend was. "I believe he said that his wife Ruth was ill but that he would try to make the celebration. I guess he couldn't get away."

Nef looked skeptical but said nothing. He stood up. "You are all my closest allies and friends. I look forward to you receiving the microchip that marks you as one of my faithful followers! It will demonstrate to all of your constituents and subordinates your loyalty and belief. Early Monday we will begin the injections." Nef turned to look at Spry and said, "My dear Dr. Shuham will be the first." The group clapped and each one started yelling that they wanted to be next. Nef raised his hand for silence and said, "You will all get your turn within the first day or two. The next privileged ones will be my faithful head of security, General Lucas, then General Sterns, followed by you—my ten regional directors—and then the rest of you. We will then open it up to the military and the GSS faithful. After that, it will be first come, first served, from the global community. They will have sixty days before the currencies will be null and void and destroyed."

The inner group applauded and cheered. Nef continued, "Those who remain stubborn and foolish will not be able to purchase the essentials for life. They will soon come to their senses. I cannot allow disruptions and terrorist actions. If anyone is defiant, they will pay the ultimate price. It is up to all of you to make that abundantly clear to all of those you meet!"

†

James had drunk a bit too much wine. He had not risen to the rank that he had by not being able to hold his liquor and knowing when to stop. Many fine officers' careers were cut short due to their lack of discipline when it came to alcohol. The wine was not ingested to celebrate the Director but to dull the pain. The emptiness he felt at losing Cindy and Chris was almost unbearable. Feeling strange, James decided to leave the celebration and return to his military headquarters. He excused himself and headed back to the office. He preferred the room that he had at the office to the suite that the messiah had commandeered for him. James really did not feel safe in either but had more power over the people around him at headquarters than he did over the GSS in the new digs for the inner circle. He missed the hidden room off of his office in Gaeta.

As James drove, he kept hearing his son say, "Crunch time is coming, Dad! You are going to have to decide, and it will affect you eternally. Please choose wisely. Things are going to get really dicey." James knew that Brad was right. Now that his destiny was set by the messiah, he had to obey, or he would not be able to help his kids anymore. He felt trapped. Pressing the button on his steering wheel, he said, "Aaron."

"Hi James, it's a bit late, isn't it? Everything okay?" Aaron asked.

"Hi Aaron, sorry about the time, but do you have a few minutes if I drop by? I want to check on Ruth, and we need to discuss Cindy further. The messiah is very concerned."

James knew that Aaron would understand that he was covering his tracks with the call because he didn't know who else was listening.

"Sure, come on over."

"Oh, I don't want to disturb Ruth. How about you come out to the car when I pull up?"

"Okay, I will be watching."

"Give me about fifteen."

"See you then."

James suspected that Aaron's home was bugged and under surveillance in case Cindy showed up or tried to contact him. The vehicle that James had was from the carpool. He selected it randomly, so he felt confident that it was safe to talk.

Aaron opened the car door and hopped in. "Hey, Aaron. It is a bit nippy out tonight, so I will leave the car running and the heater on."

Aaron shivered and said, "I can never get over these cars. You can't even tell the motor is functioning."

"Yeah. We could use a little music, and let's drive for a bit." They both knew that listening devices could pick up a conversation from a good distance, so why not make it difficult for the prying ears assigned to both of them. As James pulled out, he turned at the first block and slowed down to see if he was being followed. Headlights appeared behind him, and quickly pulled to the curb and stopped. "Gotcha," James said, smiling as he gunned the auto and turned left at the next block. James then took an immediate right, stopped, and turned off the motor.

A car came speeding past, and then a second car raced by. "Well, it should take them a while to locate us, so I really need to let you know the situation. Did you witness the sacrifice on Cybervision?"

"I started to watch, but when the sow appeared, I felt sick and turned off the ceremony. Ruth went into the bathroom and threw up. My whole family has converted to Christianity. Still, to see that shocking abomination, and to know that this diabolic act was prophesied centuries ago, was both fascinating and terrible at the same time."

"I don't understand Judaism, but even I was disgusted."

"Say, I am gathering together several of the community Jewish leaders tomorrow night at the camp community tent at eight o'clock; want to join us? I am going to present, and after today's desolation they may listen."

"Are you kidding? They see me and they will freak out that the messiah has sent his top spy."

"You could come incognito dressed as a local."

"Yeah, how long before they recognize me? Besides, don't you guys speak in Hebrew?"

"Not always, but you are probably right; it could disrupt the sermon. James, you know the truth. You have lived with this imposter for over three years and watched him develop into the Antichrist that Chris taught about."

"That is for sure and watching him evolve has been an experience I would not wish on anyone."

"You are being stubborn and using your calling to protect your family as a feeble excuse for not committing to Christ, yet you say that your freedom to help your son and daughter is being severely restricted. You are under constant surveillance. They are going to force you to accept the microchip that is predicted in the Bible and referred to as the mark of the beast. Spry has declared that the global community security number on the chips will begin with 666. If you accept the chip to help Brad and Stacey, you will be in very murky waters. You know that those who accept the mark are doomed, and demonic forces could possess you. Your following actions may be beyond your control. I haven't seen any wiggle room in scripture. It is not like they are going to drug you and force it on you." Aaron paused for a second and then looked serious. "However, because of your position, they might do that."

Listening, James responded, "Yeah, I wouldn't put it past them."

"If by helping Brad and Stacey, and the rest of your new family, you put them in harm's way, you will have taken the mark for nothing but eternal damnation. It is time to make a real decision for Christ. You can help the undergrounders as long as possible, but then you will need to flee to the desert as predicted in Revelation. You can flee with us. God will show us where to go, and he will protect us."

"How many Christian Jews are there?"

"I really don't know. It started with one hundred forty-four thousand that Jesus called out. The Bible tells us that these missionaries, and the two witnesses, will open many eyes."

James thought for a few seconds and then asked, "How are you going to protect and take care of so many?"

Aaron smirked. "You are very adept at changing the subject. I'm not done trying to get you to see the truth. Anyway, we have had a pilgrimage of Christian Jews moving south near Ein Gedi to a refugee camp that has been established."

"You mean that the false messiah has allowed it?"

"Not really. He has been told that more and more Jews are moving closer to Jerusalem to be near his statue and the new Temple. I think he likes having them congregating in a specific area. We will be an easier target for him to attack, so he has turned a blind eye to our gathering."

"Well, he has a point. How on earth will you protect so many from his wrath when he discovers that you are all Christian Jews?"

"It won't be a man who will decide our fate—it will be our Lord and Savior. He will divinely protect us, or we will join him in heaven. Either way, it will be a miracle."

CHAPTER 9

James dropped off Aaron and noticed the headlights in his rear-view mirror as he pulled away. Knowing that if he were to call his son, to keep them both safe, he would have to discard the phone following any call. James was glad that he had purchased several black-market phones. He really wanted to get to his secret room in Gaeta, but when he had tried to fly back to his Gaeta headquarters twice since Cindy's disappearance, he had been denied access to his fighter jet. He was told that the messiah had grounded his travel. The messiah ordered James's presence to help orchestrate the upcoming events. James knew that it was useless to try to get to his safe room.

Pulling into the local command center garage, James was sure that the surveillance team would not follow. He parked the car, checked out the vicinity, and quickly ducked into a dark section under a stair well. James pulled out his phone—"Brad," James whispered with a low voice. "Hi, Son, sorry that I didn't give the signal, but I can't risk a ring or buzz on this end. I have a secure phone, but it will only take a matter of minutes for the communications department to locate an unauthorized communication device and determine its coordinates. I must talk quickly. Did you see the sacrifice today at the Temple?"

"Of course, Dad. It was just as predicted over two thousand years ago. Crunch time!"

"I know. I am receiving the mark in a few days. I will be among the first to be so blessed," James said sarcastically. "He wants me to set a good example for my soldiers."

"Please don't! You *cannot* do it, Dad. The Lord will take care of us, and you can't contact us easily anymore. It will be a matter of time before you are caught, or before you accidently lead them to us. Don't you want to be with us for eternity?"

James could picture the pleading face of his son. "Of course, I do, Son. I would love to see your mom and ask for her forgiveness. I would give anything to see Chris again. I admit that I believe now. Far too much of what Chris taught is coming true. Uncle Aaron and Aunt Ruth and the kids have accepted Christ as their personal Savior."

"Praise God! Now it is time for you to accept also. All of your family and closest friends will be together forever."

"You mean that Aunt Cindy is with you?"

"She was saved by angels, and she is in a protected house. We will have her transferred as soon as it is safe. Are you ready?"

James asked hesitantly, "What do I do?"

"Bow your head and ask the Lord to forgive you your sins, accept who he is as your Savior and heavenly father, and ask him into your heart. He will do the rest. Can I pray with you?"

"Yeah, I'd like that, but you need to make it quick."

Brad prayed with his father, and Heaven rejoiced. James did not realize it, but his wife, Chris, CJ, and Archangel Michael were standing next to him with their hands on his head.

James stood up and disconnected the phone. He put the device on the cement floor and stomped it into small pieces. He then collected the parts and threw them in the trash bin before entering the building.

James felt light, as if an elephant had been removed from his shoulders. He had a smile that he could not control and swore that the area around him was brighter. He headed straight for the men's room. As he entered, he removed his military cap, and there it was, the Holy Spirit's mark. He was still smiling as he turned to leave. His staff sergeant walked into the men's room.

They stood and stared at each other. They both had the mark. James felt tears forming in his eyes and struggled to gain control. The sergeant looked as if he was in a state of shock. They spontaneously hugged and then stepped back, not sure what to do next. This was all new for James, and he figured that the sergeant had never hugged a top general in his thirty-year career. "Welcome to the family, General."

"I have never felt so peaceful and secure in my life. I just accepted and wow!"

"Yeah, 'wow' is a good response."

Another soldier walked in and saluted the general. James responded, and slapped the sergeant on the arm and said, "Please come to my office as soon as you are free, okay?"

"Yes, sir, General," the sergeant answered as he saluted James.

Smiling, the sergeant, and new brother in Christ, knocked and entered the office of his commanding general. James looked up and held his finger to his lips making a "quiet" gesture. "Well, Sergeant, I see that you are in charge of the transportation pool." As James was talking, he was printing on a sheet of paper. He held it up: ROOM BUGGED. DO NOT MENTION SALVATION. ACT NORMAL.

"Yes, sir, I am."

"Good. The messiah is concerned as to the disposition of the chips and their arrival time. He needs them by Monday morning." James continued printing. He held up another sheet of paper: WE MUST DELAY THEIR ARRIVAL AS LONG AS POSSIBLE!

"Yes, sir, I can check on the deliveries and get back to you within the hour."

James continued printing as he said, "Good. I also want you to take inventory of all troop transport vehicles and busses that we have and how many we can commandeer to transport individuals to Jerusalem for a national pilgrimage to receive the microchip and worship the messiah." James held up the new directive: I WANT ONLY CHRISTIAN DRIVERS. PICK UP CHRISTIAN JEWS AND WE WILL TAKE THEM TO SAFETY AS PER PROPHECY.

The sergeant smiled. "Yes, sir, I can get that to you by tomorrow morning, and I am sure that we have enough drivers to man the vehicles.

You would be surprised at how many eligible drivers we have in our pool."

James smiled back. He understood that the sergeant was telling him that there were several Christians in his Jerusalem unit. "That is good news, Sergeant Dunlap. Dismissed."

The sergeant saluted and left. James leaned back in his seat and tilted his head as a plan began to take shape in his head. *Brilliant plan,* James thought as his eyes squinted. *Is this really my plan? How coincidental that the first man I see after accepting Jesus is another Christian, and he is responsible for the military transportation section. Maybe I am no longer in charge. Best I listen to my gut even more now.*

James found it interesting how everything Chris had lectured about and said directly to him all those years ago was coming back. James had always acted as if he were totally ignoring Chris or giving him a hard time, but he had been absorbing the information like a sponge. Next up will be the witnesses and the quake. *We must get ready to flee or be taken to heaven, whichever is God's will.*

CHAPTER 10

The Jewish people, especially the leading religious body, were in turmoil. They had been waiting for a messiah for centuries. Thinking that the Global Order Director might be the one, they were shocked when he sacrificed a pig on their holy altar. They had already rejected Jesus whom they recognized to be a teacher, but not God and supported his crucifixion over two thousand years ago. They were confounded as to what to do. The two witnesses at the Temple wall had been preaching to them for almost three and a half years, and many of their faithful Jews had converted to Christianity. It had been rumored that one of their leading rabbis, Aaron Rubin, had confessed to accepting Jesus as the true Messiah. This news had created shock and disbelief throughout Israel. Rabbi Rubin had been teaching against Christianity for years and was a close friend of the man claiming to be the messiah, Nefas Quietus. Rabbi Rubin had served on the Knesset and had been the director of Homeland Security; both positions had been dissolved, determined as unnecessary by the Global Order Director. The Christian Jews worshiped Jesus of Nazareth. The nonbelievers claimed that the Christians started the rumor about Rabi Rubin and that it was a lie.

It was quietly announced throughout the Jewish population that Rabbi Rubin was holding a revival outside of the city in an area that had been set up as a mini refugee camp. The gathering place was designated by Nef as a camp for pilgrims to come and see the talking statue and to observe the Passover with the newly proclaimed messiah. The camp was virtually empty until the announcement of Aaron's upcoming lecture.

The camp started to fill. Under James's order, several military busses and trucks started to appear in outlying cities to transport Jews who wanted to go to Jerusalem under the pretense of receiving the mark, worshiping the statue, or seeing the messiah. The first of several meetings was to start in three days.

†

Nef leaned back in his chair. His lower jaw jutted out a small degree as he contemplated. He took a quick breath and reached for his phone. "Aaron, I understand that you are meeting with a group of your Jewish brothers in a large tent at the refugee camp. My good friend, may I ask the nature of this gathering?" Nef paused, obviously waiting for an explanation.

"Of course, Nef. We are assembling to discuss the early preparation for the coming Passover and to help orient the visitors about your new order and to help them settle in."

Nef squinted his eyes and took a deep breath, slowly letting the air escape through his teeth. "Good. Be sure and let me know how it goes. If I, or James, can help in any way, please do not hesitate to ask."

As soon as Nef disconnected, he called General Sterns. He knew it would be useless to call James when Aaron was involved; and now that Cindy had escaped, he did not trust James. Nef could not wait to get his microchip implanted into James. Once that was done, he could relax. He knew that any vessel possessing the chip would be his for eternity and under his complete control. Until then, Nef had to be cautious about the general and keep tabs on him and Aaron. He called Sterns on his private line. "General Sterns, I have an assignment for you."

"Yes, my lord and master."

"In a couple of days, I want you to send some Jewish spies to the tent meeting that Rabbi Rubin is holding in the western mini refugee camp. Have them go incognito. I want a report on my desk the next morning as to what the rabbi spoke about. It has been brought to my attention that he plans several meetings. I want to know what these Jews are plotting."

"Yes, sir. Consider it done."

"You are a good soldier." Nef disconnected.

Abaddon was standing with his arms folded as Nergal stretched after morphing out of Nef. "Still not used to possessing the earthling?"

"No, but it beats level six." Nergal looked at Abaddon and said sheepishly, "Sorry, master. I love level six! I meant that level three has a different and new set of challenges."

Abaddon squinted his eyes and puckered. "Well, when all goes according to plan, you will be on level three for eternity. Anyway, give me an update on Cindy. Have you found her location yet?"

"My lord and master, I have been trying but no luck," Nergal said as he lowered his head.

Abaddon rose from where he was standing and floated in midair as his face turned red and he began transforming into a dragon. "I don't want you to count on luck, you fool! Start torturing these pitiful human forms until someone talks. The entire area shook as he yelled, "Do you understand?"

Nergal fell face down and touched his head to the ground as he promised his master that he would find Cindy. Abaddon morphed back into a handsome man and settled back into his chair. He told Nergal to crawl over and kiss his feet and then to get back up to discuss their next step toward taking complete control of level three.

"It will not be long before I take power from the carpenter. Then I will possess the ability to know everything and to be everywhere. Until then, I must rely on idiots like you! Now do whatever it takes to get her back and to regain rule over the general and his men. Keep a special eye on Aaron and his movements as well. He may be the key to finding Cindy."

✝

The next morning the two guards that had been sent to arrest Cindy were ordered by the messiah to appear in the conference room at the new headquarters. The assembly was joined by the staff and GSS guards. Because the gathering concerned Cindy, James was not ordered to attend.

"I have been troubled by the disappearance of my top aide, Cindy Sparks. You both let me down greatly by not carrying out your orders to bring her to me. Now you have again failed to please your messiah by not finding her. This insubordination is unacceptable, don't you both agree?" The two men were on their knees before him, and their fellow guards were observing from behind.

"Yes, lord and master, we failed you," they said hoarsely in unison.

The taller guard, Sergeant Milhous, spoke with his head bowed. "We have been trying our best to locate her whereabouts, sir, but we have been unsuccessful thus far."

"Perhaps you are not taking the proper steps to cause enough desire in our constituents to want to help," Nef said with a sympathetic smile.

"Sir, you offered a reward for her return, but no one has come forward."

"So you are saying that I am cheap? I did not offer enough?"

"Oh, no, sir. I am not even intimating that. I am saying that the people don't seem to want any money, especially since they know that money will soon be worthless." Nef stood up, stared at the sergeant, and shrieked, "You fool, it will not be worthless! The money will still be in the informer's accounts. It will be represented in credits!" He flopped back down and regained his composure and continued. "Anyway, I cannot have my faithful fail me so blatantly for all to see. Sergeant Milhous, you were in charge that night correct?"

"Yes, my lord and master."

"Please lie down on the floor face down and place your hands behind you." The sergeant did as he was ordered.

Nef looked at a man standing close by and nodded. The top GSS officer stepped forward. He pulled out an axe from behind his back and raised it in the air over the soldier's head. He brought the axe down with full force. The head was severed. Some blood landed on Nef. He beamed as if he enjoyed the gore and the beheading. The room gave a collective gasp. The corporal next to the headless corpse turned white and began to gulp back vomit.

"Now, Corporal, I am about to show you that your messiah is full of mercy and love. Are you left- or right-handed?"

It was obvious to all that the corporal could barely speak. "Right, lord and master," he said in a whisper.

"Good. Now lie down and place your left arm straight out over your head." The corporal hesitated.

"Would you rather place them both behind your back?" Nef said with a laugh.

The corporal laid face down and stretched his arm out over his head. Nef nodded at General Sterns. Sterns forcibly dropped his axe on the wrist of the corporal's left arm. Blood splattered on Nef's lapel. The corporal let out a muffled scream as he grabbed his left arm.

Nef smiled. "Good, now." He looked up at his personal doctor. "Dr. Hasne, could you please stop the bleeding?" The doctor was ready and cauterized the stump for all to see. When the screams subsided, Nef stood up and leaned over the man on the floor. "Now, Corporal Hashemi, I am promoting you to sergeant. You are now in charge of locating Cindy Sparks. I give you permission to do unto others as it has been done unto you." He laughed. "Now go out and bring back Ms. Sparks, dead or alive!"

Nef hesitated. "I suggest you start with any Christians you find along the way. In fact, if you think it will help, feel free to copy my just punishment of your friend here, Sergeant Milhous. I am sure that the Christians kidnapped her. Doctor, take the new sergeant to the infirmary and see to it that he is ready to assume his duties by morning."

Nef looked around at the ashen faces of the "guests." "I want all of you to know that I can be merciful and a just judge to my flock. When I give an order, it must be carried out without hesitation. I expect all of you to assist the new sergeant." Nef clenched his teeth and hissed, "Find that woman and make these Christian terrorists pay for their crime against the global community. None of you will be held accountable for whatever you do to any Christian who may have information about Ms. Sparks, so get out there and find her!" The soldieries scattered like ants running from a foot about to crush them. General Sterns was the only follower who remained.

Nef sat back on his throne. "General Sterns, thank you for your assistance. Have you made the necessary arrangements to infiltrate Rabbi Rubin's meeting tomorrow?"

"Yes, my lord and master. You will have ears at the meeting."

"Good. Now I need to go change."

CHAPTER 11

Aaron arrived to pray over the designated tent proper. As he entered the meeting sanctuary, the hair on the back of his neck tingled. He took a quick breath. Something great was about to happen that night.

Two archangels stood next to Aaron as he knelt on his knees. "Gabriel, do you have everyone in place? We must protect Aaron. The Lord has much for him to do."

"Yes, Michael, they are in place. The tent area is well guarded."

Jewish leaders and prominent members of the community were showing up to hear what Rabbi Rubin had to say. Most felt an uncontrollable urge to be there, and they were not sure what to expect. Those that had not made a commitment to Christ were perplexed about what to do. The Global Order Director appeared to fulfill the prophecy of their coming Messiah; a ruler who would come as a conquering king and command the earth, but the sacrifice at the Temple was such an abomination that they had serious doubts.

As attendees were waiting in line, they witnessed a few Jews arrive at the entrance and suddenly become ill. They would double over in pain and had to be taken away to the infirmary. It seemed odd, but there were rumors that the stomach flu may be present.

The attendees could not see the guardian angels that touched the Jewish spies, sent by General Sterns, in the abdomen area as they attempted to infiltrate the meeting. The demons within the spies started screaming and tried to flee the inner being of their assignments. They were denied exit. Their anguish caused immense pain within their vessels.

Inside the tent the large gathering settled into their chairs as Aaron moved to the middle of the makeshift stage. "My brothers and sisters, I have asked you here tonight to share with you some important facts about our very existence. Our Torah teaches..." Aaron spoke and lectured for over an hour. The crowd was very skeptical at first, but many began to listen and show interest. Some still harbored misgivings.

One cried out, "How can you turn on us like this? We have trusted you, and you have been a terrific leader and protector of our country and religion for years. Now you have become the very thing that you have taught against."

"Yes, dear brother. I admit I was wrong, but I have found the truth. I want you all to step out of your role as stiff-necked patriots and face reality as I have!"

Three strange-looking men, dressed as if they had stepped out of biblical times, appeared at the inside of the door of the tent. Two men guarding the door stepped in front of the intruders as if to deny them entrance. The two guards bowed their heads slightly and stepped aside. As the three men began to walk to the front, a hush fell over the audience. They strode up onto the stage and stood next to Aaron.

One of the interlopers took a step forward. As he began to speak, there was no doubt as to who he was—Abraham, the father of their nation. "My children, I have come to bear witness of my fellow prophets. They share the truth. When Yahweh planted the seed that grew inside my wife, Sarah, and then into this chosen nation, I first doubted. I now see the will of our Father coming to fruition. Listen to what Moses has to say and take heed!" The man stepped back as Moses stepped forward.

"I have been sent to you to witness to the truth. Our time left here is short. We have cried out to you to listen to Yahweh's reality for well over three years, yet many of you still ignore what we say. You must listen to and follow this brother!" Moses put his hand on Aaron's shoulder.

Aaron sensed a rush of adrenalin as never before. His eyes widened a bit, and for a second he had trouble catching his breath.

Moses continued, "He has been appointed by the Almighty to lead you. The great *I AM* has thus ordered. I'm your prophet and I am here with my brother, Elijah"—Moses turned toward his companion as Elijah stepped forward next to Moses—"to carry the words spoken by the great *I AM* and the true Messiah that you rejected while he walked among you on the Earth over two thousand years ago. He wants you to be a part of his eternity, and he is preparing for his final return. If you accept the mark of the Beast and follow the Antichrist described by the disciple John, you will spend eternity with the monster called the devil, or Abaddon. Listen to your Rabbi and heed his teaching. He will lead you to the new Promised Land!"

Moses, Elijah, and Abraham walked slowly off the stage and out of the tent. The room filled with a reverent silence.

Aaron looked out over his congregation. "You have heard from our founding father Abraham and Moses, who freed our people from Egypt's bondage. They are now telling you to follow God in the flesh, Jesus, the Christ, into the new Promised Land of eternal life. Those that are ready to accept Jesus as their true Messiah and spend eternity with him, please kneel down and bow your heads." Every individual present fell to their knees. After the prayer of salvation, they all became excited as the mark of the Holy Spirit began appearing on each forehead.

"Now, my new brothers and sisters, we must begin our ministries. I'll be holding Bible study every night for the rest of the week, and then you must go out and tell others the good news!"

CHAPTER 12

Something caught James's eye. The red light on his phone was blinking. Nef was calling. James hesitated, closed his eyes and reached for the phone. He was confident that he could answer any questions or demands that Nef might have. He had prayed for the Lord to help him delay the delivery of the Abaddonic mark, and the Lord had answered his prayer.

"General Lucas, what is the delay? It has been over fifteen days. This is totally unacceptable!"

"I'm doing all I can, Global Order Director, but the logistics are crazy with ten different decisions being made by the ten regional kings. The three from the western area are the most troublesome. I'm sorry, but the chips are primarily coming out of the U.S. region and the king is being impossible. I'm also running into excessive wrangling in the religious centers of the one-world religion. The pastors are making unacceptable demands before they will receive the chips. Even though you are the messiah, the leaders want to hold onto their individual power as do the church leaders. The one-world religion pastors say that you may be the messiah, but they worship the supreme being as the ultimate god and will preach what the one-world religion teaches and not necessarily what you say."

"Those ingrates!" Nef bellowed.

A slight smile took over James's lips. "I'll keep after them and get the chips delivered as soon as possible. I'm going up north to arrange for transportation for the pilgrims to receive their marks at the Temple, but I'll be in constant contact with dispatch and will give you updates."

"Getting those chips and starting the mark insertions is top priority. I will get the leaders and pastors in line. Get those chips in our hands ASAP!"

✝

Nef frowned and his eyes became narrow slits as he disconnected from James. He called his new secretary, Molly Stein, to summon Dr. Shuham.

Spry entered Nef's office and sat down. Nef looked up from his desk. "I just got off the line with General Lucas." Nef relayed James's update to Spry. "Spry, I will not tolerate the insubordination of the ten regional kings, and your religious pastors, another minute. I am the supreme being in the flesh, and their petty lust for power will end! As one-world religion supreme leader, I want you to call the pastors to a meeting here in Jerusalem in three days. No excuse for not coming will be acceptable. If any pastors display any hesitation, send a GSS team to pick them up and deliver them to this place personally."

"Yes, lord and master," Spry said while bowing his head. He scurried out of the office to have his staff make the necessary calls. There were hundreds of pastors to contact.

Nef sat down to call each of his regional kings. The three in the Western Regions—Canada, Australia, and especially the United States—proved somewhat difficult.

Nef paused as he felt a tickling sensation as Abaddon joined Nergal inside of Nef. "I'm not *asking* you to come the day after tomorrow and to be in my office at 10:00 a.m., I'm telling you!"

"Global Order Director, I have a full agenda this week, but I could work in a short trip at the end of next week," said the king of the U.S. region.

"You insubordinate little nothing. When your messiah requests that you visit, you realize that the request is an order! If you are not sitting in front of me the day after tomorrow at 10:00 a.m., Nef's voice rose to a roar, 'I'll have your body delivered to me in pieces, starting at the ankles and ending at the neck! I am the messiah, and never forget that for a minute!"

Nef could almost see the distress in the king's eyes, and Nef could sense the insubordinate's trembling as the king started talking at a fast pace. "My messiah, I'm so sorry for any misunderstanding. I will be there as you wish."

"Your messiah and the supreme being will be pleased!" Nef disconnected and grinned.

"Molly, please get General Sterns on the line."

"Yes, my messiah," Molly said as she bowed. Molly was proving to be an excellent replacement for Cindy.

Molly left the room. A few minutes later Molly notified Nef that General Sterns was on line one. Nef picked up. "General Sterns, General Lucas says we are having problems with the chip distribution, especially to the Middle East. I want your GSS men to personally commandeer three cases from the U.S. western sector and have them delivered to the Temple. They may use any persuasive measure necessary, but have them here tomorrow!"

"Yes, lord and master."

As soon as Sterns hung up, Nef was confident that the GSS elite team would be in the air within the hour.

Abaddon and Nergal morphed out of Nef. "Nergal, I hate it when I must enter this idiot and run things because of your ineptness. Perhaps I kept you out of level three too long. Your being in level six for centuries has clouded your judgment when it comes to manipulating these humans. It has made my position weak. I'll team up with you, but you must get your act straightened out and focus on the directions that I give. If that is a problem, I can always find another."

"No, my lord and master, I will do as you say."

"Yes, you will. Now, since you are unable to locate Cindy, you must get James under control." Abaddon knew he had to treat James with some special handling. Cindy was still gone, and he had to get the chip into James if he hoped to control him and his men. "This is what we must do…"

†

Again, the red light. Doesn't he have anything else to do but keep bugging me? James reached for the phone.

"James, my friend."

"Hello, sir."

"Where are you?" James's antennae went up. Recently, anytime Nef called him "James" he knew that the Prince of Deception was up to no good. *What diabolical plot is he up to now?*

"As I told you earlier, I am almost in Tel Aviv."

"Well, I need you to turn around. I am having a gathering of the ten kings the day after tomorrow and I want you to join us."

"What's the meeting about?" James asked a little too boldly.

"Not that I really have to say, but it is to help them see clearly who is in total charge, and I want my inner circle present, so be here!"

"Yes, sir." James felt the hair stiffen on his neck. *That creep has a plan, and I know I am not going to like it.* He began to pray for guidance. As he disconnected from the Antichrist, he heard the beep of his secure burner phone. "Hello?"

"General, this is Sergeant Dunlap. I heard that the GSS is in the U.S. sector. They are pirating three cases of chips and are placing them on a jet to Jerusalem soon. They will arrive early tomorrow morning."

"So that is why he wants me back, to force me to receive the mark with the others. Dr. Shuham met with me two days ago and told me to accept the mark; otherwise, they will hunt down my children. They suspect that they are members of the undergrounders and believe that they are hiding or aiding Cindy. If I accept the mark, they will allow my family to continue as they are."

"You really believe that? I wouldn't hold my breath."

James laughed. "They even promised me that I would be the third most powerful person on the earth. They obviously did not tell me about the chips, so the director is certainly suspicious of my loyalty. He is such a liar. He would hunt down my family in a heartbeat if he thought he could. He is going to wait until he has his mark on my forehead, and I am under his control, so that he can command me to turn on my own kids. I think it is best that I go underground. If I don't, I will be made an example of for the rest of the leaders, and that will serve no one's best interest except that of the Antichrist." James reflected for a few seconds. "Sergeant, I need you to contact Captain Bartlow. I saw the mark of the Holy Spirit on the captain's forehead yesterday. He noticed mine as well. His face lit up, and I know he will be on board. Plus, he is low enough in rank that it will take a while to get the chip forced on him. He'll oversee getting Operation Transport moving. Get him a secure phone and contact me when you are in place. I'll use the code we worked out; so when I call in, you will know how to reach my new secure line. When you receive a call as to my whereabouts, tell them I am ill and still in Tel Aviv."

"Yes sir, and good luck."

"We do not need luck; we have the Lord. Now destroy your phone, and I will destroy mine."

Before James crushed the phone, he called his son. "Well, crunch time has arrived. I have the Jews' escape plan in place but unfortunately, I will not be there to orchestrate it. The Antichrist has me in his crosshairs. If I appear, he will force me to accept the mark or he will end my existence. Not that I fear death, but I know the Lord has a plan for me. I need a 'safe house' to hide in until we make our move. I'll call Aaron and fill him in as well."

Brad turned to Stacey and gave her a high-five at the excitement that their dad was going to be joining the undergrounders in a more direct way.

Brad put the phone to his ear and said, "We are sorry that life just became so much more complicated for you, Pop, but we will overcome.

I'll have a brother meet you at the intersection we discussed last night. He will have the mark on his forehead. The GSS will be out in force, so we need to get you out of Tel Aviv. I suggest that you shed your uniform and try to blend in."

"I don't look Middle Eastern, but I will try."

Five hours later Brad picked up the phone. James was keeping Brad up to date on his progress. "Hi Dad, have you shaken your GSS tail?"

"Yeah, I lost them an hour ago. They are amateurs. I brought Jewish garb in my duffel bag, and I am pulling into a drop area as we speak. I'll have to ditch the government vehicle; any suggestions?"

"There's a ravine in your area."

"Great, I'll leave a little something for them to find. I have a bag full of phones, so I can stay in touch. What's going on at your end?"

"Well, Stacey is getting big as a barn." Stacey hit Brad's arm as he laughed.

Brad handed the phone to Stacey. "Hi, Daddy. Welcome aboard. I cannot wait to see you!"

"I love you. Please be careful and take good care of my future grandchild."

"Will do. Here's Brad. You must hurry."

Brad took the phone back. "I'll wrap up. The farms are producing beautifully. Larry is traveling non-stop, but he tries to touch base often to check in on his pregnant wife. Stacey is too far along to travel. I know you're concerned about all of us, Dad. It will get more difficult with you underground and not helping direct our cause, but we will be fine."

"I've surveyed the area, and it's safe to move out. But first, I have some great news. I can still coordinate a lot of activities to help our brothers and sisters. Since becoming a Christian, I have found that we have a large contingency of Christ followers in the Jerusalem Security Unit, so I will still be able to help until the exodus. I better run, literally. Talk to you when I am in the safe house."

CHAPTER 13

Nef grabbed the phone. "General Sterns, where is Lucas?"

"My men lost him," Sterns said with his eyes tightly closed.

"What do you mean, 'lost him'?" Nef slammed his palm on his desk.

Sterns flinched. "He disappeared. They are searching for him, but he couldn't have gotten very far. He may be meeting with troops to coordinate transportation for the new believers and come to receive their mark. We lost track of him."

"You had better not lose track of the general until I say so! Find him and tell him to report to me personally. Now!" Nef shouted.

"Yes, my messiah." General Sterns hung up quickly. He called the base. "Colonel, I want you to contact General Lucas. Have him call me immediately. Tell him that the messiah wants him to personally report back to him tonight!"

"Yes, sir, General Sterns, but we've been trying to contact him all morning and he is not responding. I'm concerned that something has happened to him. He's never unavailable and has always stayed in touch in all the years that I have served with him. I contacted Sergeant Dunlap, and he said that the general was terribly ill. It isn't like General Lucas to not respond to my call, no matter how sick he may be."

"The messiah and I want him tracked down. Get your men up to Tel Aviv ASAP and help my men find him. Contact Captain Mehdi as soon as your chopper lands; he will have ground transportation for you and your men."

"Yes, sir, we are on our way."

✝

It took four hours for the search team to find the general's vehicle and its contents. It took several minutes to climb down into the ravine to get to the evidence. It appeared that the general had been kidnapped. There was some blood and a note on the front seat of the vehicle. The note left was written in Arabic and said, "WE HAVE YOUR TOP GENERAL. WE ARE THE STRONG ONES, AND YOU ARE THE WEAK. WE WILL RELEASE THE LEADER OF YOUR FALSE GOD'S ARMY WHEN THE DIRECTOR NO LONGER REQUIRES ALL TO HAVE THE MARK INJECTED INTO OUR FOREHEADS. THERE IS BUT ONE ALLAH. WE WILL CONTACT YOU AS SOON AS OUR DEMAND IS MET, OR WE WILL SEND YOU THE GENERAL'S HEAD."

The note was taken to Jerusalem for translation and then turned over to General Sterns. Sterns personally delivered the note to Nef. Nef read it and threw it down on his desk. He looked up at General Sterns. "This is nothing but deception! None of my people would do such a thing. They follow me or they follow the false messiah, Jesus, and there is no Allah. This is a trick. He has defected or is dead. Find him and bring him to me—dead, if necessary, but alive is preferred. I would love to show him, and the rest that proclaim me as their lord and master, what happens to traitors. General Sterns, you are now promoted to general over security and the GSS and are now a member of my inner circle of twelve. You may follow Dr. Shuham in receiving the mark. Your priority is to bring in the Judas who has betrayed me!"

"Yes, my lord and master. Thank you, I will not let you down!"

✝

The individual in charge of the safe house said, "General, we have to move you out of Tel Aviv. The army and GSS are everywhere. They

84

are checking every male person's papers and analyzing their faces for possible disguises. We must get you out of Israel tonight."

"That's okay, my friend. First, please call me James. I have made the necessary arrangements to leave. I need you to get me to a transport center. I have a friend who will help."

"But, General—sorry, I mean James—the transport vehicles are going to Jerusalem, not out of the country."

"I know. The Lord has called me to Jerusalem. I plan on being there when the Antichrist kills the witnesses."

"I thought no one would be able to kill the prophets."

"Better listen to the latest teachings of Pastor BL. I never thought I would say this, but can you disguise me as a woman?"

"Our make-up artist is exceptional, but you're going to give her the biggest challenge of her life." They both laughed.

✝

"Sergeant Dunlap, it's me, General Lucas," James whispered. The sergeant tried not to look startled. He was not sure how the general got to his transport, but he was sure that the Lord must have worked it out.

Sergeant Dunlap didn't know whether to be thankful, stoic, or to laugh. Laughing was out of the question; it could get them both killed, but he had to ask quietly, "How did they turn you into this, and you not be noticed?"

"Martha was a genius. She got me all feminized and then chose a horizontal-striped top. She commandeered two six-foot-six friends to escort me. I have never been happier that I am only six feet tall. To the naked eye, and from a small distance, I look shorter. She also added a few pounds on the waist and thighs to help with the illusion. Fortunately, when my escorts said we were going to Jerusalem, the major security force ignored us because the last place they would suspect me to travel to is Jerusalem. That's why they are at the plane, train, and bus stations. Now, I better get inside with the rest."

"Yes ma'am, let me help you up. Won't it be exciting to receive the mark?"

James nodded. "Don't overdo it," he whispered to the sergeant.

Once James was in the back of the transport vehicle and seated, he noticed that two-thirds of the rest of the passengers with him had the mark of the Holy Spirit.

CHAPTER 14

Nef took a deep breath. His head didn't move, but his eyes pierced into each of his ten leaders' souls. He spread out his arms. "Well, well, well, we have the inner circle together, my faithful twelve. Notice that I have discovered and removed the Judas among us. I assure you all that General James Lucas will be apprehended and I will have him and his head separated." Nef looked at General Sterns. Nef rose from behind his desk, walked around it, leaned against the front, and looked at each member directly. "I understand that some of you are a bit confused. I have received reports that each of you is making your own decisions as the king, or leader, of your respective regions. I am sure that this information was fed to me by that liar, Lucas. Just to be sure, I want to make something very clear." Nef's eyes narrowed as he took a deep breath. He screamed, "I make all of the decisions and you will obey my every wish, or your head will be joining Lucas's!" The leaders cowered like little scolded children. Nef regained his composure. He relaxed, tilted his head slightly and produced a fatherly smile. "You know that I love you all and want us to be a team, but I am not only the leader, but I am also the head with the brain. You will yield all authority to me. If you need to make a decision, call me. Now, I would like you to come with me."

Nef led the procession over to the Temple courtyard where eleven chairs had been placed in front of the altar and statue. Nef had the ten leaders sit. He then turned and walked over to the Temple with Spry and General Sterns. As punishment, and to drive home his authority, the three did not reappear for over an hour.

The general emerged from the Temple and marched directly to his seat in front of the statue. As soon as he was seated, Nef and Spry appeared. They were adorned as they were at the final sacrifice. Nef leaned toward Spry and said, "Has the global community been notified?"

"Yes, my lord and master."

Nef stepped up on the statue base, and Spry stood on the step below. Nef looked at his subjects and then the Cybervision crew. The cameras started to roll. "As your messiah, I am the supreme being in the flesh, and I have come to you to bring peace, prosperity, and security. For my subjects to receive these wonderful gifts, I want everyone to receive the holy mark. I will be the first, and your supreme holy teacher, Dr. Shuham, will administer it."

Spry stepped up on the altar. He removed Nef's turban and carefully placed it on a stool next to them. Spry held Nef's back as he leaned backwards. A numbing agent was sprayed on Nef's forehead. The chip was then injected as Spry said, "With this chip you receive the mark of the true and eternal messiah." Nef was lifted upright by Spry. He solemnly placed the turban back on Nef's head and turned toward the eleven seated leaders.

The statue began to move, and the eleven stared upward at its face. "THIS IS MY SON, IN WHOM I AM WELL PLEASED. WE WILL LEAD YOU THROUGHOUT ETERNITY." The eleven fell to their knees and bowed their heads. Nef held out his arms and looked directly into the Cybernews camera. "You have witnessed the placing of the mark. It is necessary for you to see that I am flesh like you but, as you heard, I am also the supreme being. You will now receive the mark, as will your new Supreme General of the Army and security, William Sterns. But first, I will administer the mark to your supreme holy teacher, Dr. Spurious Shuham."

The entire event was telecasted. The newscaster often made comments and was clearly emotionally affected by what he was witnessing. His voice kept cracking, and he often wiped tears from his cheeks.

†

The following morning as the ecumenical pastors gathered in the courtyard for their meeting with Nef, Cybernews interviewed the world leaders. "Did you experience any pain when you received the mark?"

One king responded, "Not at all, just a momentary pinch. What is amazing is that following the brief pinch, all of us had complete relief from the vicious sting perpetrated on us by the Christian terrorists. I felt the pain leave, but it actually was most noticeable this morning when, for the first time in five months, I didn't have to administer the salve or take any pain medication to function."

The interviewer smiled with enthusiasm and gushed, "That's exciting. I understand that you have all willingly relinquished all authority to the messiah."

The U.S. regional leader stepped forward and said, "Yes, we know that the messiah is the true king, and only through him will we, and our constituents, obtain peace, prosperity, and security. We will be fulfilling his will in all we do from now on."

The interview lasted for two hours as the kings gave glory to the true messiah. The commentator looked into the camera and closed with, "Our thanks to all of the regional leaders for speaking with the global community. I know I speak for all when I say that we cannot wait to receive our holy marks. I will be first in line as soon as the chips are ready for the general public. I understand that the pastors of the one-world religion will receive their marks and directions today. I want our viewers to know that we will be bringing this remarkable occasion to them throughout the day."

The leaders proceeded to their front-row seats, sat down, and waited in anticipation of the appearance of their messiah. The congregation had grown to several hundred pastors from all over the globe. Nef entered the courtyard in his priestly attire along with Spry. They stood in front of the crowd and were given a warm applause. Spry sat down in a chair that had been placed next to the altar. Nef held up his hands as the onlookers rose to their feet in a standing ovation. He turned and sat down in a much larger throne-type chair, and the crowd settled down.

Each regional leader stood, turned to face the audience, and gave glory to the messiah and a testimony of the previous day.

When all ten had completed their testimony, Nef stood and walked to the altar. Spry followed and stood one step below him just as he had the day before. The crowd grew silent. The air was filled with anticipation as Nef began to speak. "I'm sure that all of you watched the proceedings yesterday and witnessed the blessing of receiving the mark without pain. You also heard the regional leaders give testimonial as to who I am. I want to make it perfectly clear that you must accept that I am the supreme being in the flesh." Nef paused to emphasize his directive. "In order to facilitate the new religion that worships the true messiah, I have decided to baptize this new Babylonian religion with a new name. The Hebrew name for messiah is mashiach, pronounced ma-shy-ak. Since my new dwelling will be here in Jerusalem, I will accept the Jews' name for me. Therefore, you are to become Mashiachians, pronounced ma-shy-ak-ee-ans." Nef stopped and tilted his head upward as if contemplating something. "That is a mouthful for my faithful around the world. I'll shorten it a bit to Mashians. I think saying ma-shy-ans is much easier." Nef looked over at Spry and said, "That is less of a mouthful, don't you think?" Nef didn't wait for Spry's response. "I know that the Hebrews won't pronounce it that way, but we will. I have directed that my holy mark begins with the numerals 666. These numbers identify my loyal follower as members of the Mashians. Our new religion will be known as Mashianity, and the new headquarters will be in the Vatican City in Rome. As I have demonstrated, and the supreme being has affirmed, I am the true messiah, and I have come to rule with an iron scepter as has been prophesied for centuries."

At that statement, two men appeared from behind the statue, one on each side. The men were dressed in sackcloth. The one on the right raised his staff. Nef tried to speak but was unable. He could only stand and stare.

"I am Moses, the prophet of the one true Almighty God, who has come in the flesh in the name of Jesus of Nazareth. I led his people out of bondage and brought plagues upon the hard-hearted people serving the pharaoh of Egypt. Jesus, our Lord and your Savior, has sent us to preach the truth, but you are now listening to the great deceiver, the devil, also called Abaddon. He has come to lead you to an eternal death."

The second figure stepped forward. "And I am Elijah, the prophet of old, who also was sent to preach the truth. I brought down fire from heaven to show the power of the one and only true God. I bear witness to what Moses says. You are being led astray by this grand fraud. You have the freedom of choice, and he is asking you to make an eternal decision of death. Jesus offers you eternal life. Do not be fools."

The two men turned and disappeared behind the statue and walked back to the secure area where they had been for three and a half years. A pastor in the back stood up and boldly spoke out, "Those two made sense. We should form a committee to analyze all that has taken place in the last few days and come to a joint agreement. You cannot change the name of the one-world religion without this body of pastors' approval anyway. We believe in the supreme being as the only true god."

The statue began to move as the audience grew quiet and looked upward at its face. The lids of the statue's eyes raised as they opened and began to move along with the statue's head. It was looking over the crowd below as if searching for someone. The statue's mouth opened. Its chest heaved as the fire shot out from its statue's lips directly on the two dissenters. They went up in flames.

The four people closest to the rebels were seriously burned and had to be moved to the infirmary for treatment. When order restored, Nef again stood on the altar.

"I want all of you, including those of you watching by Cybervision, to ignore those two crazy magicians that have caused chaos for three-plus years. They have withheld rain and stolen our children. They have brought devastating war and famine. On the other hand, I have brought peace and prosperity. Do you want to choose a god that brings you pain or one that promises you pleasure and wealth? Now, those who chose me as their true messiah, please bow down before me and prepare yourselves to receive my mark."

Many fell to their knees. The statue's head started to rotate, and slowly all the remaining pastors bowed down. They had no desire to be roasted alive. The first row of pastors filed to the altar. They dropped to their knees and crawled to Nef's feet and kissed them as he placed his hand on their head and blessed them. They stood and proceeded to Spry to be baptized and receive the holy mark. The remaining rows of pastors followed. As pastors were baptized, they were allowed to baptize other pastors to speed up the process and to gain practice for their return home to administer the chip to the populace. There were still dissenters, but fear won out and all went forward while keeping a watchful eye on the face of the statue. Once the marks were administered, the vessels were filled with demons eager for new homes. The pastors, and all who were marked, lost all self-will and fell under Abaddon's total control.

That evening Nef and Spry met in the outer office. "You have made the arrangements?" Nef asked.

"Yes, my lord and master. The smaller replica statues in the one-world religion churches are being destroyed as we speak, and the new likenesses of you in different poses and garments are being placed in the positions of the old statues."

Nef thought for a second and then asked, "Did the Pope give you any trouble?"

"Not after you spoke with him. He's happy to bow down before you. He appears to appreciate life as opposed to death."

"I want the name of St. Peter's Basilica in Vatican City changed immediately to 'the Mashian Basilica' with the motto 'The Messiah Lives,' understood?"

"Yes, my lord and master."

Nef said, "We will christen it when you have everything ready. I will remain here with the supreme being's statue. I may need him to speak on occasion, but I will commute to Rome for a special communion for the global community every third Friday night. We must also get complete control of the monetary system. Announce that in sixty days all banks will be converted. The bank in the north will be the headquarters, and its name will be the Economic Center. All institutions throughout the global community will report to the Economic Center. I want the banks to be staffed by those who have the mark, including management and directors. If they want to continue working, they must accept me for who I Am."

"Consider it done, my lord and master." Spry bowed.

"Now let's go out and join the party," said a smiling Nef.

CHAPTER 15

Bowing before Jesus, Chris lifted his head to look upon the radiant face of his Lord. Chris's celestial body filled with a warmth and peace that he had never known while dwelling in level three. Chris then looked over at Michelle and said, "Heaven is like standing on a beach on the most beautiful and warm day."

Michelle looked at Chris and grinned. "But, Dad, it's like this all the time. God is so great."

The three of them looked at CJ as he ran up to them. "Gabriel's mounting an army to protect the chosen. Let's go, you two." CJ saw Jesus standing by Michelle and caught his breath. "Oh, sorry!" He dropped to one knee and bowed.

Jesus said, "It is time. I am calling the three of you to join Gabriel." Michelle gave her dad and brother a thumbs up. They turned and joined the warriors as they flocked toward where the archangel Gabriel was waiting.

The contingency of protectors bowed on one knee when their Lord and Savior appeared. Jesus turned to archangel Gabriel. Gabriel bowed and Jesus kissed him on the top of his head. Gabriel rose and gave Jesus an update. "Lord, as you know, the camps are almost ready. I have summoned an army to protect the chosen, and we have put your plan in motion."

"I know. Now, go to Babylon and warn the believers—the chosen who have denied the false messiah. They must flee Babylon and go to the desert to the encampment of safety. Tell them not to look back because Babylon's days are numbered, and its fate has been recorded. Send your army to the encampment."

The archangel Michael stepped next to Jesus. He peered into the third level and saw his two old friends at the Temple preaching to the onlookers. Jesus looked at the archangel Michael and said, "I have been communing with my beloved prophets in level three. They will be returning home soon!"

†

Nef, along with his GSS guards, walked with purpose to the fence surrounding the two witnesses. Nef moved close to one of his sentinels. The officer passed him an object. Nef placed it under his coat, turned, pulled the gate open and walked toward the prophets. The sentries stayed outside the gate and watched, amazed that the messiah could approach the magicians without fear of being destroyed by fire.

Nef strode up to Moses and Elijah and looked them both in the eyes. "I've appreciated your help until now. The two of you have played nicely into my plans, and your bold actions have given me a stage to perform on. I thought when the Almighty created you for his purpose, it was interesting how he allowed the carpenter to use you both to try to thwart my plans." Nef shrugged his shoulders. "The Almighty is about to see who the greater one is. I will start by causing you both to fail." Nef took in a breath and his eyes turned to slits as he said, "I don't need your help anymore." Nef lowered his shoulders and crossed his arms, allowing his hand to slip under his coat. "I am here to offer you an opportunity, just as I offered to your foolish and stupid carpenter, as well as Michael and Gabriel. You may both bow before me and give me your allegiance. If you do, I will spare you. In fact, I will place the two of you on my council of the inner circle."

Moses's jaw slackened and his head dropped a bit. He looked at Nef, amazed at his audacity. "You are the universal liar, the imposter and deceiver of all mankind. We would never bow before any but our Lord Jesus and God Almighty. The Lord is with us, and his Holy Spirit dwells in us while we possess these human bodies. The Lord has given you permission to do what you have come to do."

Nef clenched his teeth. "I need no one's permission to do what I want on this earth!" Nef lunged forward as he pulled out a bayonet from under his coat and thrust it into Moses's heart. With no effort, he spun around, reversed the handle in his hand, and gave a backward plunge as the blade entered Elijah's heart. He continued to stab both bodies several more times.

The guards ran through the gate cheering. They fell to their knees as they approached Nef and the two dead men. Nef turned to face the guards and pointed at Moses and Elisha's bodies. "Take these imposters to the city center and lay them in the street. Form a circle around them. Their bodies are not to be moved until I say. They are not to be buried or mourned. If anyone shows sympathy, kill them. I want Cybernews to be contacted, and I want the entire global community to witness the decay of these two bodies." Nef looked at Spry, who had followed behind the procession. "Dr. Shuham, declare this a week of jubilee. Gifts are to be exchanged in celebration of the death of the magicians and the final freedom of all global members from their tyranny." As Nef finished his statement, the sky grew black and rain poured down on a crowd that had not seen rain for over three and a half years. The crowed started to cheer and dance. Several other onlookers moved quietly out of the area and began to mourn. They bowed their heads. The mark of the Holy Spirit on their forehead was visible only to each another.

A man appeared to the clandestine group of mourners. He said in a loud voice, "Do not mourn the prophets of old. They have come to prophesy according to God's word, and their assignment is almost completed. Go now. Tell others of the good news of Jesus of Nazareth. Spread his gospel for the end is certainly nigh." Archangel Michael disappeared.

The news of the assassination of the two prophets spread throughout

Israel. A fellow believer ran up to Aaron. "Rabbi Rubin, have you heard about the prophets?"

"Please call me Brother Aaron. What has happened to Moses and Elijah?"

"The Antichrist has attacked and killed them. They are being taken to the city's center. A week of jubilation has been declared."

Aaron nodded and solemnly said, "It has happened. It was prophesied that they would be killed by the Beast in Sodom and Egypt. Our time is short. I must find James. We must finalize our exodus."

The bearer of the news looked perplexed and asked, "What do you mean, Sodom and Egypt?"

"It is from the book of Revelation. The reference to Sodom relates to the nonbelievers of Sodom and their demise due to their low sense of morality. This is reflected in the hearts of nonbelievers today. Egypt refers to the oppression and slavery of mankind prevalent in Moses's day. The same is true today; however, the slavery is to sin under Abaddon's rule. Now please, we must hurry."

While Aaron and James were preparing to save their flock, the bodies of Moses and Elijah were being viewed by the world's population. Throughout the following three and a half days, everyone who had not accepted Jesus as their Lord was celebrating like it was Christmas or Passover. They were giving and receiving gifts, dancing and singing.

Hundreds gathered around the bodies being displayed. The onlookers were throwing rocks and rotten fruit and spitting on the decaying corpses.

As noon approached, the day was still dark and rainy. Nef had ordered spotlights to be placed around the expired prophets to keep them illuminated at all hours. Suddenly the surroundings went eerily black. The line of onlookers stopped moving. The spectators looked around, confused. A strange light appeared over the area above the two dead men. There was a figure within the light, and the crowd stared in disbelief. The rotten fruit on the bodies disappeared, and the rocks mysteriously fell to one side as if the bodies were being swept clean. Appearing in the light, over each individual body, a figure could be seen blowing air into the mouths of the corpses. The figure in the light looked out at the crowd and waved his hand left to right. The sentries fell to the ground unconscious. The figure then vanished as the two dead prophets slowly stood up as if being awakened from a deep sleep. The crowd tried to scatter; but ever since the figure waved his hand, they could not move. Cybervision was televising the event as it unfolded for all to see.

Nef was celebrating with his inner circle when someone yelled out that the two dead magicians had come back to life. Nef ordered the laughter to stop and gazed in shock at the monitor. Nef grabbed the phone and commanded, "Cybernews." A voice came on the other end of the line. Nef shrieked, "Cut the news feed now! Get this off the air!" The TV went blank. Nef told General Sterns to join him, and they ran outside of the headquarters to a waiting limo. They were only a few minutes from where Nef had the bodies laid.

Nef had Sterns order a battalion of GSS forces to converge on the corpse site immediately. He had Sterns summon several busses to the site. Sterns disconnected from the call, and Nef had the limo stop. They quickly stepped out of the car.

Cybervision received another urgent call. The voice sounded like Nef's. "Sorry about the abrupt notice a few minutes ago. Please roll the cameras again on the two magicians." Michael grinned at Gabriel as he disconnected from Cybervision. Unannounced to Nef, the coverage began again as the commentator apologized for the interruption.

Nef stood in the rain and stared. The two prophets were standing as if they were expecting Nef to appear. The guards were lying in the street. The rain suddenly stopped. The clouds opened as the sun came shining through. The rays lit up the two prophets as if they were standing on a stage. The crowd that had been watching in celebration now stood starring in disbelief.

A loud voice from the heaven boomed, "COME UP HERE." The two prophets began to rise slowly toward the heavens as a strange cloud formed around them. The onlookers could not distinguish that the cloud was made up of the one hundred forty-four thousand who were proselytizing the nation of Israel.

The camera followed the action as Nef and the stunned crowd watched until the two prophets and the surrounding cloud of one hundred forty-four thousand missionaries were out of sight. The crowd began to move. Regaining consciousness, the guards shook their heads in confusion and saw some people bowing on their knees.

Nef began running through the crowd telling them to get up and that it was a trick. He noticed that the cameraman was following him and recording all that was happening. "Turn off that camera. What are you doing, you fool! I ordered the camera to be off!" The cameraman shuddered and said in defense, "But…but, sir, I was told that you called back and ordered us to start filming again. We got it all. The two dead guys going up in the cloud and everything."

Nef looked mortified. "I will have someone's head for this, you idiot. Now turn it back on and focus only on me." It was time for some damage control. Nef took in a slow deep breath and let it out between his teeth as the light of the recording camera came on. "My fellow Mashians, what you have witnessed was the trickery of the Christian terrorists' group—the undergrounders. They had help from some traitors that have infiltrated the Cybervision headquarters. I will personally deal with them. I assure you that the two deceptive magicians are dead, and I have had them removed. They will be cremated, and their ashes will be thrown in the wind. They can no longer harm or affect any of us. Consider what you witnessed on the air as a diabolical scheme aimed at tricking the global community into believing a lie. Again, I assure you that I have the situation under control. You have now experienced the rain that I have brought back for you. We will grow in prosperity and happiness. Let's now work together to grow as a community and remember the rewards offered for turning in any of these terrorists who are trying to destroy our future happiness." Nef raised one eyebrow to let the cameraman know that it was time to stop recording.

Nef grabbed General Stern's arm. "Tell your men to gather every individual who witnessed this and herd them to the warehouse where I had the statue stored. Promise them food and drink as well as a gift of extra credits in their bank accounts. Do not let *anyone* leave!"

General Sterns held up a bullhorn and loudly announced, "Ladies and gentlemen, please listen to me." The crowd quieted down. "The benevolent messiah would like to invite all of you to join us for food and drink. He will explain in detail what you saw and how the terrorists pulled off this trick before your very eyes. All that come will receive extra credits in their bank accounts as a reward." The crowd started to enter the busses that the GSS had brought to the scene. Nef returned to his limo. He knew if he could speak directly to all the observers that he could dissuade them from sharing their experiences. After all, he was the prince of mind control. His concern was about those Jews that were not committed to him. He was sure they had snuck out undetected. Nef thought, *the Jews are congregating in the town of Eilat. Soon I will vaporize those traitors and they will be out of my hair.*

Nef called Spry and told him to meet him at the warehouse immediately and to have the caterers gather up all the food and drink at their disposal.

As Spry and his team of caterers arrived at their destination, the rain clouds had formed again, and the sky had grown dark.

Rain began pouring down as Nef reached the warehouse. He shook Spry's hand as he said, "They are putty in my hands. By the time they leave this building, they won't remember a thing about those two meddling old fools going up in the air."

The warmth and love shared by all in heaven was spellbinding as Moses and Elijah reclaimed their seats with the rest of the twelve elders from the Old Testament era. The Lord Jesus morphed out from the rainbow that covered the magnificent throne. He raised his arms for silence. "I have brought my beloved Moses and Elijah back home." Jesus gave them a hug. He turned to face the congregation. "After breathing life back into the two of them, I called my chosen one hundred and forty-four thousand Jewish missionaries, who are the descendants of Abraham, Isaac, and Jacob, to form a cloud around Moses and Elijah as we rose to heaven," Jesus said as he pointed at the large crowd of missionaries. "These one hundred and forty-four thousand will play an important part in my new kingdom." Jesus smiled lovingly as he looked out over the missionaries he had called. "I've taught them a song known only by them."

Jesus nodded at the group. A beautiful chorus broke out from level seven that sounded like harpists strumming with magical fingers. The one hundred and forty-four thousand sang a new song before the throne and before the four living creatures and the elders. No one else could learn the song. The sound grew in volume until the sound filled the universe and caused the earth to begin to shake.

✝

Possessing the ability to manipulate the minds of all who had his mark, Nef took several minutes to look in the eyes of every individual attending his gathering. Once he had control of each member who had witnessed the prophets being taken to heaven, he told them to forget what they had seen as if it never happened. Suddenly the ground gave way under Nef as a major quake heaved the ground upward. Spry grabbed Nef's arm and pulled him to the doorway. They staggered out of the building and raced to the hotel, dodging buildings as they collapsed. Nothing hit Nef or Spry even though debris was falling all around them.

The quake was local to Israel and was stronger than the worldwide catastrophe experienced in the past. There was no doubt in any rational Christian's mind that this tumbler was related to the resurrection of the two prophets and their ascension into heaven. Nef had barely made it back to his headquarters. It was a newer structure and was one of the finest hotels in the region. It withstood the terrible upheaval of the earth's crust as two geothermal shelves fought for the same space, but the rest of the country did not fare as well.

Over one-tenth of Jerusalem collapsed because of the tremors, and an estimated seven thousand lives ended that day.

Thousands of fence-sitting Jews from all parts of Israel fell to their knees and accepted Jesus as their Christ. They had been hearing and ridiculing the two prophets for three and a half years while watching the evolution of their prophecies. They bore witness to the director, the man who brought them peace and the Temple as he turned into a self-proclaiming god. They observed the mark with the number 666 being forced on all of mankind and the abomination that caused desolation by the sacrifice of a pig on the Temple's holy ground. The prophets had predicted their own demise, resurrection, and the great quake of Jerusalem. It was time to decide to follow the man they rejected over two thousand years ago or to follow the man declaring himself to be the messiah. The choice was simple for most. There was only one God, and he had already come as their loving Messiah. It was time to repent or suffer eternity with a wicked imposter.

As the mark of the Holy Spirit appeared on the converts' foreheads, they began to travel to the camp where Rabbi Rubin had been holding his sermons. The camp had miraculously survived any damage or death from the magnificent quake.

Aaron continued his teaching while James began relocating the new flock to a safer refuge. James and Aaron knew that the safety of the inhabitants in the current camp was very tenuous. They were sure that as soon as the community recovered from the shock of the quake that Nef would have General Sterns and his GSS goons move in to destroy them.

When Aaron saw James walking toward the tent, he sighed. He was pleased that James had managed to disguise himself so effectively that he was free to move about the camp. James had grown a beard, walked hunched over, and appeared to be several years older than he was. He had his skin dyed darker to fit in better.

The two best friends stood together in the tent. Aaron kept reminding

James what a beautiful female Jewess he made when he first arrived. "Perhaps you should change back to that beautiful Jewish princess. After all, there were several good-looking men that fell madly in love with you when you first snuck into camp," Aaron said laughing. He loved to harass James about his first disguise. It was friendly bantering; but, growing up, Aaron seldom ever got to pick on James. James said that he was getting tired of Aaron making up for lost opportunities, which only made Aaron laugh more. "I should have taken several pictures of you when you arrived and put them on the Internet dating services for young men," he said as he raised his eyebrows. It had taken James about three nanoseconds to change into a man's garb once he had arrived at the encampment, but Aaron relished acting as if James were still dressed as a woman.

Aaron smirked as James looked at him feigning a stern general's glare. "Okay, enough humor for today—in fact, enough for good—or I will teach you that 'banana-split' wrestling hold I used to use in wrestling. Then your low voice will be no more. You will be singing as a soprano!"

Aaron hadn't had such fun in years, and James was being a good sport about it. "Okay, we need to get down to business. How many transports are returning today?" Aaron asked.

Referring to his notebook, James said, "Over a hundred, and they have been making nonstop flights to the Eilat encampment. The flight is short. We have transport trucks running back and forth as well. From there, the Christians are traveling to Petra. As soon as I heard the two witnesses had been killed, I sent word to migrate to the old fortress. At the last communiqué, all the guards at Petra had been replaced with Christian guards."

Aaron nodded and asked, "Captain Bartlow and Sergeant Dunlap are in charge at that end?"

"Yeah, and they are doing great. The chaos following the witnesses' resurrection and the quake has kept the army and GSS too busy to worry about checking on them. They have reported that they are stuck in Eilat trying to maintain control of the people and that they are keeping order so that there are no more defections to Christianity."

Aaron rubbed the back of his neck. "The Christian population will expand by several thousand. Once all the brothers and sisters from

Babylon settle in, we may overfill Petra and be forced to stretch into the outer area. Those settlers will not be very safe from the Antichrist and his troops."

"Yeah, you're right; but as Brad always says, 'God will provide.' I have witnessed God's action almost daily. Wherever we settled, the non-Christians became violently ill and developed severe stomach cramps. We shuttled them off to a hospital outside of our perimeter. Some of the sick accepted the Lord in transit, received the mark, and were fine when they arrived at the hospital. They simply returned with the missionary to the Christian camp."

Aaron nodded. "God is good! Now, we must gather the new Christian converts in the tent quickly. Put out the notice to gather tonight. We have to prepare them for our final exodus."

"I agree." James turned to leave.

The camp community tent had become known as the "tent of meeting." It was where God would speak to his children, just as God spoke to Moses when Moses came down from the mountain after seeing God in the burning bush. Oil lamps had been placed around the tent that were kept lit every night. It was a sanctuary for the converts since nonbelievers were denied entrance by the angels of the Lord who kept guard.

The final gathering was to focus on teaching the new converts and prepare them for the journey.

Aaron asked James to meet him early for prayer before any other new Christian family members arrived. James entered the tent of meeting and saw Aaron talking to another teacher. He didn't recognize him and was a bit upset that he was there. This was to be a quiet time for him and Aaron before their Lord.

James cleared his throat. Aaron turned to face James and said, "James, glad to see you could make it. This is Brother C." It was common in this clandestine atmosphere of secrecy to use initials just as James's son was referred to as "Pastor BL."

James stepped forward to shake the new member's hand. "How do you do, Brother C. It is good to meet a fellow brother in the Lord."

Brother C turned and looked at James and gave him a big hug. James stepped back. The hug was not a friendly, manly hug. Aaron and Brother C began to laugh. Brother C said, "Jimmy, you are not very friendly these days. Maybe you should have stayed a woman." The nickname "Jimmy" was what Cindy called James when she was teasing him. James grabbed Cindy and gave her a hug that he saved only for his most loved friends and family. Cindy looked into James's eyes. He had tears running down his cheeks. They were tears of joy and relief that she was okay and with him and Aaron.

James stepped back at arm's length and said, "You totally fooled me. What a disguise! Are you sure that you're okay?"

Cindy beamed. "Yeah, I'm fine. Once I was made to look like this, I was able to travel freely. Brad got word to me through the undergrounders' organization to come to this encampment for safety."

Aaron placed his hands on each of his friends' shoulders. "Well, let's get to praying; we have a lot to be thankful for! Now, if Chris were here, we would have the old A-Team together." The three of them placed their hands in the middle of the circle, grasping each other's hands. They left two spaces open. James said, "One day there will be two more hands joining us: Chris, and our Lord Jesus. We will be together for all of eternity."

Cindy spoke up, "I cannot wait to see Chris again. You know he was with the archangel Michael when I was rescued from the hotel headquarters and helped save my life."

James gasped. "Wow, I saw him on the stage with CJ when he killed the future Antichrist."

The three of them bowed and kneeled.

Chris looked on with Michael and Gabriel as he watched his brothers and sister pray. The smile on Chris's face said it all. The three best friends he had prayed for over the years were bowing before the Lord.

CHAPTER 16

An elderly looking Jewish man, wearing a kippah to cover his head, walked to another Jew standing next to the tent of meeting. Archangel Michael, appearing in his human disguise, looked around at the men and women bustling about. He glanced at Gabriel. "Gabriel, the last transport has lifted off."

Gabriel blinked. "Let's wait a few minutes and then move your army of angels to the new camp."

Michael imagined how the enemy would react to what was about to happen and grinned. They transported out hundreds of new Christians in the non-stop shuttles on the Eagle flights and in trucks by land. James had named each plane and truck with the word "eagle" in it. He dubbed the operation "On the Wings of an Eagle" after prophecy.

The returning airplanes and vehicles appeared to be full of incoming Jews but were full of angels to fool the prying eyes of the enemy spies. What appeared to be thousands of Jewish immigrants milling about the camp was an aberration.

Within five minutes the encampment was vacant.

Sergeant Vance of the GSS received a troubling report from his squad leader stationed at the outpost located on the perimeter of Camp J. He turned to his commanding officer. "Colonel, I received a very strange report from our observation team outside of the Jewish encampment on the outskirts of town, the one we cannot successfully penetrate spies into, called Camp J. Anyway, it seems to be void of any people. They are reporting that there is no activity going on within the entire area. A convoy pulled out about three and a half hours ago, and an air transport left about six minutes ago. The observers thought the trucks and airplanes were bringing in new Jews, but they must have been evacuating people."

"Sergeant, what are you talking about? There was normal movement an hour ago. Did they see any mass exodus?"

The sergeant checked his log. "Just the normal arrival and departure of transport vehicles and airplanes, which we assumed were bringing new occupants into the camp to receive the mark as soon as the injections were ready for the public at large. Now it looks like they were taking people out, not bringing them in."

"General Sterns is going to go ballistic over this. Get into the camp and confirm now!"

"Yes, sir, Colonel." The sergeant left his post.

Colonel Witt reached for his phone. He was feeling sick to his stomach. *Oh, this is not going to go well,* the colonel thought. "General Sterns, I received a very disturbing report from the observation team at Camp J. It seems that it's deserted."

There was a hesitation on the other end of the line. "Deserted? What on earth are you saying?"

"It appears that the continuous arrival and departure of trucks and planes has not been to shuttle Jews into the area for marking but to evacuate them elsewhere."

"And your team just now figured that out? Are they sure?"

The colonel began to twist the ring on his finger. "Yes, sir. My men have entered the compound, even the community tent, and all of the area is void of people."

"You mean that someone was able to get into the tent and not get ill?" Sterns asked surprised.

"Yes, sir. We checked at the Eilat airbase, and it seems that there has been a steady stream of flights in and out of Eilat. The soldiers in the Eilat area were told that the incoming Jews had orders to vacate Camp

J for safety during the quake cleanup. The documents were in order, according to the sergeant in charge."

"I want to know who the sergeant in charge is and who signed those orders!" Sterns disconnected.

Colonel Witt rolled his eyes. *This is going to be an awfully long day.*

✝

General Sterns called the messiah to update him. "Messiah, the camp outside of the city, Camp J, is totally vacant. We have kept it under constant surveillance as per your orders. The observation team has confirmed. They say that a transport plane left about twenty-five minutes ago."

Nef's eyes turned slit-like, and his complexion started to redden. He said with his teeth clenched, "What do you mean by '*vacant*'?"

Sterns explained what he had been told.

Nef hissed, "I want that plane turned around and returned to base so that we can investigate what they are up to. Meet me in the command bunker as soon as you can get there!"

Nef called Spry and ordered him to the bunker's war room. Nef stormed out of his office and headed to the elevator.

The bunker was where Nef had located the GSS headquarters. He wanted the command center on the premises of his abode where he could take control of the GSS and security force if needed. Nef and Spry arrived at the same time.

Nef entered, glancing around. The room was twenty-five-hundred feet square. To the right of the entrance was a hall that led to Nef's private war office. It was furnished simply but elegantly. The attached 12 by 12 room was his emergency sleeping quarters. Across the hall was another smaller office for Spry, also with a small sleeping area. Next to Spry's office was a third office for the commanding general. The operations center was directly in front of him. The walls were lined with several monitors. The rows of desks had keyboards and control sticks on them and were manned with GSS personnel. There was a row of observation seats with a long table. The monitors were alive with activity. Camp J was in view on monitors three and four.

Nef and Spry continued into the war room. Nef said to the officer in charge, "Has the general filled you in?"

"It was I who contacted General Sterns. The squad informed me of the situation, and I immediately called the general who in turn updated you. The general is on speakerphone now with an ETA of two minutes."

"I want to know where this flight is going and where it is now!" Nef demanded as he and Spry sat down.

Colonel Witt turned to his sergeant, who was staring at a control panel. Colonel Witt continued, "I have put all combat troops and squadrons in the area on alert. Our satellite is focusing on Camp J and moving out in scope until the plane is located. It should only take a minute or two."

The general came through the door. The troops stood at attention. Nef screamed, "Sit back down and continue your work, now!"

The soldiers sat without any response from General Sterns. The general quickly took his seat next to Spry and the messiah.

"General, and my messiah," Colonel Witt said as he bowed slightly to address Nef, "the satellite had trouble finding the plane. We crisscrossed the area several times but have finally located it. It has just landed in Eilat."

"Is there an encampment in or around Eilat?" General Sterns asked.

"We know of a camp to the south."

A soldier turned in his swivel chair and handed Colonel Witt a report. Colonel Witt quickly read it over. "It appears that the camp outside of Eilat is empty. This information says that a mass exodus has been occurring for several days."

Sterns started to respond when Nef stood up and interrupted. "Well, where did they go?" Nef was becoming enraged.

"We are not sure, my messiah." Witt took a quick step back. Colonel Witt turned to his sergeant and ordered him to scan out, looking for any movement outside of the area. The sergeant scanned out and then zoomed in on some noticeable activity. He turned to the colonel and reported, "It looks like they may be going to the Petra area, but when we try to focus on the region, the satellite loses its sharpness and the screen becomes fuzzy, much like when we were searching for the plane."

Nef glanced over at the monitors. "That is where they must be headed."

Another soldier looked up at General Sterns and said, "The control tower reported that a plane called the 'Winged Eagle' landed at the airport, and the passengers have disembarked and were loaded into transport vehicles."

Nef stood again, leaning his two hands on the table, and barked, "This 'Winged Eagle' has been flying traitors out of Camp J to Eilat for days and you did not notice?" Nef was furious. He looked at the convoy leaving the tarmac. "I want to know who is in the front seat of the lead transport, now!"

Colonel Witt looked at a log his sergeant handed him. "I have a drone with eyes in Eilat ready to launch, sir."

General Sterns stood and commanded, "Then launch it!" Nef and Sterns sat back down, and Witt gave the order. The drone was in the air in less than a minute and approaching its target in less than three. The caravan turned and headed north.

The convoy, the last one out of Eilat, had more transport units than James had planned for. Several unexpected pilgrims showed up from other parts of Israel. They said that they had a vision and were told to go to Eilat and seek out a Reverend Rubin and to follow him to safety. Miraculously, there were just enough vehicles for everyone. Aaron and Cindy were in the front seat of the lead truck. James was driving. James's focus was straight ahead as he drove safely as fast as he could. He knew that the trucks behind him were close and one mistake could injure a lot of people.

Cindy was looking up. Her eyes squinted. "What is that up there in the air coming toward us?"

James glanced up. "It looks like they have noticed our absence and have sent up their eyes."

"Eyes?" Aaron asked.

"Yeah. It's a drone that has a camera on it to take our picture. Might as well say 'cheese,'" James said with resignation in his voice.

"Should I duck down?" Aaron asked.

James stared at the road and pushed down on the accelerator a bit harder. "Too late. If we can see the drone, it has already started taking pictures. We can figure that the next drone will have more to offer than a photo."

"What do you mean?" Cindy asked with trepidation in her tone.

"Our dear friend, Nef, probably already suspects who the lead driver is, and he is probably looking at us right now. The photos are in real time and appear almost instantaneously on their screen in the command bunker. I know because I set up the center for His Majesty."

"You could have put a glitch in it for good measure," Aaron said as the drone passed over the convoy.

"Yeah, too late now," James said.

"So what do we do?" Cindy asked as she and Aaron looked at James.

"The Lord got us this far, so all we can do is keep on trucking." James appeared cool, but he noticed that his palms were getting sweaty. "Aaron, warn the others."

Aaron got on the convoy radio communication and warned the other drivers that there may be some resistance and asked everyone to pray. The drivers relayed the request to their passengers.

All the escapees understood that the request was not given lightly. They knew that there was power in prayer. Many managed to kneel in the tiny aisle.

James kept glancing up. He was running scenarios through his well-trained military brain. None seemed very good, and the outcomes seemed disastrous. James looked at Cindy and Aaron, who were also straining their eyes as they searched the skies. "We may be seeing our Lord sooner than we thought," James said.

A passenger's head stuck through the opening between the cab and the passenger section. He instructed James to slow down. The passenger had a certain authority about him that demanded attention. The stranger said, "Warn the others that you and the convoy are stopping. Sit tight and trust in the Lord. Remember Psalms 55:4: 'In God I trust; I'll not be afraid, what can mortal man do to me?' Tell the others." The canvas flap closed as the man disappeared in the back.

James looked at Aaron. "Who was he?"

Aaron shrugged his shoulders. "I don't know, but I will tell the others we are stopping, and I'll also share his verse."

James slowly brought the truck to a standstill. He then turned and peered through the opening to the back to ask the man what to do next. The man was gone. "Where is the guy who was just talking to me through the opening?"

"What man?" was the only response from the passengers.

Spry, the messiah, and General Sterns stood in front of the monitor that was transmitting the pictures from the surveillance drone. "Do you really think that the middle guy is Cindy?" Spry said as he squinted at the monitor.

"Yes, you fool, and it's General Lucas driving. Aaron, obviously, is the door-side passenger," Nef responded as he pointed to each figure on the monitor's close-up of the three persons in the front of the lead transport vehicle.

"Wow, Lucas and Cindy are wearing some kind of disguise," Spry said with a hint of admiration.

Nef looked around at the colonel. "I want that lead transport destroyed and everyone in it. In fact, I want every vehicle obliterated!" Nef turned to Spry. "Come with me. The rest of you stay here." Nef led and Spry followed as they exited the room. They went into Nef's war room office and closed the door. "Spry, give me your hands."

Abaddon, Nergal, and Decedre morphed out of Nef and Spry and into view. The dragon said, "Focus on the Gulf of Aqaba and together we will swallow up the traitors."

CHAPTER 17

James's radio crackled, and the driver from the truck at the rear said with a shaky voice, "Brother James, we hear something strange approaching from the rear."

"What are you talking about?" James said, as he pushed the button on his radio to respond.

The driver in the last transport was staring at the side mirror as his eyes widened and jaw slacked. The wave was twenty-five feet high and was roaring toward the convoy. The driver yelled in his radio, "The Gulf water is about to swallow us all!"

James yelled back, "Pray, my brother, pray. Abaddon's pursuing us with his river. Scripture warned us about this. God will save us. Trust in him!"

The driver dipped his head to look closer in the side mirror at the coming tidal wave. As he closed his eyes tightly and prayed, the area behind the truck opened like a huge sinkhole. The water cascaded into the newly formed cavity, and within seconds the water started to retreat to its origin.

†

Nef and Spry had run back into the command center expecting to witness the destruction of the terrorists. The satellite plainly showed the sinkhole, and Nef fell into his seat, shoulders slumping. As he looked at Sterns, his eyes became slits and he hissed, "Launch the armed drone."

"Yes, sir."

General Sterns clutched the speakerphone and commanded, "Send in the mounted drone now. I want the gunships loaded and in the air in two minutes and my land attack squadron in pursuit for cleanup. Arm the fighter jets in case we need more firepower. We will pulverize the entire convoy."

Nef sat back in his chair. "Spry, call our friends at Cybernews and have them send the network's chopper to get this on film."

"Yes, my messiah."

"General, I don't want these deserters to get to Petra! Have your unit at the Aqaba base move up to the northern tip of Wadi Rum and set up a roadblock on Highway 47. I want our heaviest gun-mounted vehicles facing any transport that might get through. I want them parked on and off the road and three deep. Send any tanks you have into the area."

"Consider it done, sir."

The convoy sat still in the middle of a desolate road. The three leaders in the front truck stared out the windshield watching for the inevitable. "Here it comes," James said. The drone was approaching fast. James took Cindy's left hand, and she took Aaron's hand with her right. The three were interlocked and ready for whatever their Lord had in store for them. They wanted to bow their heads and close their eyes, but they could not stop watching the drone bear down on them. None of them felt fear, but it would be right to say that apprehension was in the air. The flash was bright as the missile was launched. It was time to close eyes and pray. The transport shook, but not violently. The sound was deafening as the missile exploded in front of them. It was a strange explosion, because it did not miss and land in front of the truck; it was like the bomb hit a barrier in front of the truck.

James looked at Cindy and then Aaron. They smiled. "Michael," they said in unison. They knew that they were now in his protection. The second pass had the same result as the drone left the scene.

James watched the drone head south as he said, "Two rockets is the drone's capacity when carrying the big dogs. Nef will not give up easily, so we better sit tight."

As the drone disappeared, they could hear the blades of the helicopter overhead. James sneered as he read "Cybernews" printed on the underbelly of the chopper. He leaned forward and glanced to the right as he heard helicopter gunships closing in. "It is just like Nef to send in the news to film the execution of innocent people before he starts what he hopes to be total carnage."

As the gunships came within feet of each transport, they hovered as if to take careful aim and taunt their prey. The gunship pilots knew that the convoy was defenseless. The helicopters flew so close that one could see the pilots clearly. Their oxygen masks on their helmets resembled the head of a locust. James almost stuck out his tongue but thought better of it. He instead closed his eyes to pray for the pilot who was about to attempt to put an end to all their lives.

Cindy looked at James, and James felt her squeeze his hand a bit tighter in anticipation of a direct hit. Suddenly, the area sand began to swirl as a momentous sandstorm erupted all around the convoy. James saw flashes of light and balls of flames. *The sand must have clogged the gunship's engines*, he thought. The implements of death began to spin out of control. The choppers fell to the ground and burst into flames.

"Wonder if Cybernews got that on film?" Cindy yelled above the roar of the storm.

The monitor and the newscast relayed the new failure. The tormentors sat in silence as they watched the gunships fall to their destruction. General Sterns pushed the communication button for all in the war room to hear. "This is the clean-up squadron out of Eilat, and we can barely make out the rear of the convoy. We caught up to the target after detouring around the sinkhole. There appears to be several explosions around the target area. There is also a sandstorm like I have never seen before raging in front of us, but strangely enough it hasn't reached us yet. Should we retreat?"

"No, stay put. I will not let it get to you!" Nef yelled as he stood up. "Michael!" he said under his breath. "Send in the fighter jets and light up the entire area!"

"Yes, sir." Sterns turned to the communications officer. "You heard the messiah, send in the Adirs."

"But sir, the bombs could hit the cleanup squadron in the rear."

"You heard the messiah! Are you questioning his authority?"

The officer swallowed hard and immediately ordered the launch.

The jets were off the runway and on target within five minutes. Before they could drop their payloads, the pilots became disoriented. "I can't seem to find the target!" one pilot yelled. "Watch out, you're too close!" were the last words of the second pilot as they collided near the convoy.

After the two assassins crashed into each other, the others simply shot off their missiles and dropped their bombs. Two more jets collided on return, and none of the armament hit their intended objectives.

The sandstorm stopped as abruptly as it began. The area became silent. The wind started again but only in front of the caravan. Like a giant sand blower, the sand that had piled up over six feet high on the freeway began to be swept away. Within ten minutes the road was void of any sand. The convoy started to move again. There was no cheering, only continued prayer. The Christians thanked the Lord for keeping them safe, and they prayed for the men and women who lost their lives by following the orders of the Antichrist.

The lieutenant in charge of the rear cleanup unit called in to the command bunker as soon as he could regain contact. "Sir, we cannot pursue the convoy until we dig our way out. The sand is more than six feet deep around us. Our point has managed to crawl to the top of the sand and reported that the convoy is on the move again. There appears to be no damage to any trucks. I will keep you updated as to our progress."

Nef clenched his teeth and slammed his fist on the table but said nothing.

The fleeing line of believers regained their speed. James glanced to his right. "Nef must be reaching a crescendo of rage about now. I have no doubt that he is still a long way from giving up." James picked up his radio to communicate with the other drivers. "Keep an eye out. The Antichrist will not give up easily. Report any activity you notice."

The convoy traveled the highway for thirty minutes. James squinted his eyes. "Well, here we go again. It looks like we have another confrontation ahead."

The same passenger's head again popped out of the opening from the back of the truck. He said to stop. Aaron turned immediately to get a glance of Michael, but Michael was gone.

James and Cindy laughed. "Well, you guys have seen him, and I have not," Aaron said dejectedly.

"Guess we know who the Lord loves more," Cindy said as they all laughed.

James pushed his communication button to give a heads-up to the other drivers. "We are coming to another stop everybody, and it is time to pray again. The Antichrist is going to try to eliminate us. I guess we can give him an 'A' for tenacity." The convoy came to a slow halt.

†

An officer stood with the top half of his body sticking out of the lead tank's top hatch. He had binoculars held to his eyes and spoke into his mouthpiece. "Sir, we have them in sight. They have stopped and there is no activity. They seem to be allowing us to remove the blockade. Considering what took place further south, should we withdraw?"

Nef grabbed the radio from General Sterns. "Lieutenant, you have sworn to protect the global community and to follow your messiah no matter what, have you not?"

"Yes, my messiah, I just thought…"

"You just thought that being a coward is better than spending all eternity with me?" Nef asked in a demeaning and harsh tone.

"No, my messiah, we are ready to do your bidding at any cost. Right now, we would like to request that you use your supreme powers and help us destroy these enemies of the state."

"Fire on them and destroy every transport. That's an order!" Nef demanded.

The lieutenant, gave his final command: "Fire at will!" He loved saying that because it always made him smile. He remembered the old joke: *"Soldier, why didn't you fire?" asked the commander. "Because I didn't know who Will was."* It was his last thought.

The shell exploded as it reached the end of the mounted tank cannon. The torch set off the rest of the armament, and the tank blew into several pieces. It was as if someone had put their finger in the end of the barrel. The same scenario occurred in all the tanks and gun-mounted vehicles in the roadblock. In a matter of seconds, the massive force facing the convoy had turned into a pile of metal.

James had been looking through his binoculars when he recognized the lieutenant. James had placed the lieutenant in charge of the unit and liked the up-and-comer. He wiped a tear from his eye as the young man disappeared.

The wind kicked up again in front of the caravan. The breeze turned into a hurricane, yet none of the high-force winds caused even a slight shaking of the trucks that were sitting and waiting on the Lord. When all was done, James, Cindy and Aaron were looking at a pristine highway. The road in front of the lead truck was now free of rubble. The metal carnage was piled on each side.

The convoy proceeded without further incident and reached Petra within the hour. The trucks stopped and the Christian immigrants began to disembark. Every face was smiling as they surveyed the path to the famous fortress called Petra.

Sterns had watched helplessly as he witnessed his armor platoon being destroyed. He saw the road miraculously being cleared and the convoy proceeding as if nothing had happened. He turned from the viewing monitor and said in a frustrated voice, "We can still send them to Hades!"

Nef had to smile at his comment. *Not now but soon*, he thought.

"I can have the MIRVs launched in minutes," said Sterns.

Nef sighed, resigned to the situation and the obvious defeat. "No, if they detonate prematurely, as the missiles did over Israel during the war, the fallout could drift to Jerusalem and kill thousands more. I want Jerusalem safe for my Temple. Who knows, I might find an even bigger sow to sacrifice someday. What does the satellite now show at Petra?"

General Sterns looked puzzled. He then said in a questioning voice, "They are reporting something very strange. They must be hallucinating because they say the entire area is surrounded with white figures that look like men in the air."

Not the first time the carpenter has done this to me, Abaddon thought from within Nef. Nef stood and gave the order, "Let them be. They are not thorns in the communities' side if they stay in the fortress. I want around-the-clock observation. If anyone tries to leave or enter, they are to be captured alive, if possible, or you can bring me their heads. Find those terrorists' offspring of the Jews that are not in Petra. Concentrate on them for now. I want the undergrounders destroyed!"

CHAPTER 18

The air was pure, and the sounds of life were invigorating for the two hundred immigrants who disembarked from the convoy and were about to enter their new shelter. The transport vehicles, which were driven from Eilat and attacked ruthlessly by the ultimate force of evil, were emptied. The passengers headed toward the entrance to Petra. They exhibited a look of excitement and a radiant glow from their deep spiritual experience. They had witnessed the power of God firsthand.

James, Cindy, and Aaron remained at the end of the line. James's heart skipped a beat as he stepped through the opening into their temporary new home. He slowly looked up until his neck was crimped. The walls appeared to go on forever.

James rubbed his neck as he peered ahead. "Notice how the dusty trail curves gently downward. The trail is known as the Wadi Musa, or the Valley of Moses. See the small rock outcropping to the left and right of the path. They are small Nabataean tombs. The tombs were carved into the dry rock." James jerked his head left as he said, "Come on. Up ahead are the walls of sandstone, and just beyond is the narrow cleft revealing the entrance to the Siq, or the principal route into Petra itself."

James looked over at Cindy and Aaron and continued his narrative, "The Nabataeans, who once occupied Petra, were expert hydraulic engineers. The walls of the Siq were lined with channels and refitted with clay pipes of efficient design. The ancient pipes had been utilized to carry drinking water to the city. A dam to the right of the entrance diverted an adjoining stream through a tunnel to prevent it from flooding the Siq. It was obvious that God had protected the waterway that fed the stream since the water was clear and free of any wormwood poison or blood from the third trumpet.

Once inside the Siq, the path narrowed to little more than fifteen feet in width. The walls towered up hundreds of feet on either side. The floor, originally paved by ancient inhabitants, was now largely covered with soft sand. The Siq twisted and turned. The high walls all but shut out the early morning sunlight until, abruptly, through a cleft in the rock, James saw the first glimpse of the city of Petra. It was carved out of pale reddish sandstone. James, Cindy, and Aaron stopped and looked with admiration at ornate pillars supporting a portico surmounted by a central urn and two flanking blocks jutting out from the cliff face ahead. It was known as the Khazneh.

James had learned about Petra while attending the National War College. It was a remarkable place and virtually impenetrable from land. He knew that it was impossible for an enemy to enter the sanctuary of the city itself unnoticed. He also knew that it would not be the Romans who were going to try to destroy them. The prince of deception, who wished him and his fellow Christians dead, would use all means of firepower available to him. One nuclear-tipped bomb would do the job nicely. James also understood that the Lord could keep them all safe if that were his will. James had witnessed God's handywork firsthand.

James and his two closest friends traveled on. As they passed the Khazneh, they marveled at its intricate ornate carvings, and even more at how well it was preserved. Aaron tapped James on the shoulder and nodded toward the heart of Petra. A broad track from the Khazneh led to the main street of Roman Petra, which was paved with cut stone and lined with columns. Toward the amphitheater was an open marketplace and a nymphaeum, or public fountain. At the opposite end was the Temenos Gateway that marked the entrance to the courtyard of the Temple of Dushara.

James pointed and said, "The Temple is popularly known as the Qasr al-Bint Firaun, or the Castle of Pharaoh's Daughter." It was a large free-standing structure built of massive blocks of yellow sandstone. It had been extensively restored. "Dushara was the principal god of the

Nabataeans. His partner, the fertility goddess, Atargartis, was worshiped at the Temple of the Winged Lions over there." James pointed again. "It faces the Temple of Dushara from that low rise to the northeast of the Temenos Gateway. In Roman times, these Temples would have been taken over for the worship of the appropriate Roman gods—possibly Apollo and Artemis, respectively. In the city's Byzantine period, it was likely that they were adapted for Christian worship."

"Well, aren't we fortunate to have a personal tour guide," Aaron said.

James raised his left eyebrow and tilted his head slightly to the right and smirked.

James, Cindy, and Aaron entered into the old Temple of Qasr al-Bint Firaun and shook hands with the current pastor, Rabbi Barak. "We are so excited to have you here, Brother Rubin, and your guests as well. Please know that we have all prayed, and it is you who will lead us from this moment on. What should we do now?"

Aaron solemnly said, "Pray. That is all we can do, pray and wait for our Lord's guidance. I believe that archangel Michael is still protecting us, so we wait and pray." They all kneeled.

Nef sat and stared at the Petra area on the monitor. The screen was blurry. He decided to give up the hunt and resigned to move forward, ignoring the Jews for the time being. *I will destroy them after I take the carpenter down and they lose Michael's protection*, he thought to himself. Nef turned to Spry. "Before we have any more defectors, we need to proceed with the markings. Announce over Cybervision that if anyone has not received the mark by the end of the announced time period, they will be denied access to food and water. That will be just the start of the punishment for those who reject my protection. If they choose to join the terrorists that have caused such pain to the global community for over three-and-a-half years, they will die! Be sure that Cybernews emphasizes my intentions. Even though we are still cleaning up here in

Jerusalem, we need to get the lines moving. Start in the morning." Nef left the war room.

Nef appeared early at the marking site. He wanted to personally congratulate those who received the mark to emphasize the importance of the ritual. Spry began the microchip insertion ceremony but it became clear after two hours that the turnout would be embarrassingly minimal. Only a few hundred appeared at the morning insertion. Nef was infuriated.

The newscaster cautiously approached Nef for his comments on the turnout. He posed the question carefully. "My messiah, the number of attendees today has been light. Do you expect more to arrive to have the blessed opportunity to declare their love for you?"

Nef looked at the reporter. "My loving followers are being delayed here in Jerusalem because of the quake cleanup. I understand that the churches around the globe are mobbed with believers seeking the privilege of declaring their loyalty to me and my Mashian church." Nef paused, then added, "As a further expression of my love and appreciation for my dedicated church members, I have decided to reward the new Mashians with the honor of being first in line for all global needs. They may move to the front of any line for food, shelter, repairs, and so on. I will have the Global Social Service issue a number declaring the recipient's priority based on having the mark."

That very afternoon, fights broke out as Jews who had been waiting several hours in the food and water lines watched as other Jews with the mark showed up and immediately moved in front. Within three days, the lines to receive the privileged mark had grown to several thousand in Israel as well as around the global communities.

Nef wanted to accelerate the placement of his mark on as many as possible. He announced that those without the mark were no longer eligible to own property. By the authority of the one true messiah, Cybernews declared, any individual holding title to a home past the cut-off date for receiving the blessed mark will lose their right to own any property, and it will be confiscated and reassigned to another family. The decree was a global one. People began to show up at dawn to receive the messiah's mark.

Not all felt compelled to take a step toward hell. They had heard about the Bible's prediction, or someone warned them about the coming Antichrist and the infamous number 666. They either had heard it from the missionaries when the missionaries were spreading the truth around the globe or knew a Christian that had shared the true Christ; or perhaps they had heard about the book of Revelation in their younger years. Some simply did not want to relinquish their power to Nef. They remained undecided.

"Well, Nergal and Decedre, I told you that they would scamper to me like hungry dogs to get my mark. The global community has learned to accept a one-man rule and to rely completely on my government to survive. Even the U.S., which was under the carpenter's protection, turned on him and he withdrew. It has joined the fold. I have risen to supreme power through the camouflage of peace, prosperity, and security. I took over their banks, I gave them healthcare, and now I run the industries as well as the energy supplies. I have eliminated the hard currency and easily convinced all that a personal mark is the safest way to preserve one's identity. My mark, therefore, is simply a natural progression."

Nergal spoke up. "My lord and master, what about the Afghan warlord and others who refuse to bow down before you? He is setting a bad example for other global members in the region. He says he will bow to no man and that if Allah stood in front of him, he would not yield. The members of his circle of influence are more afraid of him than of you. He has them growing their own food, and they have access to plenty of water and have developed their own filtration systems. His fighting army has kept all GSS forces out. The demons in him are too strong to control; they even defy Colonel Odium and General Raze. The warlord is more of a disruption in the region than the Christians."

Abaddon hissed, "Nergal, we must stop this fool and set an example."

"I can have Sterns take the army of GSS forces and destroy the entire village."

"No, let's use him to further our cause and to send a message to other rebellious leaders. I will convert him and he, in turn, will convert the rest of his followers for us. If he proves to be too difficult, which I doubt, then my troops can escort him to Hades."

Abaddon and Nergal entered back into Nef. Abaddon had a plan, and he wanted to be in charge. The dissident, refusing to yield his loyalty to the Antichrist, was about to be introduced to a power he had never imagined existed.

CHAPTER 19

Nef picked up the phone. "General Sterns." There was a short pause. Sterns's voice came on. "Yes, master?"

"General Sterns, I would like to go visit a gentleman in the Afghanistan region. His name is Mir Akbar Hotaki. Have your regional GSS officer approach with a white flag of truce. Make it happen."

"Yes, sir."

Sterns relayed the command to his subordinate and within a few days a colonel in the GSS was able to start communicating with the target's closest advisor.

✝

The advisor approached his tribal chief in his leader's abode and bowed slightly. Sajad, the chief's brother and closest advisor, had learned many years ago how best to stay alive and serve his older brother. The chief had a complicated persona. He could be a determined protector, but he could also be ruthless. If he felt any treason or competition for control, he would remove the culprit's head without hesitation, brother or not. "Chief Hotaki, my brother, a Colonel Balosha from the GSS wishes to meet with you under a white flag."

"I should cut off the head of the dog and send it back. What does he want?" Hotaki replied with contempt.

"He says he would like to negotiate a visit by the messiah himself. See how important you have become?"

"I have no desire to see some make-believe god."

"But as your advisor, I would suggest that you consider your response. There could be some real financial gain here. Since hard currency will soon be eliminated and terrorist activity has all but ceased, you could use some more credits for your coffers."

"What do you mean?"

"Let him come. But, without any security, just a pilot in a two-seated helicopter. His followers will pay dearly for his return."

Hotaki grunted. "He will never agree."

"Maybe not. He thinks of himself as a god, so he may not fear anything or anyone. We will help educate him that you are worthy of his fear."

"How many credits do you think?"

Sajad shrugged his shoulders. "Millions."

"I've seen some of his magic on Cybervision. You think it is real?" Sajad noted that Hotaki showed some concern for the first time.

"Not a chance. Even though he may play a mean game of 'chicken,' if we hold tight, he and his cronies will fold, and we will be richer."

"Okay, set it up, but I still doubt he will be so stupid as to come alone."

"Well, as long as we have him, no one will risk his life by attacking. Besides, if he were planning us harm, he would have sent in his GSS army."

†

Sajad sat down across from his brother. "Our honored guest will be coming in—as we demanded—at the end of the week with one pilot in a two-seat chopper with no armament. I suggest you vacate the area until I can verify that he is alone and unarmed. Take most of your army with you so that only a few of your men are injured in case it is a trick. You might want to take some women and your sons, as well. If you do not mind, I would like my family to join you, but I will remain to negotiate and notify you if it is safe to return."

Chief Hotaki reflected for a moment. "Fine. I will reward you for your bravery and dedication and for being a true brother. Your family is welcome to join us. We will leave early in the morning in case he has something up his sleeve."

Four days after the chief's departure the remaining tribal members watched as Nef arrived. It was as ordered—a two-seat helicopter that appeared to be unarmed. Nef stepped out, briskly walked over to the apparent leader, and firmly shook his hand.

"Welcome, I am Chief Hotaki's brother and head counsel, Sajad. I hope you understand, messiah, but I must have my men search you." Nef raised his arms out from his sides as one of the guards frisked him thoroughly.

Nef was more than upset but was not about to show his true colors until the proper time. As Nef was being searched, the pilot and his chopper were also being examined. Sajad smiled and placed his right hand on Nef's back in a friendly way. "Things look good. I am glad you chose to come visit us. Now, please follow me."

Nef and his escorts entered a compound with several dwellings. In the center was a single-level-structure that looked to be over 7,000 square feet boasting beautiful stone walls—glistening white—and a front entrance displaying ten-foot-high double doors and a covered porch that extended ten feet out and wrapped around the house. As they approached the obvious home of the chief, Nef noticed that the houses closest to the palace were very plush but that as the perimeter widened, the dwellings seemed to deteriorate into small shacks. It was evident that the chief received all the funds and spent them lavishly on himself and his family.

"My kind of dictator," Abaddon said to Nergal from within the confines of Nef.

Nef was surprised at the accommodations. The interior of the palace was exquisitely decorated. The rugs were of expensive fine wool. The curtains draped from ceiling to floor and had ornate figures woven into the pattern. The furniture reflected the magnificent furnishings in the Vatican. On the wall hung a large six-foot-high portrait of a man. Nef assumed it was the likeness of the chief. The side walls were decorated with spears and ancient swords that were crossed. The courtyard adjacent to the spacious living room had a beautifully carved water treatment only steps from the porch. The windows were open, and the sound of running water as it cascaded down several tiers of rock was pleasing to listen to as Nef sat down.

Nef was impressed at how Sajad did his best to make Nef feel comfortable. *Hotaki must have quite a hold on these people,* Nef thought to himself as he smiled at his host.

As Sajad sat down he said, "May I have some tea brought for you?"

"Yes, Sajad, that would be nice."

Sajad summoned a guard to bring the tea. He whispered something into the guard's ear.

Nef asked with a sly grin, "Asking your brother to join us?"

Sajad raised his eyebrows and asked Nef if he found the trip to the hilly region to be pleasant.

The village, if you could call it that, was situated in a small valley surrounded by high cliffs. Nef knew the history of the tribe in detail. After all, Abaddon had helped shape Hotaki, and thousands more like him, from their birth.

Hotaki's tribe had been in existence for hundreds of years. It had grown to the tip of the pyramid in power and prestige. With the geography being perfect for training soldiers, without the prying eyes of the outside world, the area was known as a terrorist's paradise. Hotaki personally ran the training camps and reaped a great financial reward for doing so.

Nef looked out the window at the surrounding mountains. He understood why Hotaki's tribe had survived through the centuries of fighting going on around it. It was virtually impossible to penetrate the fortress unnoticed, and he was sure that the chief had his army high on the cliffs watching. Nef knew that the passages in and out of the compound were secret. Abaddon, while in command from within Nef, thought it was clever of the chief to have Nef screened while the chief remained in hiding. If there were an attack, he would avoid it or come down out of hiding to counterattack. "The chief is a good warlord and is very self-confident. However, his arrogance will prove to be his demise," Abaddon said as his eyes squinted and Nergal nodded in agreement.

Forty minutes later, Chief Hotaki appeared at the entrance to the parlor where Sajad and Nef were still visiting. The brother jumped to his feet and bowed his head as the chief entered the room. Nef continued to sit until the chief was close, then sat his teacup down and rose to shake hands. "You have a lovely place, and your brother has been most hospitable."

Hotaki reached out his hand to shake Nef's. "It is good to meet you, Mr. Director. Should I call you messiah?" Hotaki responded in perfect English with a British accent.

"My followers call me 'my messiah'," Nef answered in Hotaki's native tongue.

"You speak perfect Dari."

Nef responded in a mater-of-fact posture. "I speak all languages, and dialects of each language as well."

"I'm impressed. It is good to have talents. I can speak four languages. I graduated from Cambridge University and therefore have good English skills. If you prefer English, I can accommodate you comfortably."

Nef looked Hotaki directly in the eyes as he spoke in Dari. "I am just as comfortable in either language."

Hotaki locked eyes with Nef. He raised one eyebrow as he asked in English, "Why did you want to come see me?"

Nef gestured toward the chair he had been sitting in. "May I?"

Hotaki looked at the chair. He said in a matter-of-fact tone, "Oh, where are my manners? Sit, please sit."

Both men sat down. Nef leaned forward slightly and said, "We are getting close to eliminating the current different monetary systems and converting to only credits in the Central Global Bank. In order to trade in the world, one must be part of the community and a member of the new religion called Mashianity. I am here to ask you to join the universal society and to be baptized into my new religious family."

The chief sneered, stood up, and said through clenched teeth, "I bow to no man. Even if Allah were here, I would not bow. I am the chief, and no other is above me! Sajad, take this intruder into custody and move him to the prisoner quarters at once."

Sajad, who had been standing quietly in the background, stepped forward and politely asked Nef to go with him. Four armed guards appeared. Each was carrying an automatic pistol. Nef willingly agreed. In fact, Nef was enjoying the moment.

The four men escorted Nef to his new domicile. They pushed Nef into the room, closing and locking the door. The room was small, cold, and dimly lit. Nef should have been intimidated and uncomfortable; but two days later, when the chief and his brother entered the room, Nef looked up and grinned. The scraps of food given to Nef during his confinement were untouched and still sitting on a small table. Nef looked at Hotaki and continued to smile as he said, "My offer for you and your tribe to swear allegiances to me is still available."

Chief Hotaki laughed. He had the four guards and Sajad put on ski masks. They moved behind Nef and told him to sit on the floor. A guard tied Nef's hands behind him, and another guard put a black hood over Nef's head. Nef heard the door open and Chief Hotaki say, "Film this and send it through Cybervision." He leaned over and said to Nef, "When I pull off the hood, you are to read the teleprompter next to the camera and do not deviate!"

Chief Hotaki stood in front of the camera. The recording light came on. "I am the man in charge of this Afghanistan region. I am Chief Hotaki, and I am now in control of the director. I believe most of you now call him your messiah. We have captured your precious leader. We expect you to place one hundred million credits into our account at the World Bank and give us total assurance that no retaliation will be launched." Hotaki looked up from the camera and said, "Bring in the other prisoner." The door opened and the pilot from the helicopter was pushed to the floor. Two of the four guards behind Nef stepped over to the prisoner, grabbing the pilot by each arm and forcing him to his knees. Hotaki looked into the camera lens and pulled out a large machete from his belt. "If you do not acquiesce to my demands, then this is what will happen to your messiah!" The chief raised the machete and then thrust it downward onto the pilot's neck severing his head.

Chief Hotaki then removed Nef's hood. Nef ignored the pilot's headless body lying in front of him. The chief nudged Nef and pointed to the teleprompter.

Nef calmly sat and reviewed what the idiot behind him had put up for him to read. One of the guards struck the back of Nef's head with the butt of his gun. Nef's head did not move.

Nef ignored the teleprompter and said, "I am the invited guest of Chief Hotaki, his brother Sajad, and their tribal family. They have, for the most part, been most hospitable toward me. As the messiah and the supreme being in the flesh, I am loving and forgiving. There is nothing that they can do to me without my specific permission, so please don't worry. My supreme holy teacher is praying for my safe return, and he asks you all to join him. He understands that my pilot, who was just martyred in my name, will be with me for all eternity and will have a place of great honor. I want my hosts to know that I am sure they do not know what they have done and therefore I forgive them for their indiscretions." Nef smirked as the chief tried to motion for the cameraman to stop taping, but the chief was unable to move. "These fine men do not know what they are doing because they have yet to accept Mashianity as their new religion, but I will continue to share the beauty of Mashianity devotion with them. Thank you for all of your prayers and concern. We will get back to you soon."

The chief screeched, "Turn that off!" Hotaki put his face within an inch of Nef's and said, "I don't know what you think you are doing. You have forced me to send your ear to your religious teacher so he will know that I mean business." A guard stepped up to Nef and took out a knife; another guard grabbed Nef's ear. The guard holding the knife placed the blade on Nef's ear. He yelled as he dropped the knife to the floor. His palm began to welt from the extreme heat of the knife's handle. The other guard let go of Nef's ear as Nef stood up. The rope tying Nef's wrists behind his back fell to the ground. The chief and his men were unable to move. The chief cried out, "I cannot see! I cannot see!"

Nef stepped forward. He looked at each man in the room. He addressed Hotaki's brother. "Sajad, your brother has spoken his last words until I say differently. Now, please lead your blind brother and follow me."

Nef turned and walked through the door into the sunlight. Sajad was leading Hotaki, who was making muffled grunts and moans because he was unable to speak. The four guards and the cameraman followed. They were obviously struggling to disobey but to no avail.

The entire tribe was gathered outside the holding cell watching a monitor that was placed for them to view the telecast. As Nef led the group of seven down the steps and onto the common area, the tribesmen and their families fell in behind them. The chief's family moved up next to him as did Sajad's. Nef heard Hotaki's wife's voice. "What's going on? Why are we following this prisoner up the hill? Akbar, speak to me! Akbar Hotaki, what is wrong?"

"He cannot speak or see, my sister," Sajad said quietly with panic in his voice. "We cannot resist. Please cooperate."

Hotaki looked in his wife's direction. He screamed in his mind, *Go back, go back, my queen. Run from this monster. He has superpowers as I have never seen. We are in danger. Run!* Hotaki did not realize that no one in the parade could turn back. They were being controlled by new and more extreme demonic powers.

The procession walked up a winding path to the top of a high cliff at a fast clip. When Nef reached the top, he showed no sign of exertion, yet the chief could barely breathe. The rest of the tribe were heaving for breath as well.

The top of the cliff was a flat area where generations of tribal members had gathered for ceremonies and sacrifices. Nef walked to the edge and looked down. It was a two-hundred-fifty-foot drop down to sharp rocks. He saw skeletons at the bottom. He turned and motioned for the guard that had butted his head to step forward. The guard struggled but could not stop himself from walking to the edge of the cliff. Nef raised his arm and pointed. The guard jumped to his death.

The chief still could not see but heard screaming and suddenly felt ill. Nef pointed to the guard that had grabbed his ear, and the scene was repeated. He pointed to the other two guards who had set the pilot up for assassination; they involuntarily ran to join their comrades. The chief could hear their cries of panic as they fell to their death.

What Hotaki could not hear was the gnashing of teeth and the shrieks of horror as the four guards were being ushered into level six. The demons of Hades took pleasure in repaying Abaddon's tormentors.

Nef pointed to the wives of the guards, and they jumped off the cliff. The sound and shrills of the screaming wives caused Hotaki's blood to run cold. *Allah, what have I done?* he thought in dread.

Nef turned to the chief, who was shaking and had tears running down his cheeks. Nef pointed his finger at the chief's wife. She walked to the edge of the cliff. "Your wife and then your family are next," Nef said with some sadness in his voice.

Suddenly Hotaki's voice returned. The chief cried out, "No, please forgive me." He dropped to his knees and began to cry.

Nef said, "Crawl to me and kiss my feet and then my right hand. I will bless you and forgive you."

The chief crawled as quickly as he could to Nef and blubbered out, "Thank you, my lord and master." The chief's brother dropped to his knees and crawled toward Nef as all the tribesmen fell to their knees as well. Nef touched the chief's eyes and his eyesight was restored.

Hotaki sighed and his heart raced as Nef led the procession back down the mountain. When they reached the village, the messiah called Spry and instructed him to come to the stronghold and bring the area pastor to join them. He ordered Spry not to mention to anyone that he was safe. The world community was still in global prayer for their messiah's safety, and Nef was enjoying the attention.

Spry and a district pastor arrived within ten hours. During the waiting time, Nef educated the tribe in their new religion and told them what would be expected of them.

†

Nef had the chief, his brother, the cameraman, and four new guards enter the same room that he had been held captive. The camera began to roll, and Spry had arranged for the feed to be live around the globe for all to see. Nef looked into the camera lens. "My beloved Mashians, I am not only safe but doing very well. I am your loving and forgiving messiah and my captor, Chief Akbar Hotaki, has a few words to say."

Chief Hotaki stepped in front of the camera. "My fellow believers, I was shown the light and have asked my messiah to forgive me and my family. He has graciously given me a blessing and has offered to have the holy teacher of our new church join my messiah and baptize me into Mashianity for all of you viewers to see. I was a sinner and nonbeliever, and now he has shown me the way."

Spry stepped next to the chief in front of the camera. He placed his hand on Hotaki's back, and Hotaki leaned back. Spry sprayed his forehead with a numbing solution. Nef stepped within camera range and injected the chip. The room broke out in applause. Hotaki looked into the camera and announced, "My family and my brother Sajad, and his family will be baptized by the regional Mashianity pastor, and then my entire tribal community will be baptized. May the supreme being bless us all, and may we follow the messiah to the ends of the earth! I call on my fellow warlords and anyone watching today who doubt that the messiah is the supreme being in the flesh to rethink your beliefs and to bow down before him!"

CHAPTER 20

"Cybervision news Update" flashed across the screen. The commentator appeared on screen and announced, "Rumors are spreading around the world that Christians have penetrated the messiah's headquarters in Jerusalem and his military. The undercover Christian agents in conjunction with new Jewish Christian believers have successfully relocated thousands of Christian Jews to an impenetrable area called Petra in southwest Jordan. We will be confirming the veracity of this latest update as soon as we can."

Nef heard the journalist comment on Cybernews about the Christian infiltration of his government and military. He was furious. Nef grabbed his phone and called the news agency. "Get your idiot head editor, Hopkins, on the phone now!"

"Yes, my messiah, this is Dan Hopkins."

"Why are you allowing these lies about my government and military being infiltrated by Christian terrorists? I demand an immediate opportunity to set our viewing audience straight. I will be in your studio within the hour to be interviewed. Make it happen!" Nef slammed down the phone before Dan could respond.

The newscaster reviewed the statements about Petra on the air and then introduced Nef.

Nef looked serious as he responded to the commentator. "Lies. All lies. We have successfully corralled the terrorists in Petra. They are determined to cause harm to our new society. It is exactly where we want the nonbelieving radicals. I will deal with the terrorists once they are all imprisoned." Nef droned on for thirty minutes and closed. "Now, we must all pull together and apprehend the dissidents so that we can jail them in Petra. The reward for helping us find these fanatics will be worth your while. I promise!"

Nef was enraged and took action. He had microchips inserted in all military personnel and GSS members. Any that refused, or even hesitated, were eliminated. Many Christian military personnel had already fled to Petra and only a few remained to face the Antichrist's fury.

Nef called his inner circle together to discuss the situation. "Gentlemen, now we will focus on the rest of those that have gone down the wrong path. I call them the 'Jews' offspring.' You know them as Christians. If we cannot redirect their belief, we will send them to their eternity. General Sterns, how are chip insertions coming?"

"We have lines of recipients in every church location, and there is real excitement in the air. It may be hard to get everyone injected before the deadline because of the sheer numbers. We have doubled and tripled production of the chips and opened more facilities."

Nef nodded. "Good, now what about nudging along a few more by televising what happens to those Christian rebels who continue to hinder the global economic growth and threaten our peace?"

General Sterns continued, "Actually, my messiah, we have located a Christian 'study group' in London that we are planning a raid tonight. Perhaps we can invite a newsperson with a camera?"

Nef clasped his hands. "Excellent idea! Have it filmed and after we set an example of what happens to rebels, have the newsperson report directly to me as soon as possible. I will have the film edited, spliced, and broadcast it on Cybervision."

The room was relatively small and located at the end of a dark alley. The small congregation of Christians was standing and singing a hymn.

As Monica stepped in front of the group, the study group members sat down for the sermon.

Monica was a believer in her forties and had birthed two beautiful girls. She had married later in life, so her daughters were still young when the disappearance occurred. As a child Monica had attended the local church. She had not appreciated her parents insisting that she attend Sunday school and youth group. Her dad had been a serious disciplinarian, so they had butted heads regularly, especially over religion. As soon as she had left home, she stopped going to church.

Monica's husband had been killed in a head on collision two years following the birth of their second child. As a single mother, she provided as best she could. The girls were the center of her life. When the girls and her parents disappeared, she remembered the sermon she had heard as a child about tribulation. It had scared her. She was confused about the end times. Monica had listened to a sermon by a visiting pastor named Chris O'Malley just two weeks before her little girls had gone missing. He had made the end times more understandable, but she had not done anything to change her life.

Monica knew that she could keep looking for her two girls or accept the truth. After falling to her knees and praying, she began to read the Word every chance she could. She became a disciplined student of Pastor CJ and Pastor BL and was a participant of the undergrounders' society.

Monica met Stacey while she was helping Stacey set up an underground food facility in London. They had become fast friends. Stacey had introduced Monica to Brad on one of his clandestine visits. He had invited Monica to become one of his trainees as a Bible study group leader in London.

Monica's morning began with an online Bible study presented by Brad. That afternoon Monica called an evening meeting to share with her Christian group what she had learned. She was full of enthusiasm as she began her talk. "Tonight, we are going to discuss Hebrews 12:1-4. The section I will focus on is 'Let us run with endurance the race God has set before us. We do this...'"

The door flew open as a group of GSS soldiers burst through. Each combatant had a machine gun in their grip. The deadly weapons were pointing at the Christians, who jumped to their feet and quickly joined hands.

The lieutenant of the GSS squad growled, "Do not try to escape. If you do, you will be shot!" The officer in charge was a large burly man who, like all the others, had the mark of the microchip injection on his forehead.

Monica noticed that a man with a camera had entered the room. He began to film the proceedings as if it were a wedding. Monica took note that the cameraman did not have the Antichrist's mark.

A man dressed in a robe stepped forward. Monica recognized him as the area pastor for the Mashian's Church. Reverend Cromwell calmly said, "We are here to help facilitate your baptism into the true religion of Mashianity. We have brought plenty of chips. Please step outside. You will do this for your new love of the true messiah and for the good of the global community. It will also help our church succeed in meeting our projected goal of 100 percent participation of all *living* community members in the new religion."

Monica spoke up while the entire group still held hands. "We are prepared to run the race with endurance for our Lord and Savior just as we are taught to do in the book of Hebrews. We all know that the race is a faith-centered battle that requires morality and purity, something your false messiah knows nothing about. We may not be able to see the end now, but we know that when we get there it will be a finish worth running for."

Reverend Cromwell pointed at Monica. He spoke as an angry father would who was scolding his child. "That is enough of your rebellious talk. Kneel down and worship the true messiah or suffer the consequences." Monica frowner. Cromwell reminded her of her father when she was young. She was glad that he had mellowed in his later years and expressed God's love to her and others.

Monica stepped over to the other hostages, and they opened a space for her. She joined hands with two fellow believers. The group of Christians stood firm, and they all began to sing. "*Won't you come, oh Lord, and join us here as we give up our souls to you…*"

The burst of gunfire was deafening. Monica, and the two on each side of her, fell to the ground.

To the commanding officer's surprise, the singing started up again as the circle closed. What the GSS guards could not see were the three bright white objects hovering above the group and the bright light shining through the ceiling. The three martyred Christians looked down as their brothers and sisters in Christ calmly sang to Jesus. One officer screeched, "Stop that infernal noise and get down on your knees, or I will send more of you to your eternity!" No one stopped or kneeled.

The officer nodded and another burst of gunfire rang out as ten more fell to their earthly death and rose to their eternal life. The circle quickly closed. The singing continued. The officer was dumbfounded. No one had tried to run or escape. There was no panic. He looked around at his men and could see more doubt and fear in their eyes than in the people standing in the circle about to die. "Kill them all!" The room burst into gunfire, and the study group members fell to the floor.

The officer stepped in front of his men. He looked into their faces. "I'll call the cleanup crew. We will have all their bodies burned outside. First, remove their heads. We will put them up on tall spikes on display for the rest of the terrorists to see their fate."

Reverend Cromwell stepped next to the commander and whispered, "Look at their faces. They display only calm." They both turned and surveyed the expressions of the dead. The reverend pointed. "That one is smiling. Do you really want to display their faces for all to see?"

The commander turned back to his soldiers and said, "We will burn them all. We do not have time to separate their heads. Move out!"

The cameraman kept filming the carnage. He continued until all had left. As he was taking a final shot of the massacre, he sensed something and looked up.

Jesus allowed Geoff to see the large group of white-clad Christians floating just below the ceiling. They were holding hands and looking down at him with joyous smiles. Geoff fell to his knees as he saw the ceiling open. "Look to the Lord and his strength; seek his face always. Remember the wonders he has done, his miracles, and the judgments he has pronounced." Geoff looked directly into the face of an angel standing next to him. He glanced down and saw the angel's outstretched hands and noticed the nail wounds. He quickly looked at the angel's feet and they, too, had been pierced. Geoff's childhood Sunday school teachings flooded his memory. He realized he was looking into the face of Jesus.

Geoff began to cry softly and was glad that it was not his turn to receive the microchip. Geoff asked for forgiveness and accepted the true Christ. Jesus placed his hand on Geoff's head. "Go, listen to me, and do as I instruct you until I bring you home." Jesus rose in the air as he and the group of martyred saints ascended out of sight. Warm tears ran down his cheeks as Geoff heard soldiers approaching. He stood up to run but hesitated. Geoff felt God's leading—he had to trust the Lord, cooperate with the messiah, and turn the video over as directed. He wondered how long he could avoid receiving the mark of the beast as he quickly wiped away any tears.

✝

The Cybernews coverage of the rebels' massacre was broadcast around the globe. For the followers of Mashianity, it was a time of jubilee. For the Christians, it was both a time of sadness and a time to rejoice. They knew that their brothers and sisters were with Jesus. For the fence-sitters, it caused a different reaction.

Nef's plan was for those fence-sitters who witnessed the elimination of nonbelievers in Mashianity to cringe in fear and rush to their nearest church to join the Mashians to worship Nef as the messiah. Witnessing the peaceful repose exhibited by those murdered, and the spiritual singing of those whose lives were in peril, many of the undecided accepted Christianity and rejected Mashianity.

Nef was furious. He stopped broadcasting all massacres. Out of desperation, Nef ordered his communications director to orchestrate a staged raid filled with screaming and fear—with actors directed to fall on their knees, beg for their lives, and ask for forgiveness. The actors then faked a baptism into the Mashianity church. The ruse may have worked if it were not for the obvious falsity of the whole show.

After realizing the failure of the staged raid Abaddon called out his two archangels. Nergal and Decedre sat at his feet. Abaddon looked at Decedre. "I want you to have Spry announce that we are going to reward those true followers who love their messiah and are helping to bring safety and security to the global community." Abaddon reflected. "Just as I did in Smyrna centuries ago, I will put into place a ten percent reward. As you both remember, those that participated were called ten-percenters. I sent more than five million Christians to their death." Abaddon looked over to Nergal as he nodded and raised his left eyebrow. "Keep the raids going. Review each video and do not allow it to be broadcast unless it shows the panic we need. We will find some groups that will give us the authentic reaction we desire for release of the video. I want Nef to announce that if one of my true believers identifies a Christian and the terrorist is apprehended, the Mashian will receive ten percent of the Christian's credits and belongings. The rest of their personal estate will be confiscated by the Mashianity church, and our informant will be considered a global hero." Abaddon continued with his instructions. "If the family of the Christian has not reported the Christian's activity and rebellious belief and the family member is reported by another, then the entire family will suffer the same consequence as the perpetrator even if they are marked. It will behoove any family member who knows that their brother, sister, parent, or child is a Christian, or about to become one, to report the apostate to the nearest GSS office. Their loyalty is to me and not to family!"

The decree was put out on Cybernews the following day. Out of greed, many rushed to the local GSS offices to report suspicious neighbors and family members as potential Christians. Lines formed around government facilities with members who wanted to claim their ten percent. Neighbor turned against neighbor, friend against friend, and family member against family member. The Christian deaths began to climb into the hundreds and then the thousands.

CHAPTER 21

Even though he had just celebrated his twenty-sixth birthday, Brad arrived in London appearing as a seventy-five-year-old man—wrinkled face, shoulders hunched, graying hair, and a beard that was almost white. His eyeglasses were fake, and his teeth appeared to be yellowing with age. His passport was professionally forged, so he passed through security with ease.

A lady walked up to Brad, put her arms around him, and said, "Hello, Grandpa. How was your trip? The kids will be so excited to see you."

"Oh, Mary, you look wonderful. Your Nana would be so proud. I, too, am excited about seeing the kids." Mary was a perfect stranger. Brad had never met her, but the code phrase was: "The kids will be so excited to see you."

Anyone standing close enough to hear would have paid attention to the mention of kids. Children born after the disappearance were a precious commodity, and anyone listening would have ignored an old man.

The reunited grandpa and granddaughter left the airport arm in arm. None of the GSS guards paid them any notice.

Brad was soon settled in at the undergrounder's safe house. His first order of business was to thank the Lord for his safe arrival and for guidance as he performed the final touches on his sermon. Brad, still looking like an old man, easily jumped up from his knees. He had been praying for over forty minutes.

While sitting at the desk writing, Brad's cell phone rang. "Brad, this is Larry, you must not go to the seminar tonight. Geoff gave us information through his code during his news presentation about his latest raid review." Geoff doubled as a cameraman and commentator about the event he covered. "The GSS are planning a raid. They suspect that you will be there. They are bringing an entire platoon to surround the area. We are trying to notify as many attendees as possible. Unfortunately, notifying everyone will be impossible. Please do not risk the entire teaching ministry by going."

"Okay. I have been praying and knew something was up. God has indicated to me to stay put. Please tell the leaders that I will meet with them alone at the safe house so that we can pray. By the way, how's my sis and my nephew?" Stacey had taken Jimmy with her on her trip to the hydroponics seminar and had not returned before Brad left for his seminar presentation.

†

Larry looked pensive as he reflected on his son's birth. He had named Jimmy after his grandpa, James. Larry was so in love with Stacey that telling Brad the news, and accepting it himself, was breaking his heart. "We have been led to send Stacey and Jimmy to Petra for safety. Your dad will be waiting for them. An angel visited Stacey in a dream and gave her the instructions. The Lord has special plans for Jimmy in the coming millennium, and outside of Petra our welfare is in question."

Larry picked up on Brad's concern. He was not surprised when Brad responded, "I don't want to be an alarmist, but if a GSS guard sees her, they will take Jimmy and place him in a government home, won't they?"

Larry had the same concern, but children were not confiscated until their dependency on the mother for food was concluded. "She is still nursing him. That's why she must go soon."

"How soon? Are you going too?" Brad asked.

Larry knew that Brad would be apprehensive, but he also knew that Brad would support following God's direction. "I am staying to help run the underground food supply. They are leaving early next week after you return. Stacey insists on saying goodbye to you personally."

"I will be done here in two days, and then I will begin my return. Give her my love and hug my nephew for me."

"May God bless and keep you safe, my brother!"

†

It took six days for Brad to return to the undergrounders headquarters. His heart was heavy for the attendees of his seminar who had not been notified of the impending raid. Brad entered his office. Stacey, Larry, and Jimmy were waiting. Stacey gave the baby to Larry and ran to Brad and wrapped her arms around him. "Oh, Brad, if we had not received the warning, you would have been among the martyred."

Brad hugged his sister. "If the Lord wants to take me home, I am ready. I guess he has more for me to do."

Larry walked over to Brad, and Brad hugged both Larry and Jimmy at the same time. "Can I hold my nephew?"

Larry handed Jimmy over to his uncle. The baby looked up at Brad, and Jimmy's face lit up as he giggled. Jimmy had always been a happy baby. He was quick to laugh and continually gave happiness to anyone around him. "You love your Uncle Brad, don't you? Remember, I am the best. I love you, little guy, and God loves you even more." Brad kissed him on the cheek and then the forehead.

Stacey smiled and then looked a bit sad as she said, "We are still upset that the GSS martyred seventy brothers and sisters who attended the meetings in London. At least we know that the seventy are with loved ones and their Savior." Stacey looked at Brad and perked up as she added, "Have you heard how upset the Antichrist was that you were not there?" That made them all grin.

The evening wound down as the three reviewed and planned their next steps. As Stacey looked at Brad, they both had tears in their eyes. They knew that what they were about to do was the will of their Lord and Savior, but it still hurt.

Stacey said through her tears, "It is time to go." She grabbed Brad and wrapped her arms around his neck, and said, "God, please keep my brother safe and guide him in your will. I so look forward to your return and the time that we are all together for eternity." Stacey kissed Brad on the cheek, and they headed for the door.

Stacey was glad that Larry insisted that he drive her, Jimmy, and a fellow brother, Tim, to the airport. Tim had been chosen to accompany Stacey and Jimmy to Petra.

The ride was quiet. Larry held Stacey's hand with one hand and held his son with his free arm. Stacey noticed that tears had made Larry's cheeks wet, but he was not about to let go to wipe his face.

At the airport, Stacey kissed Larry for the last time before boarding, and she could see that Larry was fighting back his emotions. She poked his side and said, "Don't worry, Jesus is sending us. Do you really think anything can happen to us?"

Larry responded with a painful smile. "No, but I will miss you both so much!"

"I know, sweetheart, but we will be together soon, and this is the Lord's will."

Larry choked down a sob. "I love you both more than you will ever know," Larry said as he grabbed Stacey one more time and hugged her and his son.

"Well, you will have all of eternity to tell me, but for now please take good care of my baby brother. He thinks he is invincible. Also, I know how much he misses CJ. Now, I will be gone, too, so do not get so tied up in work that you forget to be Brad's friend as well!"

"No problem. I will treat him as my brother. By the way, please tell the general hi for me, and I expect him to take good care of my family until I see you again." Stacey nodded affirmatively as she took Jimmy. She, Jimmy, and Tim walked onto the gangway.

Larry stood at the security gate until his family was out of sight. He said a silent prayer, and a peace overcame him. Larry felt a bit empty but also very relieved. He knew from Brad's teaching what was next in the prophecies. Larry did not see how anyone outside of Petra could survive. He was content that Stacey and Jimmy would be safe. He knew that Stacey was as stubborn as her father. She never would have left if it were not for the Lord and her maternal instincts to protect her son. Larry was assured that she would arrive safely in Petra, and that made him feel confident.

CHAPTER 22

Tim and Stacey had to travel as if they were partners. Although Tim was a relatively new member of the headquarters team, they had been working on the underground hydroponics project for several months. Larry picked Tim because of his size and smarts, and he felt led by the Holy Spirit to do so.

As Tim and Stacey were passing through a GSS checkpoint, a guard stopped the two pilgrims and directed them to the entry station. The guard behind the check-in desk scowled and squinted his eyes as he demanded, "State your business."

Tim was tall, well-built, and had a handsome face. Even though his heart was racing, he calmly answered, "We are headed to Jerusalem to worship the true messiah and have our son dedicated to him."

The guard looked over the top of his reading glasses as he sat at his station. He was heavy with muscular biceps and a determined face. "Passport ID, please."

Tim handed the guard his ID.

"Your name, sir?" the guard asked as he looked up from the ID.

"My name is Timothy Marietta."

The guard kept Tim's ID.

The guard looked at Stacey. "Name, please."

Stacey passed her false ID to the guard while she was acting as if Jimmy needed her attention, dipping her head down and avoiding eye contact with the guard. "My name is Eloise Zimmer."

The GSS guard was looking at the screen of photographs of

suspected Christian terrorists. A picture of Stacey Lucas popped up. As Stacey stood facing the GSS guard wearing her blond wig, her fake teeth made her smile look as if she had very crooked teeth. The contact lenses had changed her eyes from brown to blue.

The picture on the guard's monitor was a high school picture of Stacey. The hair was dark, the nose smaller, and the teeth straight, but the guard was a trained scanner. The GSS knew that the undergrounder leaders traveled in disguise. The photos were always accompanied with computer renderings of possible changes. The guard determined that the match was definite. The official acted nonchalant. He gestured for a female GSS officer to come over. He did not want to alert Stacey of his suspicions. The female officer walked over to stand next to the guard.

The female officer was a tall solidly built woman. She had a ruddy complexion and reminded Stacey of a prison guard. It was obvious to Stacey that this woman was not the sympathetic type. The officer looked at Jimmy. She asked, "How old is your child?"

"He's eighteen months, ma'am." Stacey held Jimmy a little closer to her chest as she answered.

"You should know that the newly established age for children to be delivered to the governmental homes is eighteen months. We will need to have you go to the local Children's Home Center to relinquish your child. I will have two of my associates accompany you."

"Food has been scarce, so I am still nursing my son," Stacey pleaded.

The officer looked indifferent as she replied, "Well, they will help you wean him and get him onto cereal. He is plenty old enough to begin solid food. Our messiah has helped overcome the food shortage and increase the food supply. After you and your partner receive the microchip as you are baptized into the Mashianity church, you and your baby will have all that you want to eat."

Stacey felt like a cornered animal. She glanced at Tim. She and Tim did not know what to do. Running was out of the question, but relinquishing Jimmy was also not an option. Four guards surrounded the couple. Cooperation was Stacey's only choice.

The female GSS officer followed as the guards escorted the detainees to a private room. The female officer entered the room with Stacey and

Tim. Stacey was still clutching Jimmy. The officer closed the door and said, "Please wait in here while I arrange for you to go to the local Children's Home Center."

The female officer opened the door and walked out. She closed the door and locked the prisoners inside, turned to the guards and said, "The female and her companion may be wanted fugitives. I want you two—the officer pointed at two of the four guards—to take them to headquarters. I will notify General Sterns and the messiah that we are certain that we have captured one of the undergrounders' leaders. It will be best to let her think that she and the baby are being taken to a center. I am sure that they will try to escape, so put them in the transport that locks from the outside. Now, I don't want a scuffle in public. Too much can go wrong. Do not alarm them when you leave; act very matter of fact. Now let's get them to headquarters!"

The two transport guards entered the room with the female officer. Stacey and Tim moved close together, and Stacey held Jimmy with a strong grip. The officer said, "Miss Zimmer and Mr. Marietta, these two guards will escort you to the children's home. You can plead your case there to the commander in charge. I know him and he is a reasonable man. Perhaps he will see things in your favor. Cooperate and you will all be safe: resist, and you will lose your baby and perhaps your lives," she said with a sinister look. The officer turned and left.

One of the escort guards took a step toward Stacey. He was a short, stocky man and appeared to be in control. Stacey glanced at the second guard. He was a taller man with red hair and had a quick smile. Stacey thought that he was nice. Perhaps under different circumstances she might even try to like him. Stacey took a step back and said with as much strength as she could muster, "Touch this child and I will be forced to tear your eyes out. You will have to take him over my dead body."

The shorter guard beamed and said, "My name is Gabe." He pointed to his comrade. "He is Mike. You will be escorted to a vehicle, and then we will proceed to our destination. Please cooperate and do not cause any trouble. You can keep your son. You truly have nothing to fear."

Both guards led the three fugitives to an armored carrier. Stacey and Tim felt compelled to cooperate. The guards had guns, and Stacey could not put Jimmy in harm's way. Stacey held Jimmy tightly with her left arm as she grabbed the handrail, pulled herself up, and stepped into the back of the truck. Tim followed. Stacey looked at Tim as she heard the guard lock them in. Stacey yelled at them to tell her what was going on.

The guard sitting up front in the passenger seat pressed a button that brought the intercom to life between the cab and the transport compartment. He said, "Please, sit down and rest. We have a bit of a trip ahead of us."

Stacey looked around the compartment to see where the voice was coming from. "Where are you taking us? I demand to know," she said to a speaker located in a corner. There was no answer.

Tim took Stacey's hand. She resigned herself to the situation and sat down. She and Tim began to pray. The truck traveled for about thirty minutes. It stopped. The door to Tim and Stacey's prison cell opened.

One of the guards came in and sat down. "Perhaps a prayer of thanksgiving would be in order? You are safe. Would you like to ride up front? We have about two hours ahead of us."

Stacey looked confused. "Who are you?"

"We are in the army, and we serve one master."

"Whose army?"

"The same army as you, Stacey. Your father and his friends are waiting impatiently for you to arrive. Jimmy's to be kept safe. The Lord has big plans for him."

Tim smiled and asked, "You are angels?"

"We are. Our purpose right now is to keep you all safe from the Antichrist and his minions."

General Sterns walked up to the GSS headquarters master sergeant and questioned, "Why hasn't the transport arrived with the prisoners?"

"I do not know, General. We have been unable to contact the guards."

Sterns gritted his teeth and said, "The messiah's arriving in five minutes, and you had better have some answers!" Sterns turned and returned to his office.

Seven minutes later Nef briskly walked into the general's office. "Where are they? I want to interrogate the terrorist myself."

Sterns held up one finger after he hit a button on the intercom. He rang the master sergeant again and put the contact on speakerphone. "What is going on? Where are the prisoners?" the general demanded.

"We have no idea where they are, sir. The satellite has not located them. Their tracking device is sitting and not moving. We have zeroed in on the coordinates, and there's no transport truck where the device is located."

"You fool!" howled the messiah. "Someone has dislodged the GPS and discarded it. Get some eyes up in the air and search the roads to Petra from Eilat!"

"Yes, my messiah."

Within ten minutes the moving vehicle was located. The master sergeant rang the general's office, and Sterns put the call on speakerphone once more. "You were right, my messiah; the transport is entering onto Highway 47 toward Petra."

Nef was irate. He yelled, "Get an armed drone up in the air and stop that vehicle. I want this undergrounder captured alive so that we can get her to talk. I am sure she is Lucas's daughter, and she has a kid. That will make it extremely easy to persuade her to share the whereabouts of the undergrounders' headquarters before we kill them." Nef turned his head toward Sterns. "I want that to be televised so her father sees what happens to the families of those who defy me and leave my inner circle." Nef looked back at the intercom and slammed his fist on the table as he ordered, "Send some gunships and bring the armored truck to a halt.

Send a squadron of men to overcome the vehicle and take them into custody. I want her in my interrogation chamber now!"

✝

The truck was traveling as fast as possible. The shorter guard was driving. Stacey, holding Jimmy, sat between the driver and Tim. The taller red-headed guard was in the back praying.

The guard in the front cab was surveying the skies. He said, "Ah, guys, we have some company." A drone appeared about two hundred yards ahead and hovered. Six gunships moved to each side of the transport as it came to a stop. The guard in the cab pushed the intercom button. "Abaddon is making his play."

A voice came back into the cab. It was clear. "He is a tenacious-egomaniacal fool if nothing else. Abaddon never ceases to amaze me, but the Lord knows what Abaddon will do before he does it. The Lord says to start moving again. Let's see what they do. The Lord does not want us to send these souls to Hades unless it is necessary. You would think that Abaddon would learn, wouldn't you?"

Stacey looked at the guard sitting next to her with a puzzling stare.

"You know Abaddon as Satan, and that was archangel Michael," was all the guard said.

"Gabe? You're the archangel Gabriel?" Stacey asked with eyes wide. Tim glanced over at Gabe, and Tim's mouth dropped open.

Stacey had to ask, "Is this what you always look like?"

Gabriel grinned. "Only when I am allowed to be seen in your level."

Tim asked, "Level?"

"You will be able to ask all you want and see much more than you could ever imagine soon enough. That is all I can say."

Stacey had a million questions, but Gabriel's response seemed final. She did not want to anger one of God's archangels. Besides, they had more pressing matters at hand.

✝

General Sterns notified the command center to send a live feed from their monitor to his office. "Make sure we have eyes on the subjects so that we can watch their capture."

"Yes, sir," was the response on the other end of the line. Nef and Sterns watched the monitor with anticipation. The screen came to life. The road was desolate, and there was nothing but sand on both sides of the target. The gunships were hovering around the truck. The drone could be seen coming in from the top left of the monitor.

The sky lit up as a fireball sped towards the front of the truck. The missile suddenly veered in a wide arc back toward its launch pad. Within a matter of seconds, the explosive bomb destroyed the drone that had launched it.

Stacey said, "Did you see that? I'm glad Michael is on our side."

Tim grunted a laugh of agreement.

"You haven't seen anything yet," Gabriel added.

A voice from the rear ordered Gabe to stop. The wind around the perimeter began to blow. In a matter of seconds, a sandstorm began to rage. The truck did not move.

General Sterns stood up. He leaned into the monitor to get a better look and said, "Messiah, they are starting to repeat what happened last time on the road to Petra."

Nef fell back into his seat. He looked away from the monitor and let out a sigh of defeat. "Okay, General, have the gunships return to base."

Sterns held the receiver to his lips. "Return all gunships to base. Do not engage the enemy. I repeat, return the gunships to base."

"Sir?" said the communications operator.

Nef stood up and grabbed the phone from General Sterns. He screamed into the receiver, "I said to return to base! We do not need to lose any more gunships." The messiah stared at Sterns as if he were about to say something. He abruptly turned on his heels and left Stern's office. Nef heard a hissing voice in his head, *When I take over heaven*

*and earth, I will send Michael to the outer reaches of Hades. He will suffer
more than any other human or angel. His fate is in my hands.*

The GSS truck pulled up at the entrance to the Petra sanctuary.
James, Aaron, and Cindy were waiting with unfettered anticipation.
Stacey gave Tim the child as she ran into her father's arms. They both
started crying. They had not seen each other since James left to serve
the future Antichrist. Once James released Stacey, she stepped back to
Tim. She took Jimmy from Tim and walked back over to her dad. She
turned Jimmy's head toward his grandpa and said, "Jimmy, this is your
grandpa. Can you say 'Grandpa'?" The baby looked at James and said,
"Bompa." Everyone laughed and clapped. The name stuck and James
loved it.

James took Jimmy from his daughter and gave him a big hug.
Jimmy instinctively put his arms around his grandpa's neck as if he had
been with him forever. Aaron and Cindy both looked at each other and
winked. Cindy grinned at James and his grandson and said, "I believe
you are more excited now than when you received your first general's
star."

"I will second that statement," Aaron added.

Stacey turned back to the truck to thank her escorts. They were
gone.

Jimmy was the talk of the community. There were no other young
children, and everyone agreed that Jimmy had an unusual glow about
his face. They all knew that God had a special plan for this little guy.

CHAPTER 23

During the mission to destroy the Christian faith, the Mashian churches grew in both power and riches. Having received one-tenth of so many captured Christians' estates, the churches' coffers were immensely increased. Adorned in purple, scarlet, and gold, each worship site was determined to outdo the next in opulence. None, however, compared to the Mashian Basilica, formerly known as St. Peter's Basilica in Vatican City.

The messiah would hold his "communion of commitment" each week that was televised around the world. All church members were required to participate. Three evenings out of each month the communion was conducted by Spry as the supreme holy teacher with taped messages interjected from Nef in Jerusalem. However, once every month the messiah would appear in his priestly garments on the balcony of the Basilica. The church in Rome was the center of faith and the focus of all Mashians.

The night air was sultry and warm, the moon full and bright. The floodlights illuminated the Vatican Square, as streetlights gave light to the area avenues. Nef peeked out from the curtain to assess the size of the crowd. He glanced toward Spry and nodded toward the crowds. "Look at my people. They are here to worship *me*. It is finally as it should be." Nef raised his head slightly and took in a deep breath. "I have conquered the earth, and now my faithful will receive my personal blessing." Nef gritted his teeth and squinted as he thought, *Next, I will overthrow that imposter in heaven and take my rightful place over all levels.* He turned and stepped onto the balcony as the spotlight lit up Nef like a star on the stage. Nef looked out over the crowd. The roar of the onlookers was deafening.

The messiah's robe, decorated in gold and precious jewels, sparkled and danced in the light. Spry followed and stood behind Nef to his right. Spry was dressed in a similar robe. The crowd, estimated to be larger than one hundred fifty thousand, stood in the courtyard and streamed down the avenues lined with loudspeakers. They were all eager to hear Nef's communion message and to worship their messiah.

Upon entering the vicinity of the Mashian Basilica, each participant was given a small cup of wine and a piece of leavened bread.

Nef raised his hands. He glanced down at his feet. *I am standing in the same spot that the Pope of the now defunct Catholic Church once stood. I am the sum of all religions and churches and the only true god in the flesh.* Nef clasped his hands and bowed slowly toward the adoring crowd. As he looked up, the crowd began to chant "messiah, messiah" at the top of their voices. Nef let the mantra go for some time and then raised his hands for quiet. The crowd became reverent. Someone screamed, "We love you!" and the people cheered and applauded.

Nef allowed the adoration to go on for several more minutes and then gestured for the crowd to quiet down. The congregation grew silent. The air was full of anticipation. Nef peered out over the flock, his head turned, and he looked directly into the TV camera. Nef wanted all who would view the ceremony at their appointed time to feel as if they were in Rome with him. The televised sermon and communion were recorded so that it could play over Cybervision in each time zone at a designated time in the evening.

At the conclusion of the hour-long sermon Nef held up a golden goblet full of white wine. He turned from the camera and toward the courtyard. Nef spoke with authority and boldness. Every attendee could hear his voice clearly. "This wine represents my purity as the supreme being in the flesh. I do not need to shed blood for you because I have forgiven your sins. Now, I will drink first; then my supreme holy teacher will drink from the same cup. Please join my beloved teacher when he drinks." Nef took a drink and handed the cup to Spry. Spry turned to the camera, then to the audience. Turning back to Nef, Spry drank from the cup as the world population of believers joined him. Spry then set the cup on a beautiful golden table. He picked up a loaf of leavened bread with reverence and handed it to Nef.

Nef held up the bread and said, "This bread represents my body in its fullness. You may worship me, and by your faith in me we will live eternally together." Nef pulled off a piece of the loaf and placed the bread into his own mouth. He tore off another chunk of bread.

Nef turned to Spry. Spry kneeled. The front line of believers in the courtyard kneeled, followed immediately by the next line and then the next. The people bowing before their messiah were like a wave of water flowing out to sea.

Once all were kneeling, Nef said, "Now, eat and remember your love for me, the supreme being and your supreme holy teacher." Nef placed a piece of bread in Spry's mouth. Spry chewed his bread and then kissed Nef's hand. Nef again turned to his adoring congregation. "I bless you all. Now, bless me by going and experiencing the unbridled pleasures I have promised you."

The crowd, and Spry, stood. The congregation started to disperse as Nef and Spry left the balcony.

Once the messiah and the supreme holy teacher were no longer in view, Nef went over to a world globe placed next to his desk. He poured a goblet of wine over the orb. The wine ran down the seven continents and into a pan that was at the base of the stand. Nef laughed his diabolical and Abaddonic laugh. Through his laughter he said, "My world is drunk with sin."

The only thing growing in wealth faster than the Mashianity religion was the global economy. Virtually every man and woman made a good income. The governmental laws prevented the raising of prices according to demand, so pricing stayed steady. Everyone could buy whatever he or she wanted or needed. Excessive hoarding, which was disapproved by the church, was kept in check.

Families had learned over the two and a half years since the messiah took complete charge of the global society to live together and to help support each other as long as no one was trying to take advantage of anyone else. Fights were uncommon because the global church and the GSS police force, had tight control over the personal lives of every member.

The army rising against the Christian terrorists was made up of the Mashianity church converts, eliminating the necessity of a paid military force. Therefore, the trillions of monetary credits saved by not having a military budget were invested into the global society. This influx of finances contributed substantially to the development of the global infrastructure.

Periodically, Nef would secretly orchestrate a terrorist act to galvanize the area against Christians in general. He staged an attack on a food supply source, killed the owner, and blamed the Christians. Nef followed up his plot with a news interview on Cybervision condemning the rebels, "Yes, they are so desperate for food that they have initiated attacks on innocent Mashians who are only trying to contribute to the global community. It is a shame that these desperate zealots are still running loose. I personally ask that each of you watching me today make it your personal goal to help us apprehend all non-Mashians. If you suspect such a person, turn them in at the nearest GSS police facility. If you see or hear one of these terrorists espousing their false faith, feel free to apprehend, or even kill, the global traitor. You will receive my personal appreciation and a ten percent reward. May the supreme being bless you all and may the supreme being bless the united global community." The newscast ended and Nef winked at Spry, who was sitting off-camera.

The Christians in Petra were untouchable, but those in the global community were continually at risk. Food was still available through the undergrounders network, but obtaining the food was dangerous. Distribution was always done with the chance of detection and certain death. Being a Christian, easily identified by the lack of the mark that the chip insertion makes, was a virtual death sentence. The population of the Christian undergrounders started dwindling exponentially.

The well-paid GSS police force kept law and order. Even though the general population feared them, they also relied on them for safety. The force was especially focused on discovering Christian dissidents. If a GSS soldier thought it was for the good of the community, he had the authority to behead or torture the rebels.

The messiah often reminded his constituents that it had been only a couple of years since the demise of the terrorists' magicians in Jerusalem and that the entire world was enjoying unparalleled prosperity. Large cities, such as London, Paris, New York, Los Angeles and many more, had started to resemble the cities they were before the great quake and the devastating wars. Rome was rebuilt to its grandeur of old and was the center of trade. It was also the religious center, and the wealth of its world prominence was displayed on every new building.

Contractors, laborers, and all trades people pulled together with a common cause to rebuild the new global communities. The old third world countries witnessed new cities developing before their very eyes. They had adequate housing and food outlets with plentiful supplies throughout the regions for the first time in known history.

Nef's grip grew stronger daily. Everyone who participated in the economy had the mark of the new church.

Jesus watched closely and greeted new martyred believers into his kingdom. He personally escorted each of his children to the Temple and the throne. Each was given a white robe and placed with their fellow martyred saints under the throne. Jesus called Gabriel to come to him. When Gabriel arrived, Jesus was sitting on a rock all alone. He had a sad expression on his face. He sighed and then said, "I have waited as long as I can. The end of the second Woe has come. The third begins!"

CHAPTER 24

Jesus was walking from the Temple as archangel Gabriel kneeled before him. Jesus stopped and placed his hand on Gabriel's head. A fatherly expression formed on Jesus's face as he said, "I know your concern, my son, but please feel free to express yourself."

Gabriel looked up at his creator and stood. He squinted slightly and took in a breath. "Lord, the believers outside of our army's protection in Petra are being hunted. Although they are still sharing their faith, they are being sent here by the hundreds every day. The two witnesses are back on the throne with the elders, and the one hundred forty-four thousand are here with us. You still have many who have yet to make a final decision in level three. Who will continue the proclamation of who you are and what lies ahead for those who accept the mark of the beast?"

Jesus appreciated Gabriel's kind heart. "I know, my son. I have not given up on mankind. I will send three messengers to declare the truth. They will be from your army. I want you to be sure that my message spreads across the globe so that all inhabitants see and hear the proclamation. Commandeer Cybervision. Ensure that the angel's pronouncement is broadcast around the world." Gabriel bowed his head. Jesus commanded, "Go and do my bidding." Gabriel disappeared.

A figure suddenly appeared on Cybervision that had not been pre-approved by the communication director. The communications director called the central station and ordered that the figure being telecast be removed. The station manager said they were trying but were unsuccessful.

"Then shut down the broadcast. Turn off all solar power to the equipment!" the director demanded.

"We tried that, but the human shape is still appearing on screen," the station manager responded with a defensive voice as he pointed at the foreign figure on the monitor.

"Has the figure said anything?"

"No, sir."

Exasperated, the communications director articulated with a demanding voice, "The messiah saw the shape. He is on hold and expects an explanation. What can I tell him?"

The station manager raised his shoulders and with his hands turned palms up responded, "I don't know, sir."

From within Nef, Abaddon recognized Gabriel's lieutenant whose face filled the Cybervision screen. The figure often accompanied Gabriel when Abaddon visited level seven. He knew what the angel would probably say.

The communication director switched over to Nef and tried to stay calm as he explained, "My messiah, we have tried everything we can think of to no avail. The figure is still appearing on Cybervision all around the globe. We have had continuous calls from every station, and we are all confounded."

Nef roared into his receiver, "Keep trying!" He disconnected from the phone.

As Nef watched the monitor, the human figure started to fly through the sky and began to speak. The sound was rich and full, like a beautiful trumpet, as the angelic being said, "Fear God and give him glory, because the hour of his judgment has come. Worship him who made the heaven, the earth, the sea and the springs of water." He continued calling out as he encircled the earth.

When the figure's global travel had concluded, the screen went blank. Within a matter of minutes a second figure appeared. The second figure began to speak with a voice of a blaring trumpet. "Fallen!

Fallen is Babylon the Great, which made all the nations drink the maddening wine of her adulteries." The non-Christians were baffled at the meaning of the pronouncement, but the Christians understood the truth of the announcement. Brad had taught that God's messenger would decree what was prophesied in the book of Revelation. He stated that the decree meant that the false religion of Mashianity and the new economy would fail.

The screen went blank. Nef's fist hit the top of the desk so hard that the floor shook. He growled into his intercom, "Molly, get the communications director on the line now!"

The director came on the other end of the phone and weakly said, "Hello, my messiah."

Nef said, "I will be at Cybervision headquarters in twenty minutes. You will put me on for all to see, and I will explain the figures. You are not to breathe a word that you had no control over the broadcasts. Notify all station managers and their crews who are aware of the broadcast glitch to stay silent about the situation. Do you understand?"

"Yes, sir, my messiah."

"Good. If it gets out that I did not control the last broadcast, you and they will pay dearly!"

Twenty minutes later Cybervision broadcast a new figure. It was their messiah. Nef looked like he was in total control and at ease as he started to explain, "My fellow members of this united global community, I am your messiah; and as the supreme being in the flesh, I want to explain what I meant in the last telecast. All of you are to fear me. The fear is that of a child toward his father, a fear of respect. You are also to give glory to the supreme being, as we made the heaven and earth as well as the sea and the springs. If you do not, then the judgment will not be pleasant; and you will be severed from our society. If you revere me and the supreme being, you will be with us for all eternity. My second message has declared that I have destroyed the one-world religion and replaced it with Mashianity. Please do not be misled by heretics that are focused on destroying your faith by feeding you lies about the false God, Jesus. They will try to tell you that my announcements were foretold, but they lie! If anyone approaches you with such hypocrisy, contact your local GSS office and report the individual. Remember, you will receive ten percent of their estate. Thank you and may the supreme being bless and keep you all safe."

The telecast ended. Nef's cell rang. He could hear Spry clapping on the other end. "Great, my messiah, that presentation should stop the Christians in their tracks."

Nef stood up from his broadcast seat and inhaled deeply in triumph. With eyebrows raised and standing a little straighter he said, "Thank you Spry. I am sure that my followers will tighten the noose on the Christians. Again, Jesus is helping our cause. Now, please get back to preparing our sacraments for the next communion telecast."

"With pleasure." Spry disconnected.

Abaddon, in full control of Nef, was pleased that after three days many Christians had been reported to the GSS.

On the fourth day, the screen went blank again. Nef looked up at his monitor and said, "Now what?" Another figure appeared, and again Abaddon recognized the third angel. Nef jumped to his feet and said to no one in particular, "Enough already!"

The messenger appearing on the monitor started to travel around the globe. His voice rang out as clearly as the two messengers who came before him as he announced, "If anyone worships the beast and his image and receives his mark on his forehead or on their hand, he too will drink the wine of God's fury, which had been poured full strength into the cup of his wrath. He will be tormented with burning sulfur in the presence of the holy angels and of the Lamb, and the torment rises forever and ever. There is no rest, day or night, for those who worship the beast and his image, or for anyone who receives the mark of his name." Nef watched helplessly as the angel continued repeating his affirmation. At the conclusion of the interruption the screen went black again.

Nef called the communications director and instructed him to meet him at the station. Nef hissed, "I will be there in twenty minutes. Don't turn the stations back on until I am there!" Nef was livid. There were still some individuals living off the land who had not received his mark. He rushed to his car.

Nef arrived at the broadcast station and ran up the stairs. He entered the booth, sat down, looked at the camera, saw the red light come on and began, "I again come before my family to help you understand what recently happened on Cybervision. The Christians have figured a way to take control of our global stations and have propagated a falsehood on the community. The vision you saw was animated, and it was a lie. Besides, it is the Christians who will burn for eternity in sulfur for denying me as their true messiah. They have twisted the truth about me to make you think that the outcome of receiving my mark will result in the eternity that *they* will be in. They call me a beast. Let me ask you—am I a beast? Would a beast bring you peace and prosperity? Look at what I have built for you, members of the global community and Mashianity, and ask yourselves who you believe. Please, turn any of these terrorists in to the GSS, and let's remove these rebels who carry your destruction in their hearts."

There was, however, one problem with Nef's response; his argument did not hold true for those individuals who had seen the figure fly over their heads. Several of those who were undecided about which religion to accept, fell to their knees, repented to God, and accepted Jesus as their Savior.

Archangel Gabriel walked over to his Lord, bowed and announced, "It is done, my Lord. The angels you sent have delivered your messages. I am sure there will be many who will call on your name and will believe."

Jesus placed his hand on Gabriel's shoulder. "What was said by my three angels will call for patient endurance on the part of the saints who obey my commandments and remain faithful to me. Come with me. I must return to the Temple and the throne. It is time."

Gabriel looked confused. "Time for what, my Lord?"

Jesus looked determined as he answered, "You will see, my son."

Jesus walked onto the throne and morphed into the light. Moments later he reappeared—his face shone like the sun itself. Jesus looked over at St. Luke, who was sitting with the elders, and said, "Write this down—blessed are the dead who die for the Lord from now on; they will rest from their labor, for their deeds will follow them."

Jesus disappeared as he moved to the third level and reappeared above the clouds. He placed a crown of gold upon his head, reached down, and picked up a sharp sickle, holding it in his right hand. Then he sat. An angel came out of the Temple and shouted to Jesus from heaven, "Take your sickle and reap, because the time to reap has come, for the harvest on the earth is ripe."

The prophets, Zephaniah and Nahum, appeared and Zephaniah said, "The great day of the Lord is near, near and coming quickly."

Nahum nodded at Zephaniah and then added, "Who can withstand his indignation? Who can endure his fierce anger? His wrath is poured out like fire—the rocks will be shattered before him!"

So, he who was seated on the cloud swung his sickle over the earth, and the earth was ready for harvesting. Jesus said, "Open the Temple, the tabernacle of the Testimony." Jesus instantly appeared in the Temple. He commanded, "Send out the seven angels with the seven plagues."

All heaven could hear the shouts and cheers of the martyred saints coming from inside the Temple. They had withstood the pressure to accept the mark of the beast or to reject their love for Jesus. They had overcome the temptation for lukewarmness and tolerance of socially accepted sins. Their victory was secured by the blood of the Lamb and by the word of the Lord's testimony as to who he was—God in the flesh. They had not loved their lives so much as to shrink from death. They were under the throne and anticipated the end so that a new beginning could evolve. They were about to be avenged.

One of the four living creatures led the seven angels out of the Temple. The creature was solemnly caring seven items. The seven angels followed and were dressed in white linen and wore golden sashes across their chests.

As the seven, and the living creature, stopped outside the Temple, the multitude played their harps. Moses appeared and led them in his song, "Great and marvelous are your deeds, Lord God Almighty. Just and true are your ways, King of the ages. Who will not fear you, oh Lord, and bring glory to your name? For you alone are holy. All nations will come and worship before you, for your righteous acts have been revealed. God has exalted you to the highest place and given you the name above all names, and at that name every knee shall bow in heaven and on the earth and under the earth, and every tongue shall confess that Jesus Christ is Lord, to the glory of God, the Father."

The seven angels took a position facing the Temple. The living creature with the face of a man turned to the angels and carefully handed a bowl to each. The bowls represented that which was carried once a year into the Holy of Holies of the Jewish Temple by the high priest for the forgiveness of sins of the nation of Israel. The atonement for the sins of mankind was about to be completed.

Jesus walked out of the Temple and approached the seven angels. The first angel held up its bowl. Jesus had a crucible in his hand. He began to grind the contents of the bowl. Jesus moved to the second angel and repeated the grinding. When he completed the ceremony with each of the seven, he, and the living creature, returned to the Temple. Jesus walked up on the throne. The living creature joined the other three living creatures—one like a lion, one like an ox and one like an eagle. The living creatures and the twenty-four elders fell to the ground and worshipped their Lord as he entered the light. CJ, Chris, Michelle, and their heavenly family, as well as the other saints, bowed on their knees in worship. All sensed that the end was near and a new beginning was about to unfold.

The Temple began to fill with smoke from the glory of God. The entrance to the heavenly Temple was closed. The Tabernacle was changed from a place of mercy, through the blood of Jesus, to a place of judgment. Heaven was closed.

Jesus stepped out of the light and stood on the throne of the smoke-filled Temple. Archangel Gabriel walked up and bowed before his Lord. Jesus put his hand on Gabriel and Gabriel stood. Gabriel looked at Jesus and asked, "Lord, what about your followers on earth? We cannot protect all of those who are not in the Petra sanctuary. What will become of the new martyrs?"

Jesus looked into Gabriel's eyes. Jesus's appearance had changed. He still expressed the love of a father but the bearing of a judge. "Your concern for the brothers and sisters who have chosen my love over the easy choice of the beast is enduring. I, too, love them and I will never forsake them. One hundred and forty years after my death and resurrection, I told my prophet St. Paul to share with the Christians in Thessalonica that when I come down from heaven, as the earth hears my voice at the last trumpet, those that died because of their faith in me will rise first, and then those who are still alive will follow and be caught up to me in a cloud of angels. We will meet in the air, and they will be with me forever. Since the Temple of mercy is closed, the newly martyred saints will sleep until they hear my voice and awake. They will be at my side, just as those martyred before them. Those who survive Abaddon's rule until I return will also rise to join me in the air. We will then continue our descent to the third level to finish my revelation. I will call the living my first resurrection, and they will help populate my new earth during the millennium. That is their reward. Now, Gabriel, it's time to initiate the end and usher in a new beginning."

Jesus morphed back into the light on the throne.

A thunderous voice came from the Temple in level seven. "Go and pour out the seven bowls of my wrath on the earth!" God Almighty had spoken. Jesus walked through the closed doors of the Temple and approached the angels. He nodded and the seven angels holding the bowls joined Jesus on the cloud overlooking the earth. The harvesting sickle was again in Jesus's hand.

The first angel stepped forward, held his bowl up and waited. Jesus commanded, "Empty your bowl on those with the mark of the beast!"

CHAPTER 25

As Molly sat in her chair at the reception desk, she glanced down at her right arm. Her skin burned. She rubbed her arm, and every nerve ending began to scream. She thought, *What is happening?* She put her hands on the edge of the desk and pushed her chair back. The muscles in her legs refused to respond. Leaning on the desk for support, Molly stood and inched her way to Nef's open office door.

Nef looked up. He could see the ugly sores forming on Molly's face and her bare arms. The agony was reflected in her face, and her eyes were moist with tears.

Spry bumped into Molly as he entered Nef's office. Spry had arrived from Rome earlier in the day to prepare for the Jerusalem communion. He complained, "The poison of the sting is coming back." Molly turned and looked at Spry. Red spots were forming on his face. They both looked at Nef for some answers.

Nef said with a hint of excitement, "This isn't a result of the sting. His end is coming."

Spry asked, "Whose end?"

Nef was still looking at Spry, watching as sores spread over his face. Nef glanced down at Spry's arms, and the sores were popping out in abundance as Spry kept rubbing the infected areas. "Never mind. Things are going to get a bit dicey." Nef looked over at Molly, who was now slumped in a chair crying. "Spry, I need you to call Cybervision and get me on the air as soon as possible. I am sure that the two of you are not the only ones with sores."

Spry glanced at Molly and was glad that his inner demonic being was strong enough to keep him from suffering like Molly. Even though Decedre was a demonic archangel, his power was limited. He was able to keep Spry's pain to a minimum but was unable to eliminate the sores. Abaddon, on the other hand, had great powers and Nef was free of any signs of the plague.

Spry and Molly left—Spry to call the station, Molly to go to the hospital. Nef stood up, looked out the office window, and saw virtually everyone scratching and holding parts of their bodies. Nef knew that those who possessed his mark were seeing strange and painful lesions forming on their skin.

Nef noticed his car arriving. He looked away from the window and walked to his desk. He rummaged through the bottom drawer. He found what he was looking for—several tubes of salve used to relieve the pain from the scorpion sting. He grabbed a sack for the salve and tossed in six tubes. Nef stepped into the elevator and pushed the "Lobby" button. When the door opened, he saw that the lobby was full of employees scurrying to the exits and searching for transportation to the hospital. Nef smirked to himself and thought, *I read about the "boils" in Revelation. They are one of Jesus's announcements of what will happen prior to his second coming. What a fool he is to reveal his plan. Now I know what to do and when to do it. I will be ready.* Nef entered his limo. "Take me to the Cybervision station." Nef noticed that his chauffeur was uncomfortable and having difficulty driving. As the car moved erratically, Nef asked the driver, "Are you experiencing some sores and pain?"

"Yes, my messiah. Can you do anything to relieve this stinging sensation?"

Nef sat back into the car's plush cushion and replied, "I will be doing something to help, but for now you need to focus on my love. This contamination will pass. Soon I will be in total control, and the stinging pain will never happen again, I promise. First, we must eliminate the terrorists who are spreading this terrible virus." Nef reached into his bag. He leaned forward and handed a tube of salve through the opening in the partition. "This may help. I don't know if it will work yet." The driver reached over and took the tube. "Now, keep driving. You can put on the salve while you wait for me at the station. Be patient and remember that we will be together for all eternity."

The driver nodded and tried to smile at his passenger through the reflection in the rear-view mirror.

Nef looked out the window and observed several fender benders on the road as they traveled the short distance to the Cybervision headquarters. He could see that the pain was giving his driver more determination to get his messiah to the station and to the salve he desperately needed. The driver had the messiah's personal flag out and continuously honked his horn for people to get out of the way. He did not stop for anyone.

Nef lifted his cell phone and said, "Spry." Spry answered. Nef demanded, "Call the head of my medical staff and have him send notices to all pharmacies to locate any salve left from the sting and have the manufacturing centers retool for salve production. I have some salve with me. I will give you a tube when I return." Nef hung up the phone.

Nef entered the studio and bounced up the stairs to a waiting crew. They all had red spots and were scratching their arms. Nef rolled his eyes and sat down. The interviewer looked at Nef and asked, "Please, my messiah, can I have some salve. That worked the last time."

Nef adjusted his lapel microphone. He lied. "I don't have any salve, and I am not sure that it would work on these sores, anyway."

The regular anchor was out on assignment and unavailable, so Ralph, a rookie, sat in the anchor's seat. This was his first interview with the world leader. Nef was sure that Ralph normally would be nervous, but the pain was Ralph's priority. Ralph's face was covered with makeup to hide the red sores, but new ones appeared before Nef's eyes.

Ralph's eyes began to water as he said, "I don't think I can hold it together to ask questions. The throbbing is becoming unbearable!"

Nef grunted, "You got to be kidding me. The pain will pass, trust me. I will do all the talking." Nef looked up at the cameraman, who was bent over rubbing his legs, and said, "Point the camera toward me." The camera was set on a tripod and focused on Nef. The cameraman fell into a chair nearby.

Nef then looked up into the control booth where the producer was sitting. Nef instructed him over the connecting microphone, "When I get the sign, I will speak. Do not do anything until I am done." The producer gave Nef a thumbs-up. Nef could tell that he was in too much pain to talk.

The news producer managed to point at Nef to let him know that he was on the air. Nef looked into the camera lens and assumed a fatherly, understanding voice. "My beloved family of believers, I must warn you that the magicians are still causing anguish within our global family. Even though I have successfully destroyed the two old masters of deceit, they have taught their constituents how to carry on their work. The perpetrators of black magic have been in hiding, and they have been plotting to destroy our new order. It seems that their latest attempt to attack our believers is by producing a substance that causes sores that attack the flesh. They have obviously figured out a method to make the poison airborne. I will have our best minds discover the cure, and we will overcome these terrorists," Nef said with a set jaw.

Nef's expression changed. "We have experienced the greatest economic boom ever known on earth and have enjoyed security and prosperity like never before. That is what *I* have brought you. The terrorists that still call themselves Christians are now trying to tear down all we have accomplished ever since I have come to you in the flesh. Your first rule of order is to do your best to continue your productive contributions to the new society. Secondly, we must join together to rid ourselves of all Christians from our global community. The GSS will help in any way they can.

Although I am not sure that the salve produced as an antidote for the past scorpion poison will help, I have instructed all pharmacies to make the salve available to all Mashians who request it, for as long as the supply lasts. If we have positive responses to the salve, we will again mass produce it for my new family. Now, I must return to my duties. Pray to the supreme being for wisdom and relief. May the supreme being bless each of you, and may he continue to bless our global prosperity." The producer shut down the broadcast and fell to the ground in agony. The interviewer was lying on the floor in pain as Nef stepped over him and vacated the premises.

Nef entered his car and asked, "Is the salve helping?"

"It seems to be better, my messiah."

"Good. Take me to the GSS headquarters. I need to get some salve to General Sterns."

The lines to the local pharmacies began to grow as thousands sought relief from their agony.

†

Brad and Larry were watching the telecast in Brad's office at the undergrounders' headquarters. Larry shook his head and looked at Brad. "Did you see how the Antichrist twisted this plague into being our fault?"

Brad shrugged his shoulders. "Larry, would you expect any less from the great deceiver?"

"No, I guess not, but it really galls me. What are you going to do?"

Brad tipped his head back and closed his eyes briefly. Then he continued, "First, we are going to pray. Then I will warn all our brothers and sisters to witness only to those without the mark of the beast. I will also caution them to be extra careful when, and if, they leave their safe houses or farms. The community will do their best to identify any suspected believers in Jesus. Nef has convinced his followers that by capturing a Christian the captive may disclose where the Christians are hiding their vaccine to the boil-causing virus."

Larry grimaced and said, "What they don't know is that things are just getting started. Do we have plenty of water on board for our Christian family around the world?"

"The desalination water units will be worthless, but we have been anticipating the next bowl and have millions of gallons stored around the globe."

Larry stood and said, "Brad, we have to be sure that we get this information out to all the undergrounders. All members of our Christian family must know what's coming next."

CHAPTER 26

The second angel stepped forward, raised his bowl, and smoke billowed from the Temple as a commanding voice from the Temple said, "Pour out your bowl on all of the seas of the earth."

✝

"Now what?" Nef could see by Spry's expression that something new was happening. Because of the boils and the mounting tensions around the world, Spry relocated from Rome to be with Nef in Jerusalem.

The sores were debilitating. Every global member had tried to maintain their routine, but most failed miserably. The number of Nef's staff that had had gone to the hospital and returned home was crippling his government. In fact, the entire economy was faltering due to inactivity and a severe shortage of the salve.

Spry bowed slightly and said with alarm, "My messiah, we are receiving calls from our fishing fleet." Spry took several short breaths and paused, as if he were afraid to complete his thought.

Nef said impatiently, "And what? What's going on with the fishing fleet? Speak up!"

Spry looked sheepishly at Nef. He started to stammer.

Nef screamed, "Decedre, get control of this imbecile!"

Spry spit out, "The seas have all turned red! They say it tastes and smells like blood!"

Nef sat back in his chair. "It looks like Moses is up to his old tricks again. He pulled this 'open sores and turning water to blood' on us in Egypt thousands of years ago. Only this time, it's on a bit grander scale."

Spry said, "I'm not sure what you mean."

"Never mind, find out how widespread the contamination is, and what it is doing to the sea life."

Spry returned within ten minutes to Nef's office. He entered and Nef looked up questioningly. Spry said, "The reports are coming in from all over the globe, and it does not look good." Spry turned on his heels and left.

Molly entered the office as Spry brushed by her. She was wearing a shawl that shrouded her face and a long-sleeved blouse. She was covered with the salve to sooth the sting. It helped but the pain was far from gone. Molly said, "Messiah, there is an urgent call on line one."

Nef did not look up. He reached for the phone and said, "Thank you, Molly. You can go lie down if you need to." She nodded and left the room.

"Yes?" Nef said into the phone.

"My messiah, this is General Sterns. First, thank you again for the generous supply of salve for myself and my force. Have you heard about the sea?"

"Of course."

Sterns hesitated and then continued, "Well, the captains of my ships are having trouble maneuvering, and the engines are clogging with thick red blood. They tell me that the surface of the sea is starting to fill with dead sea life and maneuvering through it is proving impossible. There are many seagoing vessels that are trapped in the water. I have ordered our ships back to port as soon as possible. The captains have also reported that dead whales, dolphins and tons of sea life are blocking passages to rivers."

Nef's eyebrows raised as he asked, "So the rivers are not affected?"

"Not that I know of."

"In case the rivers start getting contaminated, have your men fill all water tanks around the globe with fresh water from the rivers."

"Great idea, sir. The desalination factories have reported that their pumps have stopped performing because their technology does not purify blood, only water. I have also ordered gas masks issued to all of my soldiers. The smell is nauseating the people so much that regurgitation is occurring everywhere near the sea."

Nef said, "Have all GSS and military personnel find clean river water and fill as many containers as they can find. Set up pumps to deliver the clean water to the nearest water tanks and fill them up."

"Yes, sir." General Sterns hung up.

Nef put down the receiver and sat back in his chair. He tapped the tips of his fingers together near his lips as he thought about Jesus. *I'll bet you are having fun directing your calamities from the safety of your own level. I know the rivers are next, and I know the rest of your plan. You were stupid enough to reveal your strategies and share your "bowls of wrath" in Revelation. Well, I have my own plan with a different ending for you, and I was not dumb enough to write it down.*

The second angel stepped back into the line of seven. It bowed down on both knees, joining the first angel. Jesus watched from above and observed the reactions to his judgment. He knew how each person would respond. His heart jumped with joy when new believers fell to their knees and accepted his love. He also knew which would survive until the end and which would sleep until his return. Jesus's heart felt pain for those, using their free choice that was available to mankind, who turned to the Antichrist and accepted the mark of eternal damnation.

Enough time had passed for the effect of the plague to demonstrate the power of the one true God. It was time for the next phase.

Jesus faced his seven. The third angel looked into Jesus's eyes as Jesus ordered, "Come forth and empty your bowl on level three."

The angel of water stepped forward and turned the bowl upside down as he spun in a circle. Jesus watched as the contents floated downward.

The angel stopped, returning to his position in line. He lowered himself to his knees and again looked at his Lord's face that reflected not a hint of anger, only sadness. The tears running down Jesus's cheeks were like a waterfall, and his eyes were focused on the level below. It was obvious that he was feeling pain and disappointment for those who had chosen the mark of the beast. Even though he was acting as a judge, he could not repress his compassion.

Jesus knew that he was a just God and that his word was pure. If one of his creations chose Abaddon's side, it was the human's right. Jesus, the true Christ, knew what lay ahead of them for all eternity. He had given warnings through parables and direct commands about the results of refusing the truth—eternal separation from him. It weighed heavily on Jesus's heart that any of his creations would choose to ignore him and turn to his nemesis. Abaddon had fulfilled Isaiah's prophesy in scripture that evil would be called good and good would be called evil. It had taken Abaddon centuries to complete the process, but he had succeeded, and many had chosen to ignore the good that was taught in scripture, such as loving your neighbor as yourself.

The angel of water was compelled to say, "You are just in these judgments, O Holy One, you who are and who were; for they have shed the blood of your holy people and your prophets, and you have given them blood to drink as they deserve."

Those from the closed Temple, and under the altar, also heard what the angel said. Voices in unison from the altar sang out, "Yes, Lord God Almighty, true and just are your judgments."

†

Nef looked up. He did not know what, but something was strange. He went into a trance as Abaddon and Nergal morphed out of his body. Red spots began to form on Nef's face immediately.

Abaddon recognized the two figures standing before him. They had passed him almost every day when he visited heaven. They were Gabriel and his sidekick, Amon.

Archangel Gabriel looked at both angelic demons and said, "The Lord has had the third bowl of God's wrath poured out on your constituents. It is never too late to repent. Abaddon, you were one of the Lord's greatest creations. Your pride and self–centeredness have blinded you to the truth. Jesus is God and you cannot defeat him. Accept who he is and lead your followers to salvation and not damnation."

Abaddon rose in the air. He slowly turned into the red dragon. Abaddon hissed, "Gabriel, you do the bidding of a fool. I will destroy you all!"

Gabriel frowned and then shrugged his shoulders. He and Amon disappeared and Nergal reentered Nef. Abaddon slowly returned to the handsome man as he was joined by Nergal. The red spots faded away on Nef's skin.

Nef regained his composure. The news that all the rivers were turning to blood, just as the sea had, was exasperating. He needed to hold this global community together in their support of him. Nef pushed the intercom button down and ordered, "Molly, come in here."

Molly gingerly rose out of her chair. She slowly opened Nef's office door and stood there. She could tell that Nef was waiting and was ready to yell at her. It was obvious to Molly that Nef thought better of it. She knew that she appeared very fragile and that Nef needed her there to do his bidding.

Nef said calmly, "Please call Cybervision. I want to be on the air as soon as I arrive."

Molly nodded but said nothing. She walked very slowly to her desk and said softly, "Cybervision station Jerusalem." The pain from the sores on her face and around her mouth made it almost impossible for her to talk. Were it not for the salve that Nef provided her, she would not be able to function.

Molly had plenty of pure bottled water, enough to last her for several months. She wondered what would become of her when the water ran out. She was sure that the global community must be approaching a state of panic.

†

Larry walked into Brad's office with a distinctive and fast-paced strut. He excitedly said, "Brad, have you heard?"

"About the rivers? Yeah, Larry, the Antichrist is on the news now. He's putting his spin on it. Come, listen."

"…and the Christian terrorists have only your destruction in mind. I repeat, you must find their hideouts and drive them into the open, kill them, and confiscate their water! They have caused this. As your messiah, I can guarantee that none of the rebels are suffering from the boils and that they have pure water to drink. Is that fair? Is that the kind of God you want to worship, the kind that allows these monsters who practice witchcraft and magic to scare the community?"

Nef looked directly into the camera and said with feigned love, "I bring you peace and prosperity. The terrorist Christians want to be the elite and take all that you have worked for. We will not let them!" Nef's persona changed to anger as he proceeded. "Find the Christian terrorists! Destroy them! Why do they have water that is pure and drinkable? I will tell you why. They have known their diabolical plot long enough to have stored up plenty of water before they caused the water contamination. Why don't they have the boils? Because they have the vaccine and are unwilling to share it unless you cower to their false belief. If you see anyone without my mark, follow them to discover their safe houses and then call the GSS. You will receive ten percent of all the captured Christians' belongings and wealth plus twenty-five percent of any water found to do with as you like! We are a family, and we will not let these self-righteous Christians destroy us. As your messiah, I will give you all of my support for each rebel you help bring to justice and send to their demise!" Nef looked up and said, "Praise be given to the supreme being."

Nef again looked directly into the camera. "I assure you that I have taken steps to help. All drink-manufacturing facilities are being retooled to produce liquid drinks without water in them. Production will be increased as much as needed! Your welfare is my top priority. The supreme being will bless you all for your belief and support. Now, go find the diabolical monsters who are responsible for your pain. 'Death to the Christian terrorists!'" The monitor went dead.

Larry looked at Brad. "Wow, he is out for blood. No pun intended. What are you going to tell the other undergrounders?"

Larry waited for Brad's answer as Brad thought for a few seconds and then responded, "That they need to listen very carefully to the leading of the Holy Spirit and not to go into harm's way unless directed. The next two bowls will drive Abaddon's followers into a frenzy."

CHAPTER 27

As the fourth bowl was spread out over the earth, the clouds began to dissipate and the precipitation around the globe evaporated. The ozone layer was thinned out, so the sun's rays were lightly filtered.

The Lord laid down his sickle. As he descended, his glory illuminated the entire earth. He stopped. The blinding light would last twenty-four hours a day for the appointed time. As the heavenly hosts watched, Jesus threw a great millstone into the sea of blood as a symbol of the coming destruction and judgment.

The sun shone with such intensity that everyone on the earth was experiencing the same environment as the nomads of the desert. The problem was, only a small percentage of the earth's inhabitants had any idea of how to survive in such direct sunlight. Within a few days, the sun began to scorch people.

The members of the Mashian Church cursed the name of Jesus because of the heat, sores, pain, and lack of drinkable water. They refused to repent. The messiah's followers called out for the supreme being to give them relief. None came. Air conditioners broke down from overuse, and buildings became uninhabitable. Cybervision reported that people were suffering from heat prostration and were found lying in direct sunlight with their bodies seared. Many community members were searching out deep caves for refuge from the extreme heat. The world was in disarray.

Jesus returned to the cloud above the earth. The fourth angel knelt before him as he joined his brothers. The Lord watched the peoples of earth scurrying for shade and reprieve. He thought, *Why are some humans so stiff-necked and foolish? I gave them warning! I had my prophet, Malachi, write, "Surely the day is coming; it will burn like a furnace. All the arrogant and every evildoer will be stubble, and that day that is coming will set them on fire, says the Lord Almighty." Once my rebellious children have accepted the mark of the beast, they are consumed with evil. The demonic forces have total control and can delude the vessel into believing any lies spewed by Abaddon.*

The undergrounders, hiding in parts of the city with seven hills, also known as Rome, heard the Lord. The Holy Spirit said, "Come out of her, my people, so that you will not share in her sins, so that you will not receive any of her plagues; for her sins are piled up to heaven, and God has remembered her crimes. Give back to her as she has given; pay her back double for what she has done. Pour her a double portion from her own cup. Give her as much torment and grief as the glory and luxury she gave herself. Because she boasts that she will never have to mourn, I will consume her in one day. Her plagues will overtake her: death, mourning, and famine. She will be consumed by fire, for mighty is the Lord God who judges her." The Christians clandestinely fled the city as swiftly as possible. They knew that the Lord was warning them.

The intense heat not only caused the odor of the blood to permeate the globe, but the ice caps began to rapidly melt. The blood-filled sea rose, and coastal cities began to flood. Ocean-going vessels, used to transport commerce, sat helplessly mired in the thick sea. Perishables rotted.

The extreme sun caused rapid deterioration of all machinery that came into contact with the bloody water, rendering the vessels useless.

Ships were marooned in the Tyrrhenian Sea outside of Fiumicino on the outskirts of Rome. Sailors on the merchant ships that sat dead in the sea began to wail as they witnessed Fiumicino sink into thick blood and the great religious and economic center of Rome burst into flames.

All of Rome's inhabitants ran for safety as the city turned into another Babylon. The flames reached so high into the sky that its destruction could be seen for hundreds of miles. All the ships' occupants moored outside of Fiumicino along with the merchants in the outlying cities and the viewers watching Cybervision saw the obliteration taking place. The mourning was intense. All, especially the regional leaders, witnessed the great city crumble before their eyes. There was no doubt that the cities under their control would follow suit. They cried out because they knew that the great cities of the world would never be rebuilt again to their current splendor.

The merchants realized that their livelihoods would be ruined. The great metropolis of trade was going to perish.

In the cities around the globe, the panic was intense. People ran for cover from the sun, or to find higher ground from the rising red sea, not knowing if the place they would call a refuge would become a furnace of death or their underwater burial site.

Inhabitants of the global community began to withdraw all of their credits from the bank to try to purchase the last bottles of water and any food that was still edible. The prices skyrocketed, as people were willing to pay whatever was asked. They dared not complain or take a grievance to the local price-control board. If they did, someone else would pay the asking price, and the sustenance would be gone.

As a result of the run on credits, the global bank collapsed. Nef declared that the bank would continue to create more credits, but the bank could not keep up with the demand. The credit-dispensing machines crashed, and all commerce stopped. Abaddon had been bringing about economic chaos throughout the ages. This time the bedlam was caused by his arch nemesis, and he was furious at being on the other end of the calamity.

Nef realized that the time had arrived to muster all humans to join in a march to the valley called Armageddon. He knew where Jesus would return, and he was going to be ready.

†

Giving a quick nod as his eyes pierced earth's inhabitants, Jesus concluded that the number of believers remaining on earth was complete. It was time for another wakeup call. He hailed the fifth angel. "Come forth. As I did in Egypt, I will also do over the earth. I told my prophets Isaiah, Joel, Nahum, Amos, and Zephaniah and expressed through my apostle, Mark, 'But in those days following the distress, the sun will be darkened, and the moon will not give its light.' Pour out your bowl."

Jesus's anger about Abaddon and his deception was growing to a crescendo. How the evil one had led so many to their eternal damnation broke his heart. He knew what was next and what was to be the outcome. Jesus watched as the new plague covered the world community. He protected his followers from the sores and the blood of the sea and rivers and those in Petra from the scorching sun, but what was to come was unavoidable. Jesus was prepared to see many more go to their resting place until his return. He also knew that some of his believers would survive despite the circumstances.

✝

Nef appeared on Cybervision again, declared war on all Christians, and told his community to converge on Israel if they wished to survive. The supreme being would lead them to victory over the terrorists, and they would destroy the radicals in a local valley. As soon as he finished his statement, complete darkness engulfed the globe.

Brad, Larry and all the undergrounders at headquarters were watching the newscast. Although they were deep within the ground in the bunker, they observed the total darkness take effect on Cybervision. It was no surprise to any Christian. Pastor BL's latest teaching was clear about the fifth bowl. Nef's call to arms in the valley of Armageddon was also predictable.

At the conclusion of Nef's broadcast, Larry turned to Brad. "Brad, the lesson last night was great, but I am afraid that our listening audience is shrinking fast. Reports show that we lost another three thousand this week. Antichrist's believers are taking revenge on our brothers and sisters. They are searching for them with a vengeance, and they are showing no mercy. I am worried that the only ones to pass into the millennium will be the ones who have somehow made it to the Petra fortress."

Brad leaned forward, elbows on his knees. His face seemed to sag. "I know, Brother. Perhaps you should be planning a way to get to Petra to be with Stacey and Jimmy."

Larry shook his head. "I will go when the Lord calls. Right now, he is telling me to stay put."

Brad smiled. "Well, I enjoy the company even if you are boring." They both laughed. They had confidence that the Lord was in control and that if he wanted them with him, they would be. They never shed tears for the martyred saints. They knew that they would be received warmly and would have a special place in heaven. Brad and Larry looked forward to that as well but knew that some saints must survive to help populate the new world. Chris, CJ, and Brad had taught that in Isaiah 65:8 and Matthew 24:22 that Jesus would cut short the final three and a half years of tribulation. They believed that the shortened duration would allow Jesus's followers that were still living to enter the millennium.

If the Lord had it in his plan to take Larry or Brad home, then so be it. Eventually, they would all be together for eternity on the new earth and looking into the new heaven.

CHAPTER 28

Petra was a sanctuary that had transformed into a small city. Water was plentiful. Gardens flourished and the area surrounding Petra was protected by the Lord's angels. When it appeared that the food supply may run short, the inhabitants prayed. The next morning manna from heaven would fill the gardening area.

After a pleasant dinner, Aaron sat with James and Cindy and conversed about the night's sermon. They discussed how large the Petra population was growing and the continuing demands on the essentials. James's eyebrows raised as he said, "I am amazed at the number of brothers and sisters who have made it through the barrage. Obviously, the latest plagues have opened several avenues to Petra. The Antichrist's soldiers are in such pain and agony that they can barely function."

Cindy chimed in, "I heard that they have little water and have abandoned their posts. The last plague has allowed many Christians to come to us under the cover of darkness."

Aaron tapped his two four fingers together below his nose as he leaned forward and said, "It is sad that so many people have willingly accepted the mark of the beast during good times, and now they are crying outside of our perimeter asking to be let inside our refuge. No one with Abaddon's mark can enter. Even if we wanted to allow them in, Michael would stop them. The Lord has been clear in his scriptures that accepting the mark is an eternal death sentence." The three stood and felt sorry for those that had made the wrong choice and ignored the truth.

"Come on, let's go see what is going on outside the gate today," James said. They stood and worked their way out of the city proper and up to the observation post near the outer gate and looked at the surrounding perimeter.

James, Cindy, and Aaron gazed down on an open area outside of the main entrance filled with several huts built for the overflow of Christ followers. Within the designated area there was a section filled with an abundance of lush green crops. At the center of the dwellings was a large opening several feet in diameter where the community could congregate. It was in this gathering center that manna was supplied by God and collected when necessary. The outer edge of the complex was fenced off, and there was a small opening where new inhabitants were permitted to enter in. Most believers migrated to the interior shelter of Petra every morning and did not return to their huts until later in the evening. The zone, outside the gate, was populated with hundreds of refugees milling around awaiting entrance as James, Cindy and Aaron looked on.

Taking in the scene of refuges, James said to Aaron, "It is so comforting how God is protecting our new friends from his plagues. Even though it is deathly hot and pitch-black outside, the protected area is still cool, and one can see fine to navigate about within the safe zone behind the outer fence due to God's light."

The three leaders focused on the refugees attempting to enter the Petra sanctuary. Many Mashians knocked others down trying to get to the front of the line. They mistakenly thought that they would be among the first to be let in. When they reached the entrance, they would beg. When begging failed, they became belligerent, demanding entrance. When rejected, they would start cursing and threatening. "You know," Aaron said, "I have always heard that you can choose your own sin but not the consequences."

James raised a pair of night vision binoculars to his eyes as he scanned the outer perimeter more closely. He noticed two men standing toward the rear of the crowd outside of the entrance. For some reason he strained to see one of the men's faces. He pointed. "Aaron, there is something about those two back there." James handed Aaron the

8

binoculars. "See the two in the back? They look like trouble. I can spot a reconnaissance a mile away."

Aaron spied the two and passed the binoculars to Cindy and pointed. Aaron said, "The Lord is in control. Neither he, Michael, nor his angels will let anything sinister happen around or in Petra. Now, come on, we have watched long enough. Let's get back to our people. Besides, it's time to gather for prayer."

The three left the observation point. James still suspected a diabolical plot, but he knew he had to let it go. It was no longer his responsibility to protect anyone.

†

Alexander and Leto Callis stood outside the entrance to Petra. Staring at the crowds that had gathered, Alexander began his analysis of the best way to gain permission to enter. The fortress was well lit, and he heard that the food and water were plentiful. Leto was anxious to obtain access because the trek had been long and dangerous, and they had suffered enough. After all, it was time to cash in on their entitled benefits and then reap satisfaction for the revenge they so justly deserved.

Alexander and Leto had grown up in Athens, Greece, on a street named Vonue. They were happy boys and very intertwined in their Orthodox Christian church. Alexander, the oldest, had wanted to be a church deacon when he was old enough. After that, who knew? Maybe a priest. He loved drawing pictures, and perhaps he could be an artist for the church.

Leto followed his older brother everywhere. He even emulated Alexander's artistic expressions. Sketching landscapes was Leto's specialty.

Their mother, Chara, was deeply religious. She prayed to the saints and to Christ every day. Her primary prayer was for her two boys to grow up to be God fearing and loving men. Alec, their father, was hard working and supported the church and the Greek government. He was a dedicated union member, as were his friends and associates. He believed that all men and women should be treated equal and that all should receive a fair wage. He supported all social programs. He was incredibly pleased in how the country narrowed the gap between the haves and have-nots.

When the economy went terribly south, Alec was on the picket lines fighting for the common worker and supporting the union causes. His resentment against the church began when the priests did not back the unions more vehemently. When the economy began to collapse, the concessions perpetrated on his country by the EU were devastating to him and his family. His fury toward the government and the church never subsided.

Alec's rage permeated the family structure. As his sons passed through their teen years, they started to dismiss their mother's zealousness about Jesus and the church. Their hearts began to harden. They were not interested in forgiving those that had destroyed their father's way of life.

After Leto turned eighteen, the two brothers' interest in church vanished. They did not dare let their mother know about their new night life, so the charade was on. Whenever there was a church activity, Alexander and Leto would sneak out as soon as it was safe to join their friends at the tavern. When they came in late, which was most nights, they told their mother they were at the church social doing some effective witnessing or painting portraits or landscapes for the church. She never doubted them.

One night, Chara intercepted her two sons as they tried to sneak into the house. A friend had called her to warn her about her sons' shenanigans. Alexander and Leto swore at her during the ensuing discussion. Chara scolded the boys for using course language. The debate of Christianity versus fun living began. Soon the argument included the right to live with a woman out of wedlock, the right to speak however they wish, and the right to destructive behavior whenever they felt like it. Chara remained adamant about attending church and praying.

Alexander stood tall with his arms crossed and said, "Mama, the church is old fashioned. It needs to catch up with modern times. The scriptures were written for ancient times, not today. There is nothing wrong with partying and getting a little tipsy or swearing now and then. I believe in Jesus and so does Leto, and we were both baptized. We are grown men now and have the right to make our own decisions on how we worship. It doesn't make any difference if we go to church or not."

Chara looked down at her hands. She reached for some tissue and dabbed her eyes. "But Alexander, God is the same today, yesterday and forever. You cannot thumb your nose at him or just believe what scripture teaches when it suits you. Be careful, the Lord stresses that many will not be allowed into heaven. Just because you performed a ritual as a child does not guarantee your salvation. The baptism is simply an outward expression of your love for Jesus. If you don't *truly* accept him and his Word into your heart and mind, you are not necessarily in his palm and can be in jeopardy of not having an eternal life with our Lord and Savior. I do not want to be there without my two sons. God says to fear him, like a son fears his father, because he knows that his father has authority over him as a child. God is not your cosmic bellhop that you can call on whenever you need help and then ignore the rest of the time."

"Mama don't be so dramatic. We will be in heaven with you. We have plenty of time to live the holy life. Now, we want to sow some wild oats." Alexander looked at Leto, who had remained silent on the subject. "Come on, little brother, let's head to the tavern and see our nonjudgmental friends." Grabbing their coats, the two stormed out.

Chara went to her bedroom and knelt and began to pray. Later that night she crawled into bed alone. She knew that her husband, Alec, would join her later, after he finished his nightly consumption of Ouzo.

The next morning, Alec rolled over in bed, and reached out to Chara. He found it comforting to touch her before rising. Chara was not there. Alec sat up and looked around the room and then glanced toward the bathroom. Chara was nowhere. He got up and shuffled to the kitchen. No Chara. He returned to the bedroom and could not figure out why his wife's pajamas were still under the covers. He turned and walked to Alexander and Leto's bedroom.

Alec opened the door. His two sons were fast asleep. Even though they were considered adults, they still resided at the home that they grew up in—victims of the poor economy and lack of jobs. No one was hiring and neither son could sell any of their paintings. Families were forced to live together, which was another reason for Alec to have resentment toward the government and the church. He walked over to Alexander and shook him awake. He whispered loudly, "Son, do you know where your mother is?"

Alexander whispered, "no" and rolled over, covering his head. He was fighting a bad hangover.

Alec stepped over to Leto's bed and asked the same thing. Leto responded, "No, Papa," and laid his head back down on his pillow.

Alec left his sons' bedroom and called Chara's parents. He received their answering service, "Hello, please leave a message. We will return your call as soon as we can."

Alec squinted. It was unusual for Chara's parents not to be home at this time of day. "Hello, Pappous and Giagia, Alec, here. Please call me back and let me know if Chara is with you, or if you have heard from her. She is not here. I am getting worried. Thanks."

Alec failed to hear from Chara's parents. He found out later in the day that they, too, had disappeared.

Alec had never forgiven the magicians for taking his Chara away from him. The explanation that the new director, Nef Quietus, had given following the disappearance had sounded logical. Alec had never trusted the Jews. He thought, *If it was Jesus taking his believers home before his return, he would have taken the boys too. They were both baptized and good boys. Those two terrorist magicians in Jerusalem can rot in Hades.*

Then the great quake resulting from the first trumpet that had devastated the world came. Alexander and Leto were with their friends drinking. The tavern shook violently. Some patrons, including Alexander and Leto, dove under the solid cypress tables for cover. Those that did not perished.

Alec was one of the unlucky ones. He was in a drunken stupor at home from excessive amounts of Ouzo. The ceiling of his home caved in, and a large bookshelf toppled to the ground, crushing Alec.

The boys found their father's body as they sifted through the rubble. The home was destroyed.

Again, Nef Quietus, made a good case as to why the blame fell directly on the magicians in Jerusalem. At Alec's funeral, the boys swore that one day they would seek revenge for what the Jews did to their family.

CHAPTER 29

Alexander and Leto created a shelter within the rubble of their home. The two eked out sustenance by doing odd jobs and begging. They had survived the war and the scorpion sting and supported the new order with loyal vengeance.

When the new director's economic edict was declared and then came to fruition, Alexander and Leto had their house rebuilt. It was a comfortable twelve hundred square feet, and they were happy to ask Eleni and Chryssa Hanas to live with them. The two sisters' pasts paralleled Alexander and Leto's. They, too, had lost their mother in the disappearance and their father in the war. They blamed the Jews for their loss. The four often hung out together at the tavern, and being together was comfortable. After all, Alexander and Leto needed four people per the square footage allotted them. Best to live with someone you knew. Besides, they were attracted to each other.

All four joined the one-world religion and had a double wedding: Alexander married Chryssa, and Leto married Eleni. Even though both men were budding artists, they realized that their future was in manual labor. Athens needed to be rebuilt, and they would have work enough to support their new family. Alexander entered training to become an electrician and Leto a cabinetmaker.

The economy improved dramatically when the messiah declared himself the world leader and the Mashianity Church evolved. All four were proud to call themselves Mashians. They were eager to be near the front of the line to receive the chip declaring their belief. The foursome looked forward to the Friday night communions but even more so to Saturday's full day of pleasure.

Within the first year of the new order, Chryssa had a baby girl, Zoe. She and Alexander were elated. It increased their number of credits, and they were helping the new society grow in number. Chryssa knew she had to give up Zoe in six months when she stopped nursing. When Chryssa started to get depressed about Zoe's leaving, Alexander would say, "The children's home will do an excellent job of training Zoe and caring for her. We can start on a second child as soon as you stop breastfeeding." Chryssa would relax and accept Alexander's encouraging words. After all, she knew that giving up Zoe was inevitable.

The family of four was overjoyed that they would add even more credits as soon as Eleni gave birth. She was a few months behind Chryssa in her pregnancy.

Three months after Zoe's birth, Eleni was rushed to the hospital to deliver her baby. The birth was much longer than expected. After the baby was swaddled and placed on Eleni's chest, Eleni began to have a seizure. The newborn was immediately removed from the mother, and the nurse and doctor did all they could; but Eleni died. Her three family members were devastated. The government immediately took Leto's unnamed newborn son away from him and to the children's home.

Leto felt empty and confused. The days of pleasure helped him cope. It was only two months later when he met Katarina. They were attracted to each other immediately, and while high on hashish and alcohol they decided to marry. Katarina moved in with Leto, Alexander, and Chryssa within the week. Even though the church frowned on marriage, Leto wanted to honor his mother's memory.

A month after Katarina joined the Callis' household, the government picked up Zoe. Two months later Chryssa found that she was with child for the second time. The household was elated when Katarina discovered that she, too, was pregnant.

The two newborns entered the brave new order two weeks apart. Chryssa was able to comfort Katarina when the children were taken six months later. The cycle continued as both women were pregnant within the next month. The four family members loved watching the credits grow as the population exploded around the globe.

✝

The plague of sores had almost debilitated Alexander and Leto, but they were determined to keep going as best they could. Chryssa was covered with boils and became so weak that she suffered from extreme malnutrition. Her latest pregnancy had ended abruptly.

Katarina thought the salve would get her safely through her latest pregnancy, but she was mistaken. Her spontaneous abortion was the result of her emaciated state. The two women cried, not for the loss of their unborn children but for the loss of their credits.

After the water supply around the world turned to blood, the lack of unpolluted water caused the entire global community to grow weak and unproductive. Alexander and Leto spent their time foraging for liquid for themselves and their wives.

The plague of the scorching sun arrived, and it cost the foursome dearly. From the lack of sufficient water, Katarina and Chryssa were too weak to go on in the inferno that encompassed the earth. Leto came home early and found Chryssa lying on the floor lifeless. He ran to the bedroom and Katarina's pulse was so weak he could barely feel it. Leto scooped her up into his arms and started to the nearest infirmary. By the time Leto reached potential help, he discovered a line two blocks long—people waiting for some relief. Leto struggled to hold Katarina as he pushed his way up the line. A nurse intercepted Leto only to tell him that he was carrying a corpse.

The emotional pain the two men felt was unbearable. The anguish soon turned to rage and frustration, only to be elevated when the day turned to night.

Through squinted eyes and clenched teeth Alexander said, "Leto, I heard that the messiah is asking for volunteers to join his global GSS military force. They plan to march on the Jews and the Christian terrorists. These hypocrites are behind these plagues and the millions of deaths around the world. Rumor has it that the terrorists are joining the Jews in a place called Petra."

Leto's spirits lifted as he said, "Let's go. We can travel on the transport. The heat has dropped to the low hundreds, and the flights are safe to fly now. The transport will take all volunteers to Jerusalem. First, we should go to this place called Petra. If there are Jews there, we can avenge the deaths they have caused. I know where we can get some explosives. We'll sneak into Petra and kill as many as possible in the name of the supreme being."

Alexander sneered at the thought. "If we survive, we can return to Jerusalem and join the battle in the valley outside of the city. I think it is called Armageddon."

The two brothers headed for the airport in the blackness. Getting seats on the plane was easy. Due to the preceding months of plagues, few members of the community were interested in travel.

The plane landed in Jerusalem, and the brothers found the city in chaos. Leaving the group and slipping onto a military transport vehicle to Eilat went unnoticed.

From Eilat, Alexander and Leto started on the last leg of their journey to Petra. Alexander had stuffed into his backpack several solar batteries to his flashlight. He knew that they would be traveling by foot and because the darkness was so intense his artificial light would be essential if they were to accomplish their goal. He also knew that the batteries would only last until the current power was gone; there was no sun to recharge the batteries. They had to cover as much terrain as possible without stopping and use the flashlights sparingly.

As the two brothers traversed the countryside, they picked up fellow travelers. Many were going to the sanctuary in Petra because there was a rumor that the fortress had food and water. They were desperate. One traveler shared, "My girlfriend and I heard they are letting some people in. We hear that they have food and water and the temperature is cool.

I bet they have some type of light as well. The messiah will conquer all, but we need some respite now. We will return to Jerusalem as soon as we get replenished."

Another member of the traveling group responded, "What makes you think we can enter and leave as we wish? I, for one, am going to beg. I will do whatever it takes to save my wife." He looked at Alexander's backpack and asked, "So what's in the bag?"

Alexander held onto the strap to his backpack a little tighter. "It's not anything that will help you. No food or drink. I have back-up batteries, and if you stay by me, you will be able to see the path."

"How about your brother's backpack?"

Alexander glanced over at Leto. "He has some miscellaneous items for nourishment." Alexander did not mention the explosives hidden at the bottom of the bag. "Stay with us and do not tell anyone. We will share with you and your wife."

The traveler nodded in agreement as he and his wife moved closer to Alexander and the light. The group was able to walk at only a slow pace. It took over a week of steady walking to get in the proximity of Petra and to see its glow in the darkness.

The trekker in the lead said, "There, there it is. Let's keep heading toward the light."

†

As the desperate group approached Petra, the outside perimeter had several people milling about. Alexander walked up to one and inquired, "What are you doing out here? Why don't you go inside?"

The stranger slowly looked at Alexander with his hollow eyes and said with a hoarse voice, "Stand and watch, you will see."

Alexander leaned over to Leto and whispered, "Let's observe what's going on. We need to assess the situation and not barge our way up to the front."

Leto nodded in agreement.

Alexander turned to his fellow companions as his eyebrows raised and eyes widened. "Look, they just let a couple in. Go on ahead and get some relief. We will be along shortly."

Leto looked at his brother, squinted his eyes, and tilted his head.

As the couple slowly started for the entrance, Alexander shrugged his shoulders and said, "I befriended them to use as decoys. Now we need them to do our bidding so we can better know how to proceed."

The fellow traveler and his wife pushed their way to the front and walked up to the opening to Petra. They faced a large man who had a commanding air about him. He held a staff and his face seemed to glow. "My wife and I have lost everything, and we are desperate. Please let us enter."

The guard looked at the two standing in front of him. He ordered them to uncover their foreheads. They hesitated. "Now!" the guard's voice boomed.

The two complied and the mark of the beast was evident.

The guard's voice rang out, "It is written, 'As you sow, so shall you reap.' You have made your choice. Now be gone. Your entrance is denied!"

"But, sir," the traveler pleaded, "We will gladly denounce the messiah and repent of our sins and accept Jesus. Please reconsider." They both dropped to their knees.

The guard looked into the two strangers' eyes and said, "The seat of mercy is now empty because the gate to the Temple in heaven is closed until the seven bowls are delivered to the earth. The seat of judgment is ready for the final Great White Judgment day. You may plead your case to the creator at the appointed time. Now be gone!"

Alexander and Leto watched intently. They noticed that about a dozen men had moved within five feet of the entrance. The two travelers were on their knees crying. A man moved over to them and ordered them to get up and move out of the way. The man and his wife complied, resigned with the fact that they were not gaining entrance.

The leader of the group of twelve yelled "Now!" The men rushed the entrance. The guard stepped back inside the Petra outer area. The first man to penetrate the opening immediately fell to his side writhing in abdominal pain. The second, third, and fourth fell on top of the first, grabbing their stomachs. The other eight stopped. One of the remaining bravely put his foot over the threshold of the opening, and he, too, collapsed in excruciating pain. The guard stepped forward and effortlessly picked each of the men up, throwing them outside of the entrance.

One of the remaining intruders yelled, "You hypocrites! You say you are Christians. Christians are supposed to be forgiving and accepting. You are all liars and phonies."

The guard looked at the man who was yelling. The guard's voice drowned out all others as he said, "It is written, enter through the narrow gate. For wide is the gate and broad is the road that leads to destruction, and many enter through it. But small is the gate and narrow the road that leads to life, and only a few find it. You have made your choice and it is written on your forehead. Now be gone."

Alexander and Leto continued their reconnaissance. Alexander noticed a small group of five people with their heads bowed standing off to one side near the threshold. "Leto, look at that group over there." Alexander pointed. As they observed the small group of Christians, the one guarding the entrance to Petra raised his staff and pointed toward the small praying huddle. The mob of people blocking the path between the five Christians and the entrance begrudgingly opened a way for them to pass. The group moved to the Petra opening and raised their head coverings to display the mark of the Holy Spirit. Archangel Michael beamed. He was always pleased to witness the mark of his Lord on the forehead of a fellow believer. Michael stepped aside and the five Christians entered.

"Leto, I have an idea. Alexander paused and pointed. Look at the group over there with three people slowly working their way to the front. They were bowing their heads earlier. Come on!"

Alexander and Leto inched their way toward the three Christians. As they intercepted them, Alexander told Leto to bow his head and act as if he were praying like they used to at their mother's church. Leto complied. The three Christians let Alexander and Leto into their group. Alexander and Leto's headbands hid the mark of the beast on their foreheads. As the small band of Christians moved close to the entrance, Michael lifted his staff and a path to the entrance opened again. One of the Christians let Alexander and Leto go in front of him. The first two followers of Christ entered. As soon as Alexander took his first step into the opening to Petra, he doubled over in pain, falling to the ground. Leto fell screaming on top of him. Michael let the last Christian guest step over the two on the ground and then picked the two brothers up and pushed them back out.

Alexander crawled to his feet. His face wrinkled up and his eyes squinted as he turned to face archangel Michael. He demanded, "I was baptized in the church and attended church faithfully most of my young life. I wanted to be a deacon and I believed in Jesus. My mother said that my salvation could never be taken away. Now, let me in!"

Michael shook his head slowly and said, "It is written, as my Lord said, 'Therefore everyone who hears these words of mine and puts them into practice is like a wise man who built his house on the rock. The rain came down, the streams rose, and the winds blew and beat against that house; yet it did not fall, because it had its foundation on the rock. However, everyone who hears these words of mine and does not put them into practice is like a foolish man who built his house on sand. The rain came down, the streams rose, and the winds blew and beat against that house, and it fell with a great crash.'"

Michael pressed on for all to hear, "He also spoke through his disciple Matthew about you and others like you when he had Matthew write: 'Not everyone who says to me, 'Lord, Lord,' will enter the kingdom of heaven, but only the one who does the will of my Father who is in heaven. Many will say to me on that day, 'Lord, Lord, did we not prophesy in your name and in your name drive out demons and, in your name, perform many miracles?' Then I will tell them plainly, 'I never knew you. Away from me, you evildoers!' The archangel Michael paused, looked each brother in the eyes, and said, "You have chosen the easy way and ignored our Lord's commands. As the Lord peers into your heart, he sees the truth of your love, and he sees that your love is for the great deceiver. Now, be gone!"

Alexander and Leto limped back to their observation area. Alexander pulled Leto to his side and said, "Watch for another group of those pompous Christians gathering. This time we will help them to their eternity." Alexander took his backpack off and pulled out his detonator. Leto followed suit. Soon the two brothers had armed their explosives.

A group of Christians formed outside the gate where they started to pray. Alexander and Leto moved to the group's proximity and yelled, "Praise be to the supreme being!" They pushed the detonation buttons.

Nothing happened. Alexander pushed his button again. Nothing. He looked at Michael as Michael lifted his staff and a path opened for the believers.

Alexander looked defeated. He grabbed Leto's arm. "Let's get out of here. We will go back to Jerusalem and join the army. We will still get to kill some Jews and Christians for the messiah."

Alexander and Leto walked for 200 yards. When they were alone, there was a loud explosion and a bright light lit up the darkness around the two brothers—the blasting caps came to life and sent the shock waves through the C-4 in the backpacks. After the explosion, a man stood atop a large rock and shouted at Michael, "What kind of a god do you so-called Christians worship who would kill people and cause such pain throughout the world? We worship a god that brought us pleasure and prosperity, the true supreme being."

The sky lit up as archangel Gabriel entered from the seventh level and hovered over Petra for all to see and hear. His voice rang out as he said, "Rejoice, saints and apostles and prophets! God has judged them for the way they treated you. With such violence, the great city of Babylon and the religion of Mashianity will be thrown down, never to be found again. The music of harpists and musicians, flute players and trumpeters will never be heard from her again. By Abaddon's magic spell, all the nations were led astray. In Mashianity was found the blood of prophets and of saints, and of all who had been killed on the earth."

James had returned to his home and was playing peek-a-boo with Jimmy. As Gabriel's booming voice rang out, James fell to his knees. Little Jimmy became quiet and copied his Bompa and kneeled. James, Jimmy, and the thousands living in Petra heard what sounded like the roar of a great multitude in heaven shouting, "Hallelujah, salvation and glory and power belong to our God, for true and just are his judgments. He has condemned the great prostitute who corrupted the earth by her adulteries. He has avenged on her the blood of his servants."

Aaron, Cindy, Stacey and all of God's family were on their knees as they heard the great multitude continue "Hallelujah." Then a loud voice filled the whole sky, "Praise our God, all of his servants, you who respect who he is and what power he has whether you are small or great!"

CHAPTER 30

Spry, still feeling the discomfort of the sores, slowly walked into Nef's office. He gingerly sat down. Nef glanced up and then returned his attention to his computer. Spry's face crunched up as he said, "The emergency generators are holding up and the headquarters is well lit." Spry looked at the windows and commented, "The total blackness encompassing the globe makes the windows look like they have blackout shades on them." Spry paused, looked back at his master and painfully said, "The entire globe is in total darkness. Travel is almost impossible. With no moonlight or stars, and little artificial light available, our army is forming extremely slowly. We have millions at the river Euphrates, but most of the bridges were destroyed from the war, quake, or deterioration during the extreme heat. No way to cross over. There are reports that men are sitting in the hot bloody water and gnawing their tongues in agony."

Spry formed a slight smile as he said, "I am pleased to report that they are cursing Jesus and his followers because of their situation. They are ready to move toward Israel; we simply need to help them get here."

Nef looked over at Spry. "I will call Sterns." He picked up his phone and said, "General Sterns."

Sterns answered immediately and Nef barked out, "General Sterns, get the gunships up in the air as soon as possible. Have their searchlights on. We need to light the way for our stranded volunteer army at the Euphrates. I must have their massive army in Israel. Also, prepare the large army transport planes for trips across the Atlantic to recover every able-bodied person to be brought to Israel. I need every individual able to carry a weapon to help me defeat the Christian terrorists! We need to get our military forces from around the world. Give the pilots more pain medicine and extra salve. I want every plane available running shuttles 24/7. Do you understand?"

"Yes, sir, my messiah," Sterns said with little enthusiasm from the pain.

"I want your report by morning as to how the migration to Israel will be completed. This total darkness is annoying but not anything like the sun. The heat is still intense but bearable. Have the transport and gunships load up with juices to give to anyone coming to fight the terrorists." Nef hung up. He looked at Spry. "Sterns will set up rendezvous points and gather a fighting contingency. We will bribe them with food and drink."

†

Jesus tilted his head. He sighed, closed his eyes and then opened them again. Watching the intensity of the activity in level three he said, "For the sake of my elect, I must return ahead of schedule or not one of my believers outside of Petra will survive." Jesus looked into the eyes of his faithful angel and ordered, "Pour the sixth bowl over the river Euphrates."

The angel bowed his head, turned, lifted the bowl and poured out the content.

†

The army that was milling on the banks of the Euphrates was a determined military power. Some men had succumbed to the harsh environment, but many stayed focused on the military goal—to rendezvous with their messiah and defeat the enemy.

The eastern army had devised ways to survive and continued to prepare for the coming battle. The primary lighting was torchlight.

Because of the low volume of gas, all fuel was dedicated to the reduced armor corps, which had reconfigured the engines to run on gasoline. Due to the lack of sunlight and to reduce dependency on solar fuel, the calvary was forced to abandon the armored vehicles and return to their original mode of travel—horseback. They had commandeered hay and grain from large storage facilities throughout China.

Food was becoming scarce, and the Euphrates was polluted. When possible, soldiers would use desalination units to purify water, but the sheer number of military personnel and extreme pollution made that impossible for many. Dysentery was added to the list of woes and some were forced to find relief from thirst with their own urine. Survival was critical to their cause and to their supreme being.

General Chin, the commanding general of the world's largest army, stood ankle deep in the Euphrates River. He was contemplating how to get his men and women over to the other side. He knew that the messiah needed the general's army's might to help defeat the Jewish and Christian terrorists in Israel.

Holding his torch, the general strained to see into the blackness. He glanced down. He thought that the level of the river had changed. He bent over and held the torch close to his boots. The river was now below his foot. He thought, *What is going on? Is the water level receding?* To his utter amazement, he was standing on a dry riverbed. *A minute ago, I was in ankle deep water.* General Chin raised his hands and shouted, "Praise be to the supreme being!" He began walking toward the other side of the river. As he moved closer to the middle he was still on dry land. Chin turned and began running back toward the riverbank. "Colonel Leu!" General Chin yelled into his walkie-talkie. "Colonel Leu, do you read me?"

"Yes, sir, I read you loud and clear."

The general said breathlessly, "The river has dried up. Get orders to all divisions to break camp and get our army across the river. Our supreme being has cleared the way for us to cross. We must proceed as quickly as possible before the river water returns."

The army, which had gathered at the banks of the river, began to break camp in the dark.

General Chin notified General Sterns of their good fortune. He asked his commanding officer to thank the messiah for him.

General Sterns, doped up with pain medication, entered Nef's office and sat down next to Spry. Spry and Nef had been discussing the upcoming communion ceremony.

Sterns knew he had to rally for the cause, but his normally ridged back and impeccable military posture had been replaced with slumping shoulders and a hanging head. He glanced at Spry and then addressed Nef, "My messiah, I have good news and bad. First, the good. The great army coming from the east is crossing the Euphrates as we speak. General Chin said to thank you for drying it up for their crossing."

Nef looked up at Sterns. Displaying no emotion, he said, "That was a stroke of genius; was it not?" Abaddon said to his archangel, Nergal, "I love playing chess with an idiot. Jesus has made a blunder by letting my largest contingency with the greatest killing power join the coming war. We will crush Jesus and his band of followers when they come."

General Sterns was oblivious to Abaddon's comment and responded, "Yes, my lord and master. It was a great miracle that you pulled off for Chin. We need another act of brilliance. I have received responses from all the transport units. They are reporting that the rendezvous areas around the globe are sparsely populated. After seeing what happened to Rome and still enduring the sores, total darkness, and the lack of drinkable water, people have gone back to their shelters and show little desire to fight."

Sterns was not surprised when Nef became incensed. "Go out in the outer office and call your two best generals. Get them here as soon as possible. When they arrive, report back here."

Sterns left the room.

Abaddon called out his two archangels. Decedre morphed out of Spry, Nergal out of Nef. Both bowed before their master. Abaddon looked at his two archangels and ordered, "Call on your legions to assist us."

Nergal bowed. He stood up straight and proclaimed, "From the depth of my region in level six, I call out my legions of fear and rebellion. Come forth to serve!" Out of his mouth came the demonic forces called "fear" followed by the forces called "rebellion."

Decedre mirrored Nergal and called out "obstinacy" and "greed." The area filled with an army of demonic spirits from level six.

Abaddon's eyes narrowed. He surveyed his new recruits. "Welcome, my army of frogs." He looked at Decedre and Nergal and commented, "Get it? Fear, Rebellion, Obstinacy and Greed—my FROG army." Abaddon spread out his arms as if to introduce them to his subordinates.

Nergal looked at Decedre and said with a smirk, "They look a bit like earthly frogs, don't they?"

Abaddon chimed in, "The Almighty sent frogs to torture me in Egypt. I will now send frogs to help me torture and defeat his errand boy, Jesus!" The army cheered.

The spiritual army, unseen by the human eye, waited in anticipation for orders from their Lord and God that will result in the coming victory.

Abaddon ordered Nergal to resume his control of the earthly messiah for a short time. Decedre reentered Spry as three earthly generals entered the room.

Generals Lagshmivar and Hashemi were in Jerusalem for a war conference and agreed to join General Sterns to fulfill their messiah's request. The three entered Nef's office, saluted, bowed on one knee, and lowered their heads.

Abaddon walked over to the three and he placed his hand on each as he ordered a third of the FROG legion to enter each one. Abaddon then reentered Nef.

✝

As his sores disappeared, Nef said, "You may rise and be seated." The three generals slowly stood and sat in the chairs that Spry had placed in front of Nef's desk. They all displayed sores and a very low energy level. Spry sat in the back by the door. Nef looked intently at each officer and continued, "General Lagshmivar, so good to see you again. You were a great leader in saving the global community for me in the past, and I have appreciated your continued dedication since the Great War." Nef then looked at General Hashemi, "And you, my old friend, have also served me and the global community well for theses many months. My personal thanks are in order." Nef looked at all three generals and continued, "I have an assignment for all of you. You will carry it out as soon as you can get your supersonic jets ready. You will fly to all areas of the globe to raise an army such as this world has never seen. Now that we have no light and our religious and economic center is destroyed, every able person must come to Israel. Destroying the cause of our global pain is critical to the human survival. There is a valley in which we will gather. It is called Armageddon."

Nef rose from his chair, walked around his desk, and laid his hands on each of the three generals. He beamed as the sores dissipated and the three servants sat up straight and looked at each other. Nef could see the change, and he was pleased as he saw each one sigh with relief. He stepped back and sat on the desk with one foot touching the floor. He then spoke with a strange voice. "I have given you great powers to perform miraculous signs. You will demonstrate how powerful I am by your actions, and you *will* bring me an army."

General Sterns stood up and pointed at Nef's world globe. The globe instantly burst into flames. He looked apologetically at Nef. "Sorry!" Nef raised his hand and brushed the air toward the globe. The fire went out and the globe sat smoldering.

"Never mind, General, but save your theatrics for the global populace. Whatever the three of you need to do to bring the cowards to their knees and receive their commitments to follow your command, it will be done! Tell them that I brought peace and prosperity once and I can do it again, but I need their help. General Sterns will assign your areas of responsibility. Now, go build me an army!"

Molly entered the room as the three generals left. She struggled to speak and mumbled, "I received word that the massive army from the East Region is crossing the Euphrates as we speak. General Chin said that their numbers are over 200,000,000. I thought the river was not passable."

Nef shrugged his shoulders. "I dried it up so they could join us. Contact Chin and be sure that they are bringing their entire nuclear arsenal."

Molly lowered her head and said slowly, "I will call him back." She stumbled back out of the room.

Nef clapped his hands together and looked at Spry. "Again, Jesus performs a miracle on my behalf. I love taking credit for his blunders. My army will come, and we will defeat Jesus!"

Even though it was painful, Spry grinned.

CHAPTER 31

Brad walked with a quicker step than normal as he approached the front of the room full of staff members. He pivoted behind the podium. Larry followed and stood behind him. It was time for Brad to address his followers, those present and those around the globe via Cyberspace.

Brad looked at the room full of fellow believers. "I strongly feel that today will be among my last presentations about our Lord and Savior Jesus Christ. Due to the intense persecution by the antichrist, Nef Quietus and his followers, there are not many Christians left to hear this teaching. For those who can hear or see me, I will be instructing from the book of Matthew. If you can, please turn to Chapter 13, Verses 24-30 and 37-43.

First, I would like to say that I believe the Lord is coming soon, so please ready yourselves through prayer. We have witnessed the prophecy of the Lord found in Zechariah Chapter 13, Verses 8 and 9. Two-thirds of our brothers and sisters have been martyred by the antichrist's brutality. If the Lord waits much longer, none of the rest of us will be alive to enter the millennium. The Lord prophesied through his servant Matthew in Chapter 24 and Verse 22: 'If those days had not been cut short, no one would survive, but for the elect's sake those days shall be shortened.' God also prophesied the same at the end of Isiah 65:8: '...so will I do on behalf of my servants; I will not destroy them all.' Our Lord will not be able to go the entire one thousand ninety days given for the second half of tribulation noted in Daniel, which we have covered in past studies. It is clear that we are in that prophesied time now. According to Pastor Chris O'Malley, Jesus will cut it short by about thirty days to save the one-third of his remaining saints living on earth."

Brad glanced at the door. He felt a sense of urgency as he continued, "In Matthew, Chapter 13, Verses 24-30, Jesus told his disciples a parable: 'The kingdom of heaven is like a man who sowed good seed in his field. But while everyone was sleeping, his enemy came and sowed weeds among the wheat, and went away. When the wheat sprouted and formed heads, then the weeds also appeared. The owner's servants came to him and said, 'Sir, didn't you sow good seed in your field? Where then did the weeds come from?' 'An enemy did this,' he replied. The servants asked him, 'Do you want us to go and pull them up?' 'No,' he answered, 'because while you are pulling the weeds, you may root up the wheat with them. Let both grow together until the harvest. At that time, I will tell the harvesters: First collect the weeds and tie them in bundles to be burned; then gather the wheat and bring it into my barn.' Later Jesus's disciples asked what the parable meant."

Brad paused and raised his eyebrows as he looked out at his audience. They wanted the answer to the disciple's question as well. "So, in Verses 36-43, it says: 'His disciples came to him and said, 'Explain to us the parable of the weeds in the field.' He answered, 'The one who sowed the good seed is the Son of Man. The field is the world, and the good seed stands for the sons of the kingdom. The weeds are the sons of the evil one, and the enemy who sows them is the devil. The harvest is the end of the age, and the harvesters are angels. As the weeds are pulled up and burned in the fire, so it will be at the end of the age. The Son of Man will send out his angels, and they will weed out of his kingdom everything that causes sin, and all who do evil. They will throw them into the fiery furnace, where there will be weeping and gnashing of teeth. Then the righteous will shine like the sun in the kingdom of their Father. He, who has ears, let him hear.' This is what his Word teaches, and we know that God cannot lie. We are in the very last days and…" A man with a glow about him appeared in the doorway. He stood tall and was dressed in an unusual manner. His voice was both commanding and gentle. "All of you need to move outside. Please come." Brad stepped down from the podium. Larry followed closely. Brad, Larry and archangel Michael led the flock out of the building into the illumination of their Lord as they ascended toward heaven.

James, Stacey, and Jimmy had taken up residence just off the common area in Petra. The outdoor communal gathering center was where the people met and prayed and enjoyed each other's company. Stacey was out with other young women visiting. Her father was playing with Jimmy inside. "Bompa, who talk?" Jimmy managed to say. James listened. He also heard a voice. It was coming from within. "Go outside of the dwelling to the open air. It is time!" James picked up Jimmy and headed for the door.

As James entered the common area, he saw everyone leaving their structures and heading for an open area. His eye caught Stacey's as she moved to his side and took his hand. Her face had a strange but beautiful glow about it. James looked at Jimmy's face, and it shone as well. He looked around and noticed that everyone was starting to glow. He saw Aaron and his family. Cindy was with them. They moved toward each other, and the entire Petra population started to float upward. "Just as I thought, it's happening just prior to the festival of Sukkot, as predicted," Aaron yelled over to James. James smiled and then looked down. The common area was moving away from his feet. As they cleared the cliffs surrounding Petra, he looked into the sky and saw other lights moving up in the far distance. James beamed as he saw his friends and noted the look of pure joy on Aaron's face.

As the group from Petra converged in an area high above Mount Zion, Cindy said, "Look," as she pointed upward. James saw a large number of people dressed in white and kneeling.

James said loudly back to Cindy as the rest of the clan looked up, "They must be the dead in Christ that were martyred in the last months since the Temple closed. Scripture says that they will be resurrected first and then we follow."

The archangel Michael was floating near and said, "Yes, they have come out of the great tribulation—they have washed their robes and made them white in the blood of the Lamb. Therefore, they will be before the throne of God and serve him day and night in his Temple, and he who sits on the throne will spread his tent over them. Never again will they hunger; never again will they thirst. The sun will not beat upon them, or any scorching heat. For the Lamb at the center of the throne will be their shepherd—he will lead them to springs of living water—and God will wipe away every tear from their eyes." With an upturned face, Michael continued, "I must join my Lord. I will see you soon." He disappeared.

Joining the martyred saints were the one hundred forty-four thousand, and behind them were the rest of the saints from under the altar. Believers, taken to the seventh level over the many years, followed them. The angels of the Lord surrounded all. James felt someone grab his arm. It was his son, Brad. After Larry hugged Stacey, he took Jimmy. Brad embraced his dad and then looked up at the action coming from the heavenly realm.

The Petra occupants noticed the saints, the one hundred forty-four thousand, and the believers above them began to part in the middle. As they gazed into the crowd, a light appeared that was like the sun rising in the early morning on a clear day. Then they saw why everyone was kneeling.

James saw that the gate to level seven was standing open. There before him was a beautiful white stallion. The rider's eyes were like blazing fires, and on his head were many crowns. There was a name written across his sash that no one could read, and he was dressed in a robe dipped in blood. His name was the Word of God. The armies of heaven, led by Michael and Gabriel, were following him, riding on white horses and dressed in fine linen—white and clean. As the procession moved closer to James, he noticed that the lead rider had "King of kings and Lord of lords" written on his robe and thigh.

✝

After riding through the heavens to the prophesied mountaintop of Zion, Jesus stopped. As he dismounted, he stepped onto Mount Zion with the one hundred forty-four thousand standing alongside of him. The Jewish missionaries had Jesus's name and the Almighty's name written on their foreheads.

Michael and Gabriel remained on their horses behind Jesus. As the saints watched from above, the army of angels joined Michael and Gabriel.

Jesus and his chosen moved with swiftness to Megiddo as Jesus looked toward the valley of Armageddon.

When Jesus arrived, the western end of the valley looked as if the sun had risen. Wherever the Son of Man appeared, the area shone brightly as if it were midday. Jesus looked over the vast valley. The far end was filled with Abaddon's army, which retreated to the shadows of the battlefield. Jesus could see the determination on the faces of his enemy.

An eagle flew through the air shouting, "Woe! Woe! Woe! to the inhabitants of the earth."

As the eagle flew out of sight to make its announcement to the world, Jesus looked up. He said in a loud voice, "All the birds flying in midair, come gather together for the great supper I will prepare for you. You may eat the flesh of kings, generals, and mighty men, of horses and their riders, and the flesh of all people, free and slave, small and great." The sky began to fill with large vultures.

Nef sat, breathing through his clenched teeth, facing Jesus from more than fifteen miles away at the opposite end of the valley. He was on his red stallion, and next to him was Spry, sitting on the big gray steed. Abaddon, from within Nef, was peering at the carpenter he had pursued for centuries—since the beginning of mankind. He felt excited. Abaddon thought to himself, *Now Jesus is on my turf and the Almighty is a bystander—observing from level seven. My time has finally come! The*

first time Jesus came as a carpenter, I had him crucified. This time I will not let him go. I will put him where he belongs—a special place I have for him in level six.

Nef, controlled by Abaddon, was firmly in charge while Spry, controlled by Decedre, was sitting on his horse to the antichrist's right. As the supreme spiritual leader, Spry was dressed in his priestly robe. Gog, Nef's king from Russia, was at Nef's left atop the black stallion. Nef's generals surrounded him along with Chief Hotaki, who was present as a reward for all the converts he had brought to Mashianity.

The regional directors, or kings, were standing behind the generals, who now bowed before their messiah.

Nef said loudly, "It will be thrilling to throw Jesus and his followers into Hades for eternity. Perhaps we will visit them often for sport." They all laughed.

Nef took note of his army. The Asian contingency, the eastern army led by General Chin, was two-hundred million strong. General Comrade Sergey Lagshmivar led the army from the Northern Region, and General Ahmad Hashemi led the troops from the Southern Region. The supreme general of the armies, General William Sterns, led the Western contingency. Abaddon looked out at the generals and confirmed that all were filled with his demonic legions.

Before the army was strategically placed, Nef had his generals gather for their final instructions. "General Lagshmivar, have you placed your troops in those caves over there and over there?" Nef pointed to the areas where he wanted the army from the Northern Region.

."Yes, my messiah. They are ready."

Nef nodded. "Good, when you receive my signal, you will attack from both sides."

General Lagshmivar nodded his head that he understood. He said, "The element of surprise will cause the terrorists to panic. Incredibly wise, my messiah."

Nef looked at Sterns. "General Sterns, you will lead your men down the center of the valley, following General Chin, and take the intruders head-on." Nef looked at Chin directly. "General Chin, you will lead the battle charge. First, send your deadly armor corps." Nef paused. "The appearance of your tanks looks like a lion's head, and the large gun barrel out the rear looks like it sends fire out of its tail." Nef smirked. "That should give the enemy pause. Have your cavalry follow the tanks and then your foot soldiers."

Nef turned his attention to General Hashemi. "The army from the Southern Region will circle around and flank Jesus from the rear, so wait until Jesus has engaged with General Chin and then move in."

Nef surveyed all of his generals. "You must wait for the initial aerial strike to settle. It will be a reign of terror on Jesus and his followers. Be sure that all soldiers are dressed in toxic-safe gear."

Nef dismissed his generals, who mounted their horses and headed for their armies.

Nef commented to Spry, "The soldiers dressed in their battle gear appear as if they are strange-looking praying mantises on the prowl. The masks make the soldiers look inhuman."

Nef sat tall on his stallion. He reviewed his plan in his head. *My battle strategy includes the launch of satellite-guided smart bombs to initiate the attack. The precious drones are at the ready to do my bidding.* Nef glanced to his rear imagining the launch pads his army had established.

Nef looked back over the valley and thought, *Since the Asian army has the most attack transports with fuel, they are on notice to move forward first, following the missile barrage. Next, the elite commandos are to ride into battle on horseback. I must use horses since fuel is so scarce. The black veil that Jesus laid over the earth, preceded by the scorching sun and total lack of water and normal wind patterns, has reduced fuel production to zero, thus my cavalry is proceeding on horseback. When I am victorious, I will have the power to return the atmosphere to normal because the Almighty will be on my side. He will give me the special powers that Jesus has, and the sun and moon will be as they were before the carpenter disrupted normalcy to try and punish my believers.*

With an expression of calmness, Nef continued visualizing his coming battle. *Jesus's followers, who survived the bombing will enter the contaminated valley to face my faithful believers. They will be crushed by Sterns and Chin's army. As the enemy focuses on the frontal attack, I will send in Lagshmivar from the sides. Hashemi will close any escape from the* rear. *When the chaos settles, they will all bow before me, and with their tongues they will confess that I am their lord!*

✝

Nef raised his arm and dropped it hard as he yelled into his two-way radio, "Launch the first wave."

Several nuclear-tipped warheads launched simultaneously from behind the Gilboa mountain range. The sky filled with what resembled shooting stars that were targeting Megiddo. Nef looked around with great expectation as he brought his binoculars to his eyes to watch the massive explosions. The warheads were small but potent.

Nef yelled to Spry, Gog, and Chief Hotaki, "Brace yourselves, the fireworks are about to start, and you may feel gusts of hot wind." Nef knew his troops would experience a blast of air but not to the point of causing physical damage. He was confident of the outcome. The tips, perfected to have great precision, would deliver deadly pinpointed consequences. Nef had his army dressed for the fallout, and they would be safe.

From within his human vessel Abaddon knew he could not kill angels, or Jesus, any more than Jesus could kill him, but he could show his dominance over the people and the earth and kill Christian undergrounders with Jesus. Abaddon thought, *The Almighty will see my supremacy, and he will demote Jesus and put me in my rightful position as the reigning king over all three levels.*

After perceiving Abaddon's thoughts, Jesus looked up and shook his head at Abaddon's naivety and pride. He took his right hand and waved it from right to left over his head. No one around Jesus took cover or even cringed for fear of impact. They knew they were with the Lord of lords. The army of angels surrounded the area of Megiddo.

CHAPTER 32

Nef's heart was beating fast as he anticipated the initial kill by the barrage of falling stars. *This is going to be a nice little introduction to what I have in mind for the carpenter and his stupid sycophants.* He watched as the first flame arched downward, followed by the rest of the wave of deadly nuclear-tipped missiles.

As the entire Abaddonic army looked on, the blitz bounced over Jesus and his followers like rocks skipping across a pond. They picked up speed, made a 180-degree turn, and headed back toward Nef. He stared at the coming dirty bombs.

Nef heard Chief Hotaki say, "Messiah?"

Spry responded, "Uh-oh."

The coming onslaught lost steam and abruptly fell toward earth. The Mashian army watched as the guided missiles exploded harmlessly in the middle of the valley of Armageddon. There were no soldiers in the bombs' path; but as the deadly shells were detonated, as they landed on the hard earth, the sound was deafening. The surrounding air and smoke were sucked in, forming mushroom clouds that rose several feet in the air. The wave of blasts followed and flattened the surrounding area, and the intense heat could be felt throughout the valley. Craters opened as the air filled with smoke, dirt, and radiation. The concussion from the hot wind caused thousands to stumble backward as men and women in green contamination protective gear fell and toppled like dominoes. Had Jesus not contained the damage, all of the enemy would have been destroyed.

Nef's eyes squinted as he yelled into his two-way radio. "Abort all launches. I repeat, this is your messiah. I am ordering you to stand down. No more missiles are to launch! Do you read me?"

A voice came over the two-way radio in Nef's hand. "We read you loud and clear. All launches are canceled."

Chief Hotaki said, "Good choice. Next ones might get closer. Then we'd glow in the dark." Spry started to laugh but thought better of it when Nef's eyes narrowed at him. The look on his messiah's face was not a pleasant one.

Nef's excitement and anticipation of the carpenter's demise started to wane. Looking through the binoculars, he saw no damage to his arch nemesis. Out of frustration he raised and dropped his hand. The valley filled with his troops charging toward Jesus. The eastern army marched first. Their tanks with breastplates of fiery red, dark blue, and yellow colors led the charge. From a distance, the front of each tank looked like the head of a lion. The tanks had short barrels that began to launch shells toward the opposite end of the valley. The tanks had larger barrels out of the opposite end of the turrets that resembled snakes with heads. Many tanks would stop, swing the turrets around, and lob larger shells. The smell of sulfur infiltrated the valley as Nef watched the explosions of deadly bombs hurling toward Jesus.

As the missiles came closer to where Jesus sat on his stallion, Jesus held up his hand and waved his arm from front to back. The shells no longer struck the ground but turned up and over Jesus's head toward General Hashemi's army as it attempted to flank Jesus. The surprise barrage of friendly fire took deadly aim. The results were devastating for the army from the Southern Region.

With a second massive onslaught of deadly missiles approaching, Jesus yelled, "return," and with a mighty shout his army of angels turned the shells toward the lion-faced tanks. They propelled back to their origins.

The cries of attack and determination for destruction soon gave way to cries of pain and retreat. With a raised hand and a shout, Jesus commenced an annihilation of over one-third of Abaddon's militia in a matter of seconds.

Jesus inspected the carnage before him. He gently pulled the final scroll from his chest plate and opened the last and seventh seal.

Jesus, along with his army, watched Abaddon's hordes stumbling in disarray on the valley floor.

There was silence for thirty minutes as the armed forces in the valley regrouped. Nef was screaming frantically into his two-way radio and barking commands as some semblance of order began to coalesce.

Generals Chin and Sterns could be seen riding back and forth encouraging their soldiers as battalions reorganized and faced their common enemy—Jesus. The next charge began, slowly at first, and then the attackers moved with frenzy.

Gabriel moved his white stallion next to Jesus and lifted a golden censer. It was filled with the prayers of all the saints, smoke, and topped off with fire from the altar.

Michael kicked his horse, moving to the other side of Jesus. Michael held the seventh bowl in one hand and a sickle in the other. Jesus looked at Michael and reached out his left hand. Michael lifted the sickle and placed it in his Lord's hand.

Jesus looked out over the valley as it overflowed with the attacking enemy. He lifted the sickle over his head. His voice could be heard across the valley of Armageddon region as he said, "It is time to swing the sickle, for the harvest is ripe. Come, trample the grapes, for the winepress is full, and the vats overflow, so great is their wickedness. Multitudes, multitudes, in the valley of decision! For the day of the Lord has come in the valley of decision." The titanic army of angels was unleashed on the attacking mortals.

From above, as the followers of Jesus were observing the utter defeat of Abaddon, Brad looked at his father James and then at Aaron. "I remember teaching a class on what he said. It was a quote from Joel, Chapter 3, Verse 13. We need to observe what is coming next, because from out of his mouth will come a sharp sword to strike down the nations."

"Bompa," Jimmy said, pointing up to level seven. They all looked up and saw an angel with a trumpet. They heard the trumpet blast. "It's the seventh and final trumpet," Larry said.

After the seventh angel sounded his trumpet, there were loud voices in heaven that filled the earth's atmosphere. Brad and all of Jesus's followers heard the following words: "The kingdom of the world has become the kingdom of our Lord, and of his Christ, and he will reign forever and ever."

†

Jesus looked up into heaven as he listened to the decree. He turned back around and wiped a tear from his right eye. He looked and nodded to both of his archangels. Gabriel lifted his golden censer, and Michael lifted his bowl.

Jesus commanded, "Release them into the air!"

Michael poured out his bowl, and Gabriel did the same with his golden censer. The Lord sat stoically as the rest of his army turned to look up as they, and all inhabitants on the earth, heard a voice originating from the Temple. The Almighty's thunderous voice roared from the throne, "IT IS DONE!"

Flashes of lightning, rumblings, and peals of thunder exploded in the atmosphere around the earth. The ground began to shake and heave. An earthquake, unlike any other, tore at the very fabric of the earth's crust.

In that instant, tsunamis swallowed up whole islands, and the tallest mountains crumbled from the violent force of God. God remembered Babylon the Great, representing the sinfulness of mankind, and gave her the cup filled with the wine of the fury of his wrath.

For the few who still had access to Cybernews, they heard a shaky voice on the air as a reporter said, "This is your global news update for those who can still hear or see me. The city of Babylon has split into three parts and has been consumed by fire. Some have described it as if fire and brimstone have rained down from heaven. This beautiful religious center for the defunct one-world religion is no more. All the inhabitants are presumed lost. The heat from the fire was so intense that it was felt for miles. The news correspondent reporting from Armageddon quoted our messiah as saying that he will send in first responders as soon as the heat subsides in Babylon and as soon as he defeats the terrorists on the battlefield. I have spoken with the head of security, and he is concerned that there will not be enough rescue personnel to meet the need. More on this calamity as soon as we have further updates."

The remaining soldiers in the valley of Armageddon regrouped once the ground settled. The generals were determined to continue their pursuit. The charge towards Jesus's army resumed as millions rushed on with their demonic powers.

Jesus held his right hand up, looked to the sky, and nodded his head. First, there was a rumbling like that of a bowling ball rolling down an alley. Then the sound of a roaring avalanche as the sky turned dirty gray.

The attacking army slowed. They stopped as they turned their eyes to the skies. From a distance high above, they observed small balls of snow forming. As the balls fell towards earth, they grew. The demon-filled warriors' eyes widened as they witnessed huge hailstones over a hundred pounds each falling from the sky. The possessing demons fled from their human vessels as the huge ice balls hit their intended targets as the bodies would split apart. The remaining Mashians cursed God for the plague of hail because the calamity was so terrible.

The hail relentlessly continued as the blood was beginning to flow throughout the valley floor. Combatants, including the general and the king of Russia, Gog, ran like scared rats to hide in caves in the surrounding hills. Out of fear from facing Jesus they yelled out for the rocks to fall on them and kill them.

General Sterns witnessed the carnage in the valley and started running for the hills, crying out for the rocks to fall on him and hide him from Jesus. He knew that he was about to suffer the consequence of his decision to follow the demonic messiah. His fate was sealed.

Nef watched the hailstones as the black cloud moved toward him, Chief Hotaki, and Spry. The large frozen snowballs fell on the three, ending their lives. Abaddon morphed out of Nef, changed into the red dragon, and roared in defiance as his entire armed forces were annihilated. Not one soul survived. The decimated bodies filled the valley floor as the blood rose to the bridles—almost four feet high—of the few remaining horses. Abaddon realized that no member of the Mashian religion was still alive since the destruction was worldwide.

Cybervision fell permanently silent as the inhabitants of earth prepared for judgment.

The human bodies of Nef, Spry, and Chief Hotaki lay crushed on the ground. Their horses lay lifeless next to them with vultures perched on their heads eager to fill their bellies. Abaddon and Decedre stood and stared at Jesus as he and his two archangels approached them from midair. The red dragon rose up and roared in defiance but was unable to flee.

"It was by the words that our Lord spoke that your religious following was destroyed," Michael said to Abaddon. "No one can withstand the truth of the Word. Where our Lord is, there cannot be lies or darkness!"

Michael dismounted along with Gabriel and both archangels bowed to one knee. Jesus, still mounted on his great white, looked at his archrival and said, "What Michael says is true. The two of you are banished to a new prison that will be sealed in a lake of burning sulfur below. Abaddon, you have manipulated humankind over the centuries and led my creations to their destruction as their Antichrist. And as for you, Decedre, you will join your master because, through your miraculous signs that you performed on Abaddon's behalf as his false prophet, you caused my beloved children to choose eternal doom rather than eternal light." Jesus raised his hand in front of his face and waved it from left to right. The ground in front of them opened.

Michael and Gabriel threw Decedre into the pit. His cries echoed as he descended.

Gabriel turned, walked to his mount, and removed an object. He approached his Lord and handed Jesus a chain.

Jesus swung it in the air like a cowboy roping a steer. He flung it and the heavy chain wrapped around Abaddon. Abaddon changed helplessly from a great red dragon into a crippled, defeated demonic angel, no longer a handsome being.

Jesus pointed to the bulge in Abaddon's sash and motioned his hand back toward his own body. The bulge ripped from its secure space and flew to Jesus's hand as he took possession of the keys to Hades. Michael and Gabriel shoved Abaddon into the pit. The legions of demons that Abaddon had called on to join him and to possess the members of the Mashian church stood helplessly by as they watched their leader's sentence be carried out. Jesus looked at the hordes of demonic angels and ordered them to follow Abaddon into their new prison. They had no choice but to obey.

As the very last inhabitant entered Hades, the gorge closed and a gate to the pit formed. The gate had a lock. Jesus dismounted. He walked to the edge of the Abyss and knelt on one knee. He placed the key into the lock as he heard Abaddon scream, "This is not over. I will be back!" Jesus turned the key.

Jesus stood, walked to the edge of the great valley of Armageddon, and gazed out. Surveying the scene, he appeared as the sun itself and bellowed in a loud voice, "It is time to feast!" The black buzzards, caracaras, condors, and tawny vultures gathered in such mass that the sky turned dark. In one swoop, the dark sky dropped to the ground as the birds began their assigned task. Christians, who had not died and had survived the tribulation, were dressed in nuclear protective gear, ready to continue the process when the birds finished.

✝

As the host of Christians, saints, prophets, and angels watched the process going on below, Brad said to his dad, "All that we are watching was prophesied some three thousand years ago by the prophet Ezekiel in Chapter 39. In parts of Verses 9 and 10 Ezekiel prophesied, 'Then those who live in the towns of Israel will go out and use the weapons for fuel and burn them up—the small and large shields, the bows and arrows, the war clubs and spears. For seven years they will use them for fuel. They will not need to gather wood from the fields or harvest it from the forests because they will use the weapons for fuel.' As we see the results of the war below, we can conclude that Ezekiel was referring to radioactive energy. Armageddon will be a special area set aside for the contaminated debris left over from the war, and the valley will be called the Valley of Hamon-Gog, the burial place of Gog's army. 'On that day I will give Gog a burial place in Israel, in the valley of those who travel east toward the sea. It will block the way of travelers because Gog and his hordes will be buried there. So it will be called the Valley of Hamon-Gog.' People may be "blocked" or required to travel around the valley because this area will be too contaminated for travelers. By centralizing all the nuclear waste, it will facilitate the cleansing of the outlying land. In Verse 12 Ezekiel told his readers that it would take seven months to bury all the bodies. This lengthy time of seven months is due to the time-consuming process of handling radioactive material. In parts of Verses 14 and 15 Ezekiel further wrote, 'Men will be regularly employed to cleanse the land. As they go through the land, and one of them sees a human bone, he will set up a marker beside it until the gravediggers have buried it in the Valley of Hamon-Gog. And so, they will cleanse the land.' Note that the bone is marked for disposal and not simply picked up. Only professionally trained gravediggers who can handle radioactive material can bury the bones in the designated radioactive dump."

James patted his son on the shoulder. "That is interesting. The Lord our God laid out so much for us to know and to help us understand what was to come before, during, and after his second coming. I was a fool for so long. I can understand how magnetic Abaddon and his ways were. It was your love and encouragement that opened my eyes to the truth and brought me to my knees."

"That may be true, Dad, but many standing and watching with us came to the Lord without prodding. They believed and obeyed as well. The Holy Spirit calls, but it is up to each individual to heed the call and resist the temptations presented to us by Satan." As Brad finished his comment, the A-Team family watched with anticipation of what was to follow—the millennium.

CHAPTER 33

The crowd of saints surrounding their Lord looked into level seven. Hearing what sounded like the roar of a great multitude in heaven shouting, "Hallelujah! Salvation, glory, and power belong to our God, for true and just are his judgments. He has condemned the great prostitute who corrupted the earth by her adulteries. He has avenged on her the blood of his servants." Again, they shouted, "Hallelujah! The smoke from her goes up, forever and ever."

The twenty-four elders and the four living creatures fell and worshiped God, who was seated on the throne. They cried, "Amen, Hallelujah!"

Then a voice came from the throne, "Praise your God, all you his servants both small and great, you who respect him as your Father!"

Following the celebration of the victory of Jesus over evil and sin, the believers joined Jesus as they took up residence on the earth. When Jesus walked into the Temple in Jerusalem, it lit up as if the sun were rising within its walls. The curtain to the Holy of Holies, where the high priest entered once a year to offer up the sacrifice for the sins of the nation, tore in half just as it did when Jesus died on the cross. This time Jesus walked onto the holy ground in the Holy of Holies and sat down on the throne by the Arc of the Covenant, sitting now as God in the flesh in his rightful place.

As the Lord sat, all who were outside awaiting his commandments could hear his voice. "As I promised you through my servant, Micah, 'You, Bethlehem Ephrathah, though you are small among the clans of

Judah, out of you will come for me one who will be ruler over Israel.' Well, I have come, and we will be in total tranquility throughout the world. In Isaiah 2:4 my prophet, Isaiah, spoke on my behalf and described this period as a time of peace where man will 'beat their swords into plowshares and their spears into pruning hooks. Nation will not take up swords against nation, nor will they train for war anymore.' I will fulfill my promise; then those of you who choose to love me above all else will dwell with me for eternity."

James's eyes widened and his mouth slackened as he looked at Aaron. "Who choose to? Who on earth would *not* choose to love him after seeing him in his true glory?"

Aaron looked back at James and replied, "Remember Adam and Eve? They walked and communed with God. They had a perfect world and only one command—do not eat of the tree of the knowledge of good and evil. Satan convinced them it was their right to defy God and eat whatever they wanted to, so they ate the fruit of the forbidden tree. Sin was introduced into the garden of Eden, and it took many centuries for God to bring us back to a peaceful world without Satan's influence."

"Oh, yeah. I guess we have our work cut out for us. We know from Revelation that Satan will be released again and we must get the flock ready to resist his deceptions."

Jesus continued, "The martyred saints from the second half of the tribulation will reign and dwell with me for a thousand years as my priests. Those raptured and those who remained on earth through the tribulation and stayed faithful to me will populate the earth as we enter the millennium. You will know that I, the Lord your God, dwell in Zion, my holy hill. Jerusalem will be holy—never again will foreigners invade her inner sanctum. From this day forward, the mountains will drip new wine, and the hills will flow with milk. All the ravines of the world will run with water. A fountain will flow out of the Lord's house to water the valleys. The feasts practiced in my honor by the twelve tribes of Jacob who made up the Jewish nation will be celebrated again, and it will be required to participate in the Feast of the Tabernacles every year. Now, everyone that I saved from the wrath of Abaddon and his followers may go out and repopulate the earth for the next thousand years. I will be your God, and you will be my people. Go in peace!"

†

During the first years of the millennium the inhabitants of the new order settled into a life of peace and beauty. The A–Team became a growing family and spent a great deal of time together laughing, praying, and worshiping their Lord and Savior. They took part in every celebration and took every opportunity to interact throughout the harmonious world.

Cindy loved to visit the Temple and commune with her daughter Penny, who went to be with the Lord at such a young age. Penny now served Jesus as a priest in the Temple. Chris and Michelle saw Paul and Caroline whenever they visited the Temple as they, too, served as priests.

Brad, CJ, and Michelle had met and married their perfect mates. They all were starting their own families with God at the center of all activities.

The weather during the millennium age was consistently perfect. Enjoying their new environment, the A-Team family was walking through a wooded area and noticed a wolf snuggled next to a little lamb. The lamb's mother was close by, showing no sign of fear. They saw a leopard and a goat lying together as friendly companions. Stacey and Larry held Jimmy's hand as they watched a calf being born as a lion rested nearby. It gave the newborn and its mother no concern. Jimmy walked over to the animals. He knelt, cradled the newborn calf, and began to pet its head. Carefully helping the infant calf to stand, Jimmy led the calf back to its mother. He then coaxed the calf, its mother, and the lion over to where Jimmy's mother was standing.

Stacey was holding Jimmy's baby sister. She placed her cheek on her daughter's soft hair and then hugged her. Little Ashley was now two years old. Stacey looked at the lion and held Ashley's hand out to pet the creature. She then put Ashley on the lion's back and held her there. Ashley giggled and Stacey pulled her back to her chest. Stacey moved over to the new mother cow and petted her lovingly. She noted that as the calf was born, the mother had shown no pain. She reflected on how pain-free her daughter's birth had been. She smiled as she thought how wonderful it was to be under the Lord's rule—no pain, grieving, fear, or killing of any kind. It was utterly amazing.

As Chris watched Jimmy with the animals, he looked at James and Aaron. "Remember how nonbelievers used to ask, 'How can a God allow all of this death and destruction in the world?' I would answer that it was Satan's rule that was causing the pain; it was never God's desire. Humankind chose Satan over God as Adam defied the Lord's command and chose to eat the fruit of the tree of knowledge. For many generations humans have suffered the consequence of Adam's decision. I explained to them, that we have the right of self-will and can choose God or the world. Satan has his time, but one day the Lord will return to earth and bring life on earth back to what he created in the beginning—a world full of love. You only have to accept, repent, and rely on the Holy Spirit for guidance and keep God's command to love one another as yourself.' Well, here we are in a sin-free world."

Aaron took deep, calming breaths as he noted his beautiful new environment. "Yeah, Chris, but remember, this is the millennium and not the new earth. This new sin-free period lasts but a thousand years. At the conclusion of the millennium the earth's surface will be destroyed by fire and a new earth's surface will be formed by God and will become our eternal home.

Jimmy's education during the millennium came from several different sources. Schooling was not dissimilar to the old-world teaching, but now the focus was on God and the living Christ. Jimmy was a young apprentice for the earthly priesthood and studied under Chris and Aaron.

Years passed by as the younger generation evolved into adulthood.

The older age group basked in the new culture of love and peace, as the young were fascinated with every facet of life and freedom.

Jimmy was maturing into a bright young man. He had a reputation throughout the community as one of the youngest persons to survive the great tribulation after Jesus defeated Abaddon and reclaimed the earth and its people.

The first generation to populate the earth following tribulation had seen God's glory firsthand. Remaining true and enthusiastic about their love for Jesus, they were excited about kneeling and praying to him every day and traveling to Jerusalem for feasts to honor and worship him in person.

Many of the subsequent generations that followed took everything for granted. It was commonplace to see a cow feed alongside a bear without fear and to see their young lie down together. The meat eaters of old like the lion now ate straw—like the ox. Mothers never had to worry about their children's safety. A baby could play in a hole that was home to a cobra, and the cobra would never harm the child. The earth was truly a land of plenty. All foods were readily available for picking or harvesting. The thought of consuming meat was grotesque to the new generations. Raising and nurturing families was pure joy.

Jimmy knew that some of the following generations would begin to waver and question the current system. His parents, Larry and Stacey, and his mentors, Chris and Aaron, had trained him well in prophesy. Jimmy's Uncle Brad had warned him repeatedly about the coming rebellion.

Jimmy evolved as an outstanding spiritual leader traveling throughout the land preaching and warning the people against complacency. "Stay fervent for our Lord, who both loves us today and redeemed us from the sins of the past. One day he will create a new earth and heaven for our eternity! Over seven hundred years before our Lord and Savior came to earth and was born in Bethlehem, the prophet Isaiah prophesied about our beautiful and sin-free life during the millennium. One day this utopia can be taken from you if you do not remain faithful. Look to the valley of Armageddon—the smoke spoken of almost a thousand years ago still rises to remind us of the evil that was overcome by Jesus!"

Jimmy's entourage included his parents, his grandfather James, Aaron, Cindy, Chris, his Uncle Brad, Aunt Michelle, and all their families.

The A-Team would often meet at the Temple to pray, prepare for their next mission trip, and commune with Jesus. Knowing well what was to come, the revival of the old church of Laodicea, where the congregation grew complacent and lukewarm toward God, would raise its ugly head again. They would often discuss how important it was to emphasize to the population the importance of keeping their Lord at the center of their lives.

James, and most of his age group, lived to be over a hundred and fifty years old. Even with the corrupted bodies they had from the past sinful age, they lived longer due to the new and healthy environment. James's death was a celebration, as it was a promotion into the Temple to be a priest for his Lord. He also found joy in joining his lifelong friend, Chris, who was already serving in the Temple.

Soon after James began his duties in the Temple, Aaron and Cindy passed away and were promoted to join Chris and James in the Temple serving the Lord. The A-Team was in full complement again as a force for their Messiah.

Before they became sainted priests for Jesus, James and Aaron's children, and their contemporaries, lived to be over two hundred years old. The children raptured with the church of Philadelphia, and the children born after, walked as mortals until an average of five hundred years old.

Jimmy and his peers understood the wonders of their Savior. Their hearts beat daily for their Lord. The new generations born into the kingdom of the millennium lacked the personal knowledge of the true power of God. They had not had the opportunity to witness the Lord defeat sin. Therefore, the following generations that lived until the conclusion of the thousand-year period did not have the strong faith that the previous generation had.

✝

During the sinless millennium age, the birth of a child was painless, all the people were compatible and without strife, and the weather was perfect. With no wars and abuse, the population explosion had grown exponentially by the end of the millennium. It was greater than the pre-tribulation population after thousands of years under the tyrannical and sinful rule of death and destruction by Abaddon.

Prior to Jimmy's death and moving to the Temple priesthood, he heard rumblings of young people that were complaining about the daily prayers to Jesus. He also heard that they did not appreciate being required to observe all the feasts. There was no pride or hatred like there was under Abaddon's deception, but boredom and wonder were growing.

Jesus was sharing with his priests when Jimmy brought up the subject of the current population's protests. Jesus looked sad. "I witnessed this restlessness in Adam and Eve and therefore allowed Abaddon to tempt them. They elected to adopt sin over holiness. I must allow the same choice for the current population. I cannot bring into existence the new heaven, earth, and a new Jerusalem with people who prefer evil over good. When the thousand-year time is at its conclusion, I must know who is truly ready to be part of my eternal church and who is not. Free will must be honored!"

CHAPTER 34

Jesus looked at Michael and Gabriel. He nodded. The three of them walked out of the Temple and stood looking out over the courtyard. Jesus turned to Michael. Holding up a key, Jesus commanded, "When you open the Abyss, stand back and let Abaddon go free. Tell him he is free to deceive those who are open to his lies. Also, let him know that when he has completed his quest, I will see him and his converts at the Temple. Abaddon can bring those whose hearts are not truly mine to face me. I will send them all to their eternal damnation." Jesus paused and closed his eyes for a moment. He held out his hand. "Now, go to the valley." Jesus handed Michael the keys to Hades, turned, and walked slowly back into the Temple.

As Jesus entered the Holy of Holies, his head sagged. He sighed and his shoulders drooped forward. The tears were forming in his eyes. He peered up into level seven and lamented, "I gave them all they ever asked for and still many will choose the way of Abaddon."

Jesus wept for the souls of those who would choose sin over his gift of eternal forgiveness.

†

Michael and Gabriel stood at the door of the pit, looking at each other. Michel bent over. He placed the key into the lock. The ground turned to liquid sand just as a cavern to level six opened.

As Abaddon rose, his chains fell off and he faced his two enemies.

234

He smugly said, "So the carpenter has come to his senses, has he? Things are not going as well as he thought they would? Well, he can continue to occupy my Temple's throne or accept his failure and return to heaven. Tell the carpenter that I will see him soon; and if he is willing to return to level seven, I will consider allowing the earth to return to the mid-tribulation era when he interrupted my rightful reign over level three and leave him alone. If, however, he remains on *my* throne, I will crush him!"

Michael stared, void of any emotion. He knew that Abaddon was delusional and a great deceiver whose pride would not allow him to accept reality. "Jesus said to tell you that you are free to deceive those who are open to your lies and that when you have completed your quest you are to bring your converts to the Temple."

Abaddon's nose wrinkled and his eyes turned to slits as he hissed, "Tell your precious Lord that he had better clear out. I will be coming, not because he says to, but because I will be taking back my Temple!" Abaddon turned and yelled into the Abyss, "Come up and we shall go to the four corners of the earth and tell these pathetic carpenter followers what they are missing. We will give them an opportunity to eat of the tree of knowledge again!" The angelic demons rose from the pit with the purpose of corrupting the souls of every living human. Abaddon had coached his sycophants in how to identify potential victims who had the seed of disobedience or rebellion in them.

Over the last thousand years the names of cities and regions had remained the same from the age before the tribulation. Many large buildings had been demolished or had deteriorated over time. There was no need for shelter from the elements. Days and nights were consistently beautiful. Changing seasons no longer existed. Jesus's light and life-giving properties kept the environment perfect. Although talents and abilities varied, everyone worked together in harmony so that all tasks were done with ease and community cooperation. There were no wages or job titles. The emotion of ambition was displayed only when desiring to help one's neighbor or follow God's commands.

Children were eager to learn, expanding their minds and understanding the planet Earth that they inhabited. They questioned everything but never the sanctity of Jesus and his Temple. Prayer, while facing the direction of the Temple, was mandatory three times a day. Feasts were a time of celebration, and all were required to attend the local area of worship. The grumbling of dissatisfaction or unhappiness was kept in check and shared only in private gatherings until the new teacher and his disciples started preaching.

Upon Abaddon's release from the Abyss, his goal was to take back control of the earth. He was determined to corrupt the attitudes and way of life of the residents of his kingdom by propagating lust, greed, laziness, wrath, envy, pride, and, most of all, blasphemy against the Holy Spirit and truth of Jesus. He traveled throughout the major areas of influence as his minions attempted to evangelize the world.

Not long after Abaddon's release, he visited the Golan Heights region. In the city of Na'ran a group of young men had gathered for daily prayer. A late comer ran up to his friends and said, "Come on, you guys, there are a couple of men speaking at City Center, and they sound exciting."

Timothy Quinn, a descendant of Larry and Stacey Quinn, showed concern that his friends were considering abandoning their prayer time to go listen to some speaker. "Hey, guys, before you forsake our prayer time, you better be wary of any false prophets who make promises that seem too good to be true. My ancestors taught of a time when Satan led mankind astray during the tribulation era would return at the end of the millennium to re-introduce sin."

Timothy's friend, Shane Albright, was curious about everything. Shane was a born leader, guiding the group as to what activity they should perform during the day's free time. As Shane was about to lead the group away to investigate the prophets, he looked at Timothy, rolled his eyes, and sighed. He said, "Oh, Timothy, you are so old school. Don't you want some excitement? A little modification of our daily lives can't hurt."

Timothy retorted, "Change that is not sanctioned by the Father can destroy you. You would be wise to reject anything being taught that is not from our Savior. Remember that Jesus is the Alpha and the Omega." Timothy's voice rose in pitch and his face crunched up as he pleaded, "His word never changes. It's that attitude that got the pre-tribulation generations into trouble and brought on their destruction."

Shane shrugged his shoulders. "Suit yourself. It can't hurt to simply listen." Timothy's friends turned and ran toward City Center.

Timothy watched his friends run off as he bowed down toward the Temple region and began to pray. His deepest prayer was for protection of his family of friends.

†

As Shane and his companions arrived at the rally, they worked their way up to the front of the crowd that was congregating. It was apparent that the orator standing on the platform was getting ready to give a presentation. The handsome man possessed by Abaddon stepped up to address the crowd.

Shane, and his band of brothers, listened as the speaker said, "What you have here is wonderful. Your lives are easy, and you have perfectly fine rules to follow. However, your day-to-day routine is mundane. Each day is basically the same." He lifted his shoulder and tilted his head. "But what if you did something new, something exciting, something challenging and different? What if you do not feel like bowing toward the Temple evert day? Do you think it is fair to be punished if you break some silly rules? You did not make the tenets; why should you be bound by them?" Some listeners looked at their companions and nodded in the affirmative. Others frowned. "Did anyone ask you for your input into the decrees of the land? Knowledge is sacred. Shouldn't we all have as much understanding as Jesus? Don't you think that is fair? We have the right to understand and know what Jesus knows!" More people began to nod in agreement as others covered their ears and left the gathering.

The prince of deception continued, "I see that some prefer burying their heads in the sand and ignoring the truth. Let them go. Again, I ask, is it right to judge someone else if they believe another way? They should have the right to believe the way they want. Look at this beautiful tree. It produces fruit unceasingly. Have you never considered that it, too, has life-giving properties? Perhaps it should be held in esteem, even worshiped. If you prayed to the tree and then ate from it, maybe you, too, would be special." The man possessed by Abaddon stepped back and allowed the assembly to shout their approval.

The presenter raised his hands to quiet down the gathering. He moved to the front of the stage. "I had a man ask me if I thought it was okay to be with another's wife. I asked him if he would love the other's wife. He said he would. So what is wrong with following your heart and being with someone you love. The other man or woman can find another. The oppressive rule that you all live under is unfair and has no pleasure in it. We can make a difference! I plan to lead a march on Jerusalem and on the Temple. I want to challenge the leaders to give us our rightful opportunities to fuller lives."

The remaining crowd seemed mesmerized. Demonic forces morphed into all whose inner light had dimmed. The possessed onlookers began to applaud. Others knelt to pray to the Lord for forgiveness for standing and listening to such blasphemy. The number cheering was far greater than those kneeling.

A young man kicked a woman that was on her knees. She fell onto her side and those around her laughed. The woman looked up at Shane and cried out, "How can you listen to this profanity? Jesus is our Father and has given us a fulfilling life—"

Shane slapped her, bent over, and tore her clothes. His two friends began to beat her. Others saw what they had done, and they too began to kick and attack those faithful to Jesus. For the first time in a thousand years anger, jealously, hatred, foul language, and even death had come back into existence.

Abaddon's ministry of deceptive enlightenment had taken him all over the world, and his words had pierced millions of hearts. He and his henchmen arranged for a worldwide convention near Jerusalem. All the faithful were called to attend. Pilgrimages began from every part of the globe.

The special day arrived on the outskirts of Jerusalem. Abaddon slowly walked to the podium. He looked out over the vast sea of people and cleared his throat. The clapping and cheering subsided. His voice boomed over the huge area as he reiterated the unfairness of the current government, "We have the right to do as we please and to enjoy life as we see fit. It is time to stop being puppets under Jesus's rule! We should be allowed to pray when and where we want and not be required to attend meetings and feasts. It is only just that we keep what we produce and not be forced to share it with others. Passion and love are special. Why should we be confined in what and whom we share them with? If someone does you wrong, isn't it only right that you should be able to retaliate? We need to rise together and force Jesus and his leaders to listen to us or be overthrown. We should rule our own lives. Come, let us march to Jerusalem and meet with Jesus at the Temple to demand change!" The crowd roared with excitement and support.

Abaddon's human vessel stepped down off the stage, and the crowd parted. He and his disciples headed toward Jerusalem, leading the protesters that numbered in the millions.

The march to the Temple was monumental. The attendees had come from all four corners of the world, and Abaddon had whipped them up into a frenzy.

Jesus assembled his priesthood. With arms crossed and holding on to his shoulders, he forced a smile. Even though Jesus, as God in the flesh, knew that prophecy was about to be fulfilled, it still caused him deep sadness. He looked at his faithful and said, "Abaddon is marching toward our Holy City. Those that have willingly received his deception are joining him. Their numbers are like the sands on the seashore. It pains my heart to know that so many are coming and that they will meet their just reward—eternal condemnation. In the beginning, the Almighty and I, as one, created a beautiful garden, the garden of Eden, and then we created man. I walked with Adam and communed with him. We created for him a companion, Eve, and together we evolved into a family. Then, I allowed Abaddon an opportunity to test our creations' free will. They failed.

As time passed and evil became paramount, I heard the cries for help from those who remained faithful to me. I, therefore, developed the Jewish nation. From Abraham came the twelve tribes of Jacob and the heart of my people. I gave them my laws to follow and instructed them to tell the world that there is only one true God. They failed to follow my direction. I then came to earth to sacrifice myself for the sins of those who accept me through faith as their Savior.

The Jewish nation rejected me as their Savior, so I offered my salvation to all mankind. Many accepted my love, both Jew and Gentile. I referred to this time as the age of grace through faith. It, too, failed because of the unfaithful who practiced compliancy and chose to serve the world and to ignore me. In my Word I warned of the seven years of tribulation, the imprisonment of the great deceiver, and the following thousand years of peace. Even the millennium failed.

It will soon be time to create a new heaven and earth for my faithful bride. Together we will dwell in heaven on earth for eternity. You have all blessed me by choosing me over your own selfish desires. It was my joy to come to earth and to take upon myself your sins and then to come back to redeem you. You have chosen wisely. Now, I must go out into the courtyard and greet our coming invaders. They shall see the power of the one true God!"

As Jesus stepped into the middle of the courtyard, his body rose slowly up in the air and hovered over the city of Jerusalem. He turned in a circle and saw the vast number of souls who had followed their new leader and surrounded the city. Many carried harvesting sickles, clubs, and their staffs as weapons. The look on their faces was one that Jesus had not seen in a thousand years—anger and hatred.

The sky, which had been beautiful for the millennium, began changing to a threatening dark gray. There was a strange rumbling above. None of the invading army had ever seen the sky this way or heard the sky resound with thunder. It frightened them. The Abaddonic generals and demons kept their vessels from fleeing.

Suddenly, a great sound filled the entire sky. "You have made your final choice, and your names shall be blotted out of the Lamb's book of life." The aggressors looked at each other with puzzlement.

The sky lit up with a firestorm. The army of Abaddon was utterly consumed by the fires from heaven. Abaddon and his demonic forces were left standing naked. Jesus said to his angels, "Throw Abaddon back into the lake of burning sulfur with the false prophet. They shall be tormented day and night for ever and ever!"

Michael and Gabriel moved to each side of the defiant rebel. Abaddon screeched at Jesus, "You do not have the right to control me! I have always been more cunning and powerful than you. The Almighty will come to my rescue, you will see!" Michael grabbed Abaddon's right arm as Gabriel secured his left arm. Together they started to drag Abaddon toward the Abyss.

Jesus appeared in front of the three and ordered his two angels to stop. He walked up to Abaddon and looked him in the eyes. Abaddon immediately averted Jesus's gaze.

Jesus said, "You have thought of yourself as equal or superior to me. Throughout time you have chosen to reject my deity. You have never looked into my eyes. Now look and see!" Michael forced Abaddon to look into the face of Jesus and deeply into his shining eyes.

Abaddon instantly displayed a look of shock as his eyes widened and his mouth dropped open. "It is you, the Almighty," Abaddon said in a whisper. "You are He. I see the two of you." Abaddon's knees buckled. He fought no more. He had to accept the truth.

Jesus said, "Yes, I Am, that I Am." He nodded and stepped aside. His two soldiers continued to escort Abaddon to the threshold of eternal destination.

As Michael and Gabriel pushed Abaddon into the Abyss of torment, they could hear Abaddon's cries of pain. His defiance had dissolved. Abaddon could no longer bark orders. He could only join in the gnashing of teeth and torment in the eternal lake of fire.

CHAPTER 35

Jesus looked into level seven. The light of heaven intensified as the earth and sky fled from his presence. Jesus proclaimed, "It is time to begin the final judgment!" At the Lord's announcement, the twenty-four elders, who were seated on the throne before God, fell on their faces and worshiped God, saying, "We give thanks to you, Lord God Almighty, the one who is and who was, because you have taken your great power and have begun to reign. The nations were angry, and your wrath has come. The time has come for judging the dead and for rewarding your servants, the prophets, and your saints and those who reverence your name, both small and great. It is time to destroy those who destroyed the earth."

The Abyss opened and the entire host of sinners rose from Hades and joined the believing saints.

Jesus took his seat on the great white throne, Gabriel and Michael standing on each side. Jesus announced, "I will separate the sheep from the goats—those that accepted me through faith and those that rejected me."

All the nations gathered before him, and he separated the people one from another as a shepherd separates the sheep from the goats. He put the faithful on his right and the unfaithful on his left.

Jesus looked to his right. "Come, you who are blessed by my Father; take your inheritance, the kingdom prepared for you since the creation of the world. I was hungry and you gave me something to eat, I was thirsty and you gave me something to drink, I was a stranger and you invited me in, I needed clothes and you clothed me, I was sick and you looked after me, I was in prison and you came to visit me."

James Lucas stood humbly with the rest of the A-Team clan at the front of the gathering. He asked loudly, "Lord, when did we see you hungry and feed you, or thirsty and give you something to drink? When did we see you a stranger and invite you in, or needing clothes and clothe you? When did we see you sick or in prison and go to visit you?"

Jesus looked at James and then at the vast audience standing before him. "That is a fair question. Truly I tell you, whatever you did for one of the least of these brothers and sisters of mine, you did for me."

The saints moved closer to the throne. Jesus stood up from his seat, still with his attention to his right. "I have given you promises that are about to come to fruition. You accepted who I am through faith, believing that my crucifixion paid for your sins and my sacrifice resulted in your justification for receiving eternal life with me. I promised you, the members of my church, that you would be my bride and that I will give each of you something precious at our wedding."

Jesus took in a deep breath and relaxed his shoulders. "Because you have overcome and did my will to the end, I will give you authority over nations. As the redeemed from sin, you will be dressed in white. I will never blot your name from the Lamb's book of life but will acknowledge you before my Father and his angels. I will write on you the name of my God and the name of the city of my God, the New Jerusalem, which is coming down out of heaven from my God, and I will also write on you my new name."

With a happiness in his voice Jesus said, "You will be able to commune with God and will be called his offspring. Now, if you are the Father's children, then you are heirs of God and co-heirs with me. We shared in the suffering and we will share in the glory." Jesus had a tear in his eye—a tear of joy—as he looked out over his future bride.

Jesus held out his hands and said, "My bride. I sent my angels, and they weeded out of my kingdom everything that caused sin and those who did evil. You, my righteous, will shine like the sun in the kingdom of our Father."

Jesus sat down. "I have before me three books. First is the Book of the Law with the names of those of you who were living during the Old Testament age before I came as a sacrifice for the sins of mankind. You who strived faithfully to live by the law and those of you who were called to be my prophets and judges and followed my commands will be honored. Although you will not be part of my bride, which I have promised to only my Christian followers, you will spend eternity with us in love. Second is the book of deeds and motives. Within this book are your deeds and motives, both good and bad." Jesus noticed the apprehension displayed on his congregant's faces. He closed the book and spread out his arms, exposing the scars as a result of being nailed to the cross. "There is no need for me to review your deeds and motives or to judge you accordingly. I died for your sins and transgressions. I took them upon myself as I offered the final sacrifice to save you from your sins. There is no need for any accountability for any wrongdoing. Your good deeds are noted and I accept them as an act of love toward me, and your names are in the Lamb's book of life and will remain there for all eternity."

Jesus looked over his congregation. "Our new world will be pure and void of sin and death." The heavenly hosts sang with joy. St. John walked onto the throne area and announced, "The last enemy to be destroyed by Jesus is death!"

The A-team gave each other high fives and began to sing with the angels.

St. John raised his hands to quiet the believers. Silence filled the air. "Now it is time for what we have all been anticipating. Please follow me through the portal where we will await the new heaven and earth."

There were shouts of joy and cheers of excitement as the throngs of believers began to follow St. John.

Jesus turned to face the nonbelievers, or goats, on his left. He gravely looked down at the Book of the Law. His eyes left the pages and as he gazed at the sea of those who had not acknowledged that there was but one true God or ignored the commandments of God. Desperation was written on each face.

Jesus took in a deep breath and slowly exhaled. "All of you who populated the earth before I came as the Savior and who did not endeavor to observe the laws given to the Jewish nation by God Almighty are under a curse, for it is written, 'Cursed is everyone who does not continue to do everything written in the Book of the Law.' You have failed. I answered your cries for help while you were being persecuted by the enemies of Judaism and sent you prophets and judges who saved you from bondage. After years of prosperity and freedom, you became complacent and returned to worshiping pagan idols and ignoring the one true God."

Jesus then lifted the book of deeds and motives for all to see. "It will be by this book that you from the Old Testament age who did not faithfully try to live by the law will be judged. In addition, those of you who were pharisees and abused my Law and misused it to rule over others unjustly will feel my wrath. Your deeds and motives have condemned you. My angels will now escort you to the Abyss and the second death."

Jesus looked at the next group to be judged. Crying and whimpering could be heard breaking the silence. "Because those that I just addressed from the Old Testament age failed in fulfilling their specific mission or purpose—to be a light and to proclaim God's message among all the nations, as described in the Torah—I ushered in a new age, the age of grace. It was a time where you could believe in me through faith, turn from sin, receive the gift of forgiveness, and dwell with me for eternity. Those who rejected my gift will be judged accordingly."

Jesus held up the second book—the recordings of all deeds and motives. "As you stand before me, I will bring every deed into judgment, including every hidden thing, whether it is good or evil. Those of you from the New Testament period of grace who claimed to be Christians but whose deeds and motives proved otherwise have condemned yourselves. In my Word, I commanded you to 'love your neighbor as yourself.' I decreed, 'Love your enemies, do good to them, and lend to them without expecting to get anything back. Then your reward will be great, and you will be sons and daughters of the Most High.'"

Jesus slowly looked at the condemned sinners. "You chose to judge others harshly if they disagreed with your agenda. That judgement will lead to your second death. I had my disciple St. Matthew write, 'Do not judge, or you too will be judged. For in the same way you judge others, you will be judged, and with the measure you use, it will be measured to you. Why do you look at the speck of sawdust in your brother's eye and pay no attention to the plank in your own eye?' It is your actions, not your words, that speak the truth that is in your heart."

Jesus looked at the third book, the Lamb's book of life. "All of mankind's names initially appear in this book. However, because those of you standing before me rejected my offer of salvation, your names have been blotted out of this book. You will not be spending eternity in a new world of peace and love."

Jesus sat back down on the throne of judgment. He looked out at the vast audience and proclaimed, "Do not look shocked at my sayings. I warned you in my Word. I made it clear that the only way to receive eternal life is through me. In the Bible, St. John quoted my declaration, 'I am the way and the truth and the life. No one comes to the Father except through me.' You heard the truth and chose to ignore it. You have declared freely your own fate."

Jesus continued, "And now I will address those who claim to have had a relationship with me." The angels herded another group forward who sheepishly moved to face the judgment seat. Jesus's face reflected disappointment and hurt. "When you were in the presence of my faithful, you professed that you were a Christian. Then when residing with nonbelievers you returned to the way of the world and to sin. You intellectualized my teachings to fit your lifestyle and debated my truths to twist their meanings. You are hypocrites. You elected to ignore the parable I taught through my apostle St. Matthew: 'Therefore everyone who hears these words of mine and puts them into practice is like a wise man who built his house on the rock. The rain came down, the streams rose, and the winds blew and beat against that house; yet it did not fall, because it had its foundation on the rock. But everyone who hears these words of mine and does not put them into practice is like a foolish man who built his house on sand. The rain came down, the streams rose, and the winds blew and beat against that house, and it fell with a great crash.' You did not heed the foundation I laid out for you."

One of those judged cried out boldly, "You say you are all loving, that by grace I am saved. I did accept you. I repented and was baptized. I know I stumbled and fell back into the world of sin, but I thought nothing could pluck me out of your hand. This is not right. I did what I was supposed to do."

Jesus raised his hands to his chest and rested his chin on them as he leaned forward on the throne. "I looked back at your life. You did those things. I came into the world as your Savior. I died for your sins and returned to redeem you from a sinful place. I asked only one thing from you, that you love me more than the world and sin. The acts you performed demonstrated no evidence of love. I knew you would stumble. However, with my love for you and your love for me, you should have kept persevering. I told you in my Word what I expected from those who love me. In Colossians 3:8 St. Paul wrote, 'But now you must rid yourself of all such things as these: anger, rage, malice, slander and filthy language from your lips.' Your actions showed that the world of sin meant more to you than your dedication to me. You were never in my hand because your heart was never mine. Your actions showed your true love was for a world without me in it. You chose and now you will receive a just ruling."

The man standing before Jesus persisted. "But if you love everyone, how can you send some to Hades? That makes you the hypocrite."

There was a collective gasp throughout the remaining crowd. Jesus sat up straight. "It is out of love that I must condemn the unfaithful because I love my bride, the church, and I must be sure that they can never be contaminated again. I allowed Abaddon into my garden in Eden, and he polluted Adam and Eve. I tried to protect Abraham's descendants, the Hebrews, but they disobeyed me and became tainted.

I allowed Abaddon to infiltrate my age of sinless peace and he caused many to fail. Because of my love for my bride, the church, I will not allow sin in the new heaven and earth. You are not welcome in my eternal kingdom!"

Jesus motioned for the third group to come forward. They reluctantly obeyed. The mark of the Beast was still prominent on the foreheads of those resurrected bodies who worshipped Nef, the false messiah, during the great tribulation. Jesus spoke, "During the tribulation period you chose to worship the throne of the Beast, the serpent of old, the devil. With your allegiance displayed on your forehead, you persecuted my believers and blasphemed me. You shall be judged for your deeds."

Those who gave allegiance to Abaddon at the end of the millennium age were ordered to step up. The same fate awaited them as those with the mark of the Beast. Jesus looked into the heart of the accused and declared, "I gave you peace and love. There was no temptation, evil or hatred among us, but in the end, you chose sin over truth. You elected willingly to defy my commands and me. You desired hate over love."

†

The question posed by Jesus was, "Did you strive with love to live by the Law as a Jew? Did you accept me as your Savior and repent of your sins as a Christian; and if so, what evidence and motive did I see in your heart?"

Jesus closed with his final comment. "May I remind all of you of the many times I had placed you in situations where you would hear the gospel, have a chance to give to others in need sacrificially, help the unfortunate overcome hardship through faith, openly witness to others, and proclaim your love for me knowing that you may be persecuted or become an outcast." The audience remained silent, hanging their heads.

The condemned could not argue with truth and were marched off to their second death.

When Jesus had completed his judgment of the goats, he walked over to the lake of fire and gazed into Hades. On seeing the face of

Jesus, the cries grew silent. Jesus commanded the inhabitants to bow down and pay homage to the Christians who had remained faithful to him. They obeyed.

Jesus then closed and locked the door to the Abyss. It was sealed. Jesus held up the key and blew on it. The key turned to ash, and the wind scattered it throughout the earth.

CHAPTER 36

There was jubilation at the anticipation of the wedding feast and the coming fulfillment of the prophecy of a new heaven and earth.

James hugged Aaron. "If the new earth and heaven are anything like these newly resurrected bodies we have, I cannot wait." James stepped back and flexed his muscles. He looked to be twenty—no blemishes, and the pain from his war wounds were gone. He felt vibrant and had a deeper energy and well-being than he had experienced in all of his earthly life. His senses were heightened severalfold. If he wished, he could communicate without talking.

James turned and put his arm around his dad, whose body was perfect and whole again. Bradley, too, looked as if he were twenty years old.

Cindy said with a bubbly light voice, "Look at me and my Penny. Now these new bodies are a thing of real beauty." They all laughed.

Cindy no longer felt a sense of guilt about her folks' absence. Her parents unfortunately had accepted the mark of the Beast. They were proud of their daughter's high position in the new order and the accolades and favors they had received. Even after Cindy disappeared, they had been eager to receive their marks. When Cindy had called to witness to them, they had rejected her comments as brainwashing and encouraged her to go back to Nef. They had chosen to be a member of the new religion rather than the true faith. Cindy was confident that they would have turned her in had they known where she was hiding. It had caused her pain, but Brad had told her that each person had to make their own decision as to which path they desired. Therefore, Cindy had focused on those who were still willing to listen.

On the other hand, Aaron's parents were in heaven with him. As attendees at Aaron's first Jewish community assembly after the earthquake in Jerusalem, they had observed the presence of Abraham, Moses and Elijah in the tent meeting. Falling to their knees as the three patriarchs left the hall, they had dedicated their lives to Christ. They had been integral players in the Petra fortress. Now they basked in the light of the Almighty with Aaron, Ruth, Benjamin, and Naomi.

Chris jumped into the mix and said, "I cannot wait for the wedding banquet and to see the new earth, the new heaven, and the new eternal homes our Lord will have for us."

CJ added, "I wonder what he will have us doing. I know it will be stimulating and exciting. I have always loved to build things. Maybe I can be an artisan. I loved preaching as well, so maybe I will get to be a teacher or priest."

"As for me," Chris said, "I want to serve as a priest at Jesus's side!"

As Caroline put her arms around CJ and Paul, she looked at Paul for his comment. "I have been with our Lord since my birth. He has taught me so much. I look forward to the endless possibilities he will open to us all."

Stacey said, "The Lord gave me a talent for running things and organizing things, so maybe I will be a mayor of a town. After all, he promised that some would reign over nations. They will need someone to run towns, right?"

"Right, sis, and you would be a perfect mayor, and maybe I can help," Brad added.

Their mother, Annette, sighed. "You both will be very busy, that I know."

As they were enjoying conversation, Jesus approached the A-Team clan. They all fell silent.

Jesus made his request, "Chris, James, Cindy and Aaron, please join me." The four bowed. Jesus's eyes turned soft and filled with an inner glow. He touched each on the top of their head and called them his future bride. "The Almighty and I would like the four of you to assist Michael and Gabriel. We need the saints to rest in a holding area while we combine the third and seventh levels. It will take us six earthly days to accomplish the rebirth of earth and heaven. We will return for a celebration on the seventh day. You will help minister to the saints, as you have done in the past. Feel free to solicit any help that you may require. We will supply you with manna and living water while we are working on your new eternal home. I may look a bit different when I return, but the focus of our eternity together will be love and peace. Now, blessings on you." Jesus disappeared, but his light still shone brightly.

Chris looked at Cindy. "Eternity is starting!"

The host of believers loved watching the evolution of the new earth. James's dad stood by his son and said, "I remember flying over Mt. St. Helens when it erupted. The plane dipped and the ash rose so fast I was worried that the engines might clog. The devastation was total, but out of the horrible volcanic explosion and destruction arose a lush and beautiful landscape."

James looked at his dad. "Yeah, Dad, God's doing much more. I think it is amazing that Jesus has let us retain knowledge from our old life. It helps us remember why our Lord had to die for us, and what we learned will help us on the new earth."

Chris heard Bradley's comment and turned to face him and James. "Well, the earth was destroyed by flood in Noah's day. It was fascinating to hear Noah talk about his experiences and how God rejuvenated the earth after the water receded. This time he is destroying the surface by fire, but, unlike following the flood, there will be no sin to debase or tempt his people. The father of lies is silenced for all eternity."

Just then, a man stepped next to Chris and put his arm around him. Chris glanced over, stepped back, and bowed his head. It was St. Peter. "Hey, don't bow to me. I am your brother. You only bow to our Lord." Peter stepped back to Chris and put his arm around his neck again as they faced toward the new earth. Peter continued, "You are right about the fire. Our Lord had me write, '…by God's word the heavens came into being and the earth was formed out of water and by water. By these waters also the world of that time was deluged and destroyed. By the same word the present heavens and earth are reserved for fire, being kept for the day of judgment and destruction of the ungodly. But the day of the Lord will come like a thief. The heavens will disappear with a roar; the elements will be destroyed by fire, and the earth and everything done in it will be laid bare.' What we are witnessing together is the fulfillment of our Lord's prophecy. I cannot wait to see it when they are done."

✝

On the seventh day, a great being appeared standing at the portal to the new earth. His being brightened the entire level much more than before. The new being was exalted and exuded warmth and peace. It was the most incredible figure ever viewed. All fell to their knees. Cindy leaned toward Aaron, "God, the Almighty, has appeared!" James and Chris overheard her.

"What do you mean?" Aaron whispered back.

James and Chris leaned in to listen to her response. "There is no longer a need for a separate Messiah or a Holy Spirit. We are looking into the face of the one true living God, the face of a loving father. There he is, God Almighty!" Tears were running down her cheeks. Her three friends took a deep breath. God was now with them! God had the crucifixion nail scars. "He is appearing in Jesus's resurrected body. They are one and the same now."

A man stood up and his statement echoed throughout. "A thousand years before our Lord came to us as our Savior, I cried out, "Give thanks to the Lord, call on his name; make known among the nations what he has done. Sing to him, sing praise to him; tell of all of his wonderful acts. Glory in his holy name; let the hearts of those who seek the Lord rejoice. Look to the Lord and his strength; seek his face always.'"

Cindy quietly said, "I prayed for Jesus's return and the creation of the new earth so that I would be able to look upon God's face. Remember, anyone who looked upon God's face before now died. The time is now, and our prayers are answered! Look upon the face of your God and reap your reward!"

Chris nudged James as he gazed at the face of God. "That was King David who spoke. He is now our brother." Tears of joy ran down both men's cheeks.

The Almighty spoke, "There are those who say that God's children have been expecting this day since I walked on Earth. Many implied that the day would never come. They challenged Judaism, and Christianity, and then me, questioning why I would take so long to fulfill my promise, again intimating that I did not exist. I gave the answer to these doubters in my Word as I told Peter to write: 'First of all, you must understand that in the last days scoffers will come, scoffing and following their own evil desires. They will say, 'Where is this 'coming' he promised? Ever since our fathers died, everything goes on as it has since the beginning of creation.' But do not forget this one thing, dear friends: With the Lord, a day is like a thousand years, and a thousand years are like a day. The Lord is not slow in keeping his promise, as some understand slowness. He is patient with mankind, not wanting anyone to perish, but everyone to come to repentance.' I took as long as possible because I wished that none would perish. You have all chosen wisely with both your heads and your hearts. I will show you your new home after we have some time of rest."

At the end of the rest period, the Lord stood in front of the love of his life and spoke, "After I returned to you, we closed the portals during our last day so none of you could see the new creation until now. We would like to invite you to join us as we step onto the new Earth and behold the coming of its crown, the new Jerusalem." The Lord dropped his left arm to his side loosely and swept his right hand from right to left and back. The new level that held the eternal new Earth came into view for all to see.

Ruth took Aaron's right hand with her left and held James's left hand with her right. James, in turn, took his right hand and held Annette's who took Chris's hand. Soon the entire A-Team and their families were holding hands as they beheld the carpenter's ultimate handiwork.

CJ was mesmerized as he took in the breathtaking view of the glorious mountains and valleys.

Michelle said, "I have never seen such vivid colors."

Cindy, who was holding Penny's hand as well as Caroline's, said, "Look at the new heavens!"

Interrupting the A-Team's comments, the Almighty said loudly, "Now my church, soon to be bride, and my honored guests from the Old Testament era, behold, I have combined levels three and seven to give you a new heaven and earth. Since I am a loving God in whose image you were made, there will be no tears. I do not want my beloved bride to be unhappy but be glad and rejoice forever in what I have created. For you, my bride, I have fashioned Jerusalem, the Holy City, to be your gift, and *you* will be my joy." God swept his hand from right to left.

"When you behold our new city, you will see that there are twelve gates made of pearl, each named for one of the twelve tribes of Jacob. Those of you of Jewish descent will enter the new city through the gate named for your Jewish tribe. My bride-to-be will enter through my tribe's gate of Judah for as it is proclaimed in Hebrews, I came to you through Mary and was born into that tribe. You will all join at the center of my Holy City where the wedding ceremony and banquet will be held. Now, follow Abraham. He will show you the gate through which you will enter." The Lord God disappeared.

CHAPTER 37

The throng of excited followers of God stood waiting anxiously. The atmosphere was filled with a loud shout. Looking up, they saw the Holy City, the new Jerusalem, coming down from the new heaven. As it approached, its enormity became more and more apparent.

CJ said, "Oh my, look at its size."

Aaron said, "The new Jerusalem will come down and settle in the Middle East. God gave Moses the Promised Land, and Israel occupied only a tiny portion of the land promised by God. The new Jerusalem will cover most of the Middle East. It will be immense. To put it in perspective for those of us originally from the U.S., the footprint of the city would reach from Seattle, Washington, to Fargo, North Dakota, to San Antonio, Texas, to San Diego, California, and back to Seattle. If the new city had different stories of twelve feet per story, the city would have thousands of floors."

Cindy piped up. "Wow, I hope I'm not the only cleaning lady." Everyone laughed.

Brad said, "The city is also called the 'bride of Jesus,' the same as we are."

Michelle added, "It is the most beautiful city I have ever seen or could imagine."

Chris announced, "Just like in the pre-tribulation era, the church was a building, but the church was really its congregation. The new Jerusalem is a city, but, again, the actual new Jerusalem is the people. That is why the glorious city is adorned as a bride.

With every jaw slackened and eyes almost bulging, everyone watched in awe as the city settled onto the ground.

The new Jerusalem had great high walls and twelve gates. There were three gates on the east side, three on the north side, three on the south side and three on the west side of the city. The wall of the city had twelve foundations, and on them were the names of the twelve disciples of Jesus. As the amazing architecture settled softly onto the new earth, the trumpet sounded and the populace surrounding the new Jerusalem became quiet.

A booming sound came from within the new structure. The future inhabitants of a brave new eternity could not see their God sitting on his throne, but they heard him say, "Now the dwelling of God is with his believers, and he will live with them. They will be his people, and God himself will be with them and be their God. He will wipe every tear from their eyes. There will be no more death or mourning or crying or pain, for the old order of things has passed away. I have made everything new!" The listeners kneeled in reverence. The creator of all things continued. "It is done. I am the Alpha and the Omega, the Beginning and the End. To the thirsty, I will give water without cost from the spring of the water of life. You have overcome and have inherited all this. I will be your God, and you will be my family. This is the home of righteousness. You may enter."

The non-Jewish saints prepared to walk through one of the northern gates. As was written in the book of Hebrews, all saints were adopted members of the tribe of Judah, so they gathered in front of the gate titled "JUDAH," the name of Jesus's Jewish tribe.

Aaron looked at James, Cindy, and Chris and said, "My family will be going through the LEVI gate. We will meet you at the bride's gathering place." The generations of Aaron's family migrated toward their gate.

As Aaron's family members passed by on their way to their assigned gate, the remaining generations of the A-Team looked up at the twelve steps to their gate with great anticipation. Each step was an extension of the Holy City's twelve foundations. James, Cindy, and Chris, followed by their clans, proceeded up the steps. To the left of the gate, and standing on each step, was the disciple for which the foundation was named. The A-Team members walked over to the first disciple and gave Peter, the rock, a hug as each passed. They proceeded up the remaining eleven steps, showing their love and respect to each man who died a martyr's death for his Savior. Standing on the last step was St. John. Because of God's calling to write Revelation, John was spared a martyr's death.

Hugging each new brother and sister, John would open his left hand, palm up, and jester to the open gate. After the adopted saints and Jewish members of Judah had entered, the twelve disciples of Jesus dispersed to enter through their tribal gate along with their own families.

A regal angel stood guard. James walked through the gleaming gate, wide-eyed. The beauty took his breath away. He thought to himself, *As it said in the Word, this place shines with the glory of God. Its brilliance is like that of jewels.*

Decorating each foundation of the city's walls were precious stones. The first foundation was jasper, the second was sapphire. The third was chalcedony, the fourth emerald, the fifth sardonyx, the sixth carnelian, and the seventh chrysolite. The eighth foundation was beryl, the ninth topaz, the tenth chrysoprase, the eleventh jacinth, and the twelfth amethyst.

The city measured fourteen hundred miles in length and width, and fourteen hundred miles high.

Aaron looked at the walls and said, "They must be at least two hundred feet thick. The new city is a perfect cube, the same as the Holy of Holies was in the old Temple. This will surely be the new dwelling place of our God!"

As if on cue, a beautiful and thunderous voice spoke for all to hear. "As you enter our new city, I want you to know that on no day will my Holy City's gates ever be shut for there will be no night here. The glory and honor of the nations will be brought into the city. Nothing impure will ever enter it, nor will anyone who does what is shameful or deceitful, but only those whose names are written in the Lamb's book of life." The entire congregation was kneeling and looking up as they heard God's voice. When he finished, they slowly rose and continued their journey in the great city.

"Look at the walls!" Chris said as he startled James who was still in deep awe.

"They look like precious stones!" Cindy chimed in.

Annette took James's hand. "The streets are of gold, as pure as glass!"

Jimmy stepped up, "Hey, Bompa, St. John told me that after the banquet we should come back and visit the original garden of Eden. Don't you think that it would be fun to see?"

"Sounds cool," said Larry.

James gave the thumbs up.

Jimmy added, "Then we can go to the new Temple."

Chris interjected, "Jimmy, did you forget that there is no new Temple in the city? Jesus said in

Revelation that the Lord God Almighty and the Lamb are the city's Temple."

"Oops, you are right. Forget I said that. We will be the bride of the new Temple. How amazing is that!"

James grinned, turned, and yelled for the attention of his clan. "We must be getting to the

banquet. We do not want Jesus's bride to be late. We have eternity to sightsee." The family applauded with excitement and started singing songs of praise as they continued their journey to the center of the great city.

†

As the saints entered the bride's gathering place, Cindy and Aaron were excitedly talking at the front edge of the crowd. The rest of the A-Team's clan was chatting amongst themselves. Cindy glanced around. "The bride is made up of thousands. We are adopted sons and daughters into the tribe of Judea, and the rest are Jews who accepted Jesus as their Messiah."

"Yes. We are often referred to as 'completed Jews,'" Aaron said as he noticed the angels distributing fine linen to each bride. The wedding garments were bright and clean.

As they quickly clothed themselves in the new garb and gathered back together, Aaron whispered to Cindy, "These wedding clothes represent our character and righteous acts before God."

Penny nudged Cindy and pointed upward. "Mom, look!" The bride collectively saw the bridegroom appear in the sky. He no longer had fiery eyes or legs of bronze; the final judgment had long since passed. His face shone like the sun, glowing with strong, loving features. Jesus was encircled with an incredible rainbow. He was dressed in a white robe with pomegranates of blue, purple and scarlet yarn around the hem, and his prayer shawl covered his shoulders. As he floated down, his feet touched upon a raised mound.

Cindy smiled as she leaned into Aaron. "Look at the three special guests that are joining him on the mound. That's Abraham, the rabbi who will conduct the ceremony."

"Yes. And look, it's Jesus's best man, John the Baptist, standing next to him. I see that John is holding Jesus's marriage contract in his hand. It spells out his obligation to his bride—us!"

Abraham and John the Baptist were dressed in white robes and wore a white *kippas* on their head.

Cindy tilted her head and looked admiringly at the fourth person on the mount. "And we agreed with our husband-to-be that our maid of honor should be Rachel, Jacob's wife. Doesn't she look lovely?" Her white robe was a bit longer, than the other robes, and she wore a white-flowered wreath atop her flowing hair.

Penny stuck her head between Cindy and Aaron. "Isn't this amazing? I am so excited."

Cindy lit up with anticipation as she observed Jesus smile at the entire bride. The air around Jesus filled with angels that were holding veils. Jesus reached out and took a veil from one of the angels and walked from the mound to Mary, his earthly mother. He placed the veil on her head, kissing her on the forehead and cheeks. Cindy sighed as she watched the act of love and kindness. Jesus then moved to Mary

Magdalene and repeated his gesture. When Jesus reached Cindy, she felt the veil placed on her head, and his kiss on her cheek was divine. Cindy took Jesus's hand and felt the scar on the palm of his hand.

Tears of joy filled her eyes as she looked into God's face.

"My scars will always be there as a reminder to you and me of what I did to redeem you as my bride for eternity." Jesus stepped back and moved on.

Cindy turned and watched as her future husband covered Aaron's head with a veil and kissed him. The warmth and sense of fullness was nearly overwhelming as Jesus covered James and each member of the A-Team family.

Cindy maneuvered close to James. He looked at Cindy and whispered, "I've received the best crown a person could dream of."

The love and peace on James's face said it all. How blessed were the bride members.

The bride remained reverently quiet. Once all bride members were veiled, they sighed with anticipation as the gates to the ceremonial gardens were opened.

CHAPTER 38

James and the rest of the A-Team heard a shout from the angelic multitude, "Hallelujah! Blessed are those who are invited to the wedding supper of the Lamb!"

Dressed in fine white linen, the A-Team and their Christian brothers and sisters kneeled to
worship their future husband.

Jesus looked over his bride-to-be. "Rise and rejoice for we are to celebrate!"

The wedding party rose and formed a line made up of several columns. They quietly paused to wait for their cue to enter the arena.

Rabbi Abraham and Jesus led the procession. Closely behind was Jesus's best man, John the Baptist.

The great procession was announced by a loud and beautiful sound coming from a group of angelic trumpeters.

Old Testament patriarchs and God's angels made up the guest list. The guests became very quiet as the wedding procession entered the celebration arena.

The bridegroom's party walked slowly to the section covered by a huge canopy. They turned to face the entrance. A chorus of angels began to sing "Hallelujah" and a wedding song that filled the universe with the announcement of a heavenly union.

That was the signal for the bride to enter and join their beloved. Rachel was the first to cross the opening. She was followed by Mary, the mother of Jesus, the twelve disciples, the apostle Paul, the martyred saints, Cindy and her A-Team family, and the rest of the bride.

Jesus had followed Cindy's progress closely during the age of grace and throughout the tribulation. He knew she would be at their wedding. He now focused on her as he noticed her looking around at the beautiful open area. He heard her say, "Penny, look at the guests. They are from the past, before Jesus came to earth. They are wearing white robes. Look, in the front row; it's Daniel and Jacob. They are our brothers now. How exciting!"

"That's right." Jesus could tell that Cindy was listening to him as she looked directly into his eyes. "They will be there for you as mentors and friends and as siblings for eternity."

"Mom, this is the best day ever!"

Jesus listened to Penny's comment and said to her, "You make my heart sing, Penny. You and Paul have been with me the longest of the A-Team and you both are such a blessing to me." Paul, Chris's son who died at birth, heard Jesus's comment and his face lit up.

As the procession moved slowly, Jesus could hear the thoughts and comments of each one of his bride members.

Jesus stood facing the adoring audience.

Abraham shouted, "The *bride* has arrived." The room filled with shouts of praise and tears of joy as the angels began to sing a song of praise. After a short time, Abraham lifted his hands for quiet. "Everyone, please remain standing and hold the hand of the person next to you." The participants obeyed.

The air surrounding the bride filled with the booming voice of Abraham shouting, "Hallelujah, for the Lord God Almighty reigns. Let us be glad and give him glory!" The bride joined with the angels and sang songs of praise as all eyes were on the bride.

Jesus returned the admiring gaze of the bride. He thought, *It is finally time for me to take my bride. I created my bride with love for this very day. My bride is pure and worthy, and soon we will be one, just as the Almighty and I are one.* Jesus was full of happiness and anticipation. He knew the eternal future would be full of adventure, love, and communal blessings.

As the bridegroom stood with Abraham and John the Baptist, reverent silence filled the new Jerusalem.

Jesus's heart became lighter as he observed Cindy's response to the beauty and the presence of her new brothers and sisters in the arena area. He saw Cindy glance to her right and left. The huge area was filled to its capacity.

Full of contentment, Jesus was delighted that the residents of his new Jerusalem were amazed with their new bodies and minds and the exquisiteness of the new world he had created.

Jesus's thought was interrupted as he heard what sounded like a great multitude, like a roar of rushing water and like loud peals of thunder. The multitude was shouting, "Hallelujah! For our Lord God Almighty reigns. Let us rejoice and be glad and give glory! For the wedding of the Lamb has come, and his bride is ready!"

A silence filled the universe.

Abraham spoke loudly so that all could hear. "Dearly beloved, we are gathered here to celebrate the eternal union of Jesus and his bride." Abraham paused and said, "I hold in my right hand the sealed and witnessed marriage contract between the bridegroom and the bride." Abraham lowered the contract to look at it, then looked at the bride. "Jesus promises that there will be no tears of sadness forevermore and that he will love, feed, respect, and cherish you for eternity." Abraham paused as the significance of the contract was absorbed by everyone. "You promise to love, support, and treasure Jesus for eternity." Abraham spoke for several minutes more and paused.

A flood of angels entered under the canopy, each carrying a cup of wine. They distributed the drink to each bride member. Abraham lifted a carafe and watched the wine flow into Jesus's cup. Jesus thought, *This represents the blood I shed for my bride-to-be when I died for their sins. It has been commemorated for thousands of years through the act of communion, but now the wine represents my bride's eternal sainthood.*

Jesus looked at his bride, smiling broadly. As he spoke, his voice resounded throughout the cosmos. "I will betroth you to me forever. I will betroth you in righteousness and justice, in love and compassion. I will betroth you in faithfulness, and you will acknowledge me as your

Lord and husband. Let us drink together." As Jesus sipped from his cup, he was remembering that time in the mid-8th century before his first visit to earth when he had given those words to his prophet Hosea to write down. He looked at Hosea and nodded.

Abraham sat his cup down and addressed the onlookers, "According to Jewish tradition, I would like to introduce the seven guests who will read the seven blessings. Sarah, Jacob, Esther, Ezekiel, Noah, David, and Solomon, please join us." The seven rose and walked to the front of the canopy. Sarah stepped forward and recited a blessing, followed by each of the patriarchs.

As each one gave a blessing, Jesus thought back to the Old Testament age when those guests had carried out his callings. He respected them for their openness to be used by him to lay the foundation for the salvation of mankind. Although they would not be part of his bride, they would be honored throughout eternity.

Each blessing focused on the new relationship with Jesus, the love and joy that all would now experience for eternity, and the new husband who redeemed his new bride and honored guests.

Abraham again raised his cup and offered a toast to celebrate the blessings. Jesus and the bride drank together.

Following the toast, Abraham looked at Jesus and said, "And now does the bridegroom have something precious to give his bride to seal the marriage?"

Jesus looked out at the sea of blissful eyes who looked at him with anticipation. He said, "I do."

The area under the canopy was flooded with angelic deliveries. Each angel carried a white stone dangling from a gold chain and placed it around a bride's neck.

"I have given each of you a white stone with a new name written on it, known only to the one who received it. It is given in love, and you will be reminded of my eternal commitment every time you see or feel it. With this stone I thee wed and call you my bride."

Jesus turned, lifted his cup, and then placed it on the ground. He said, "In keeping with tradition, I will stomp on the cup." Jesus raised and lowered his foot, shattering the cup. Jesus smiled enthusiastically and everyone knew to yell "*Mazel tov*!"

The special guests, angels, and bride cheered as Jesus walked from the front of the canopy and began hugging each of his new brides. After he had greeted each one, he led his new bride to the place of the wedding feast.

✝

Chris gasped when he saw the splendor of the setting for the wedding feast. The perimeter was lined with lush green foliage protected by large redwood trees reaching several hundred feet into the air. The plants danced in a calm breeze of fragrances that reminded him of both spring and summer. Every plant was in full bloom, and the canvas of colors was almost more than his newly expanded senses could comprehend. He slowly gazed over the open terrain that was covered with a sea of tables dressed in fine white linen. Each displayed a centerpiece of beautiful white lilies.

Chris led the A-Team to a table. Chris's son, Paul, sat down to his left with Caroline on Chris's right. He leaned forward and smiled at CJ sitting next to his mother and looked to his left to acknowledge Michelle sitting by Paul. "This venue is almost exactly as God led me to teach about the wedding. I love my new husband so much!"

"And I love you. I love my whole bride with all the love I possess and will for eternity." Jesus bobbed his head toward Chris from the head table.

Chris was not surprised that Jesus could hear his thoughts. He had always been able to do that. But he was elated that now he could also communicate with others through thought with his new body and mind. It was exhilarating.

Chris saw Jesus's disciple, St. John, rise from his seat at the head of a formal table at the front. The table was almost seventy-five feet long and four feet wide. It was not covered with white linen but instead had a two-foot gold inlay running the length of the center of the table.

Jesus was seated in the center with Abraham to his left and John the Baptist to his right. The rest of the seats to his right were occupied by his disciples and to his left were the prophets all dressed in white satin robes. The prophets wore a white *kippas,* on their head and the disciples wore their wedding veil.

"Silence. Can I please have silence?" St. John said. There was not another sound as all turned toward the front. "Those of you not seated, please find a place." The rest of the party filed into a seating arrangement.

St. John opened both hands, palms up, giving the go-ahead for the angels to inundate the wedding feast. They placed objects in front of each individual. Chris was energized when he saw what was before him—a cup of red wine and some unleavened bread. He leaned over to CJ. "This is it. Jesus is about to fulfill his promise to his disciples, and we get to participate."

The Lord invited each guest to join him in communion before the banquette dinner commenced. They sat quietly. "We shall continue to share together for eternity. As you did during the age of grace, you will continue to perform this in remembrance of what I have done for you. Now, please take a piece of unleavened bread and hold it in the palm of your hand." Each participant did as instructed. Then Jesus declared, "I am the bread of life. Whoever comes to me will never go hungry. As you eat, remember that this represents my body which was given for you. Through me you will have abundant life and my eternal love, for I Am who I Am. Now, eat."

The adoring group partook together.

Chris's heart beat faster as Jesus lifted a cup of wine. "I promised my twelve, and you, that one day we would drink this cup of praise, for I have restored you to the eternal garden where you will dwell as one with me. We will live together forever. You will drink this in remembrance of our marriage covenant." They drank and began to sing praises to Jesus. He raised his hands for silence. Jesus's chin rose a bit, and his eyes widened as he proclaimed, "Let the banquet begin!"

Thousands of angels entered the banquet area and served a magnificent feast.

Chris turned to Caroline. "This tastes heavenly."

"Well, this is the new heaven on earth," Caroline said as she scooped up another bite of food.

The celebration was on!

†

The light in the A-Team's surroundings intensified. "Our Lord is coming," Brad said to James as everyone turned to look.

As Jesus approached, the clan lowered to one knee and bowed. "Rise, my bride, and let us sit together. I want to share with you how your eternal lives will be anything but boring. Your opportunities in our new heaven on earth are endless." The clan elders sat with Jesus and listened as he enlightened them on what to expect. When Jesus finished, he said, "Now, go and explore our wonderful Holy City and then go out and begin your eternal lives and all that it will offer you. For now, I must go to visit with another clan and share the good news with them." Jesus disappeared.

James stood and said, "Before we go to our new home, let's see this wonderful place. We are going to the original garden of Eden." The clan cheered and clapped. They began to sing as they headed north.

†

James was communing with his family while standing on the streets paved with gold while in route to the garden. The disciple St. John and the prophet Zachariah walked up to the A-Team and pointed at the river. It appeared as clear as crystal as it flowed from the throne down the middle of the great street of the city. St. John said, "It's called the water of life. Jesus once said, 'If you knew the gift of God and who it is that asks you for a drink, you would have asked the Christ, and he would have given you living water, but whoever drinks the water I give him will never thirst. Indeed, the water I give him will become in him a spring of water welling up to eternal life.'"

Zechariah nodded in agreement and then added, "The river will flow outside of the city to supply the rest of the new earth. As it was prophesied in the book of Revelation, 'On that day, living water will flow out from Jerusalem, half to the east and half to the west.'"

St. John acknowledged what his friend had said. "Please feel free to drink," said St. John.

Everyone walked to the riverbank, scooping up a palmful of water to drink.

Michelle spoke first. "The feeling it gave me was far beyond the quenching of thirst. It was more like an energy boost on overdrive." They laughed and realized that their resurrected bodies were regenerating as they stood together.

James said, "Well, this does make sense. Jesus came back from the dead in a resurrected body, and he ate and drank with his disciples; so we, too, will eat and drink."

"Yes," St. John said. "Jesus drank then, and he will drink with us throughout eternity. He will also eat with us." St. John pointed to the trees along the banks of the river of the water of life.

On each side of the river stood the tree of life, bearing twelve crops of fruit. Zechariah said, "My fellow prophet, Ezekiel, wrote about these remarkable trees. 'Fruit trees of all kinds will grow on both banks of the river. Their leaves will not wither, nor will their fruit fail. Every month they will bear fruit because the water from the sanctuary flows to them. Their fruit will serve for food and their leaves for healing.'"

St, John added, "I also wrote in Revelation that his name will be on our foreheads." St. John pointed to James's forehead. James looked at Chris and then Aaron and smiled as he gazed on Jesus's name on their foreheads. James noticed that each member of the family had the name of Jesus written on their foreheads. "We will be with our Lord, who will reign for ever and ever."

They all bid St. John and Zechariah farewell and proceeded on their journey. The clan experienced continued feelings of awe as they toured the garden of Eden and the rest of the huge new Jerusalem.

It soon was time to leave the Holy City and relocate to the area that Jesus had told them about. They all gathered together.

The A-Team family bowed down and gave praise to Jesus. James, Cindy, Chris, and Aaron moved to the front of the clan and formed a circle, as they always had done as youngsters. They placed their right hands in the center, one on top of the other. Since becoming Christians, they left a space open that represented Jesus's participation in their ritual. As they stacked their hands, they felt a warmth and were aware of a presence in the open space. They withdrew their hands, stepping back to bow down.

"Please remain standing and put your hands back in the center." They obeyed and the newest member placed his hand on top. The four A-Team members saw the nail scar visible on the top hand.

Cindy whispered, "Our circle is now complete."

Looking into the face of Jesus, James said, "Thank you for giving us the greatest gift of all time—eternal life with you!"

With joyful adoration the entire clan cried out, "Amen!"

Rev 1:3
"Blessed is the one who reads the words of this prophecy
and blessed are those who hear it and take to heart
what is written in it, because the time is near."

AUTHOR'S NOTES

The word "Revelation" means apocalypse, or the revealed or disclosed. In the Bible Revelation is the name of the last book in the New Testament, and it represents the completion of God's Word.

The Bible consists of sixty-six books written by more than forty God-inspired authors over a period of a thousand years. Their words are clearly written by divine design. The accuracy of the writings from the Old Testament has been confirmed by the texts found in the Dead Sea Scrolls that were discovered in a series of twelve caves around the site originally known as the "Ein Feshkha Caves" near the Dead Sea in the West Bank (then part of Jordan) between 1946 and 1956 by Bedouin shepherds and a team of archeologists. Every fact evidenced a master plan and anticipated things to happen in the future.

There are over three hundred prophecies written about Jesus's birth, life, death and resurrection that were expressed several hundred years before Christ came on the scene. Every prophecy was fulfilled to the letter. Christ's death on the cross was prophesied at a time when the common method of death was stoning (crucifixion had not been developed). His death among criminals, his dying words, his rising from the dead on the third day, and much more were described centuries before Jesus's birth. If so much was fulfilled by Christ's first coming, why would there be any doubt about the prophecies of Christ's second coming.

There are 8,362 Verses of prophecy in the Bible, yet this topic of prophecy is the most neglected area of study. It is not surprising that many people refer to Revelation as a confusing book of doom. To the non-Christian it appears to be science fiction filled with fairytale-like frightening events. Jesus spoke of this confusion when he said in Luke 8:10, "The knowledge of the secrets of the kingdom of God has been given to you (believers), but to others (nonbelievers) I speak in parables, so that, though seeing, they may not see; though hearing, they may not understand." The prophecies Jesus spoke of will become clearer to believers as the time of Jesus's second coming grows near. Perhaps that is why Jesus gave Daniel the response he did in Daniel 12:8-10, "I heard, but I did not understand. Then I said, 'Oh my Lord, what will be the final outcome of these things?' and He said, 'Go your way, Daniel, for these words are closed up and sealed until the end. Many will be purified, made white, and tested, but the wicked will grow even more wicked, and none of the wicked will understand, but the wise will understand.'" Jesus was telling Daniel that his vision of the tribulation period will not be understood until the end-times. Daniel wrote his book around 530 BC.

The book of Revelation was written by St. John. The vision Jesus gave his disciple during the first century could be a vision of events taking place during the twenty-first century. We must remember that the vision seen by St. John in AD 95 was interpreted by St. John according to his knowledge of his current first century environment. Therefore, St. John described his vision in the best way he could, not truly understanding what he witnessed. For example, St. John would not be able to interpret 9/11 accurately in the first century. He had no knowledge of planes, skyscrapers, etc. As we study Revelation in the twenty-first century, we can better understand the events that St. John described.

Revelation makes it clear that Christ will return to redeem humankind. There will be a thousand years of peace on earth in accordance with God's promise to Israel. The wrath of God will not fall on true believers. The Antichrist will be real, and his persecution of dedicated Christians will be worldwide. God will conquer and rule, and there will be a final judgment for Abaddon, his demons, and those who chose not to follow the Law during the Old Testament and those who chose not to accept Jesus as their savior during the age of grace. The only area of debate among knowledgeable born-again believers is when the rapture will occur, as to whether it is at the beginning, middle or at the end of tribulation. After many years of studying rapture, I have decided to pray for pretribulation, but prepare for post tribulation.

Revelation is not a book of doom but a book of victory. It is not a book of fear but of ultimate love. God will do all he can to bring each of his children to the realization that Jesus is the only way, even if takes some exceedingly difficult reminders. The book of Revelation should be studied with the anticipation of Christ's return and the fulfillment of the prayer Christ taught his disciples: "…your kingdom come; your will be done, on earth as it is in heaven" (Matthew 6:10).

9 781489 735973